T0278234

"Bob Ostertag is our companionable chaperone at his meetings with men. His intimacies and distances with mass murderers and queer saints have sex at the core: the highways and byways of male desire. Ostertag guides us through this phantasmagoria, the welcome and unwanted violence, the erotic spaces, the activism, the deaths, the life changing encounters, the profundity of orgies. What arises is a portrait of Bob, the man himself, tender explorer of love in more forms than you can imagine." —ROBERT GLÜCK

"In *Encounters with Men*, Bob Ostertag writes about the men he has known. He writes of love and loss, artists and cops, rapists and friends, leather daddies and shy immigrants, the closeted and the uncompromisingly out, military guys and go-go dancers. Ostertag manages to create an image here of manhood that could only be seen by a gay man who's lived through several generations of queer life and politics. Anyone who wants to know about masculinity from quiet emotional strength to outright villainy should read this book." —ALEX DIFRANCESCO

Also by Bob Ostertag

Facebooking the Anthropocene in Raja Ampat:
Technics and Civilization in the 21st Century

A Home Yoga Companion

Sex Science Self: A Social History of Estrogen,
Testosterone, and Identity

Raising Expectations (And Raising Hell)
Co-authored with Jane McAlevey

Creative Life: Music, Politics, People, and Machines

People's Movements, People's Press:
The Journalism of Social Justice Movements

ENCOUNTERS WITH MEN

Encounters With Men

BOB OSTERTAG

BLACK LAWRENCE PRESS

Black Lawrence Press

Executive Editor: Diane Goettel
Book Cover and Interior Design: Zoe Norvell

Front Cover Artwork:
David Wojnarowicz
Fuck You Faggot Fucker, 1984
Four black-and-white photographs, acrylic, and collaged paper on Masonite
48 x 48 ins.
121.9 x 121.9 cm
Copyright Estate of David Wojnarowicz
Courtesy of the Estate of David Wojnarowicz and P·P·O·W, New York

ISBN: 978-1-62557-089-5

In June of 2023, Black Lawrence Press welcomed numerous existing and
forthcoming Nomadic Press titles to our catalogue. The book that you hold in
your hands is one of the forthcoming Nomadic Press titles that we acquired.

Published 2024 by Black Lawrence Press.
Printed in the United States.

Table of Contents

INTRODUCTION

Many, though not most, of the encounters described in this book are sexual. Men pursue sex with men in all kinds of ways, many of which do not involve emotional intimacy, and some demand emotional distance. For me, sex with men is more like a crow bar with which to quickly pry away the layers of life's detritus and put my heart close to the heart of another. I tend to fall in love with the men I have sex with, for good or bad. That's the way I'm wired, and that wiring runs deep. I have never been ashamed of this, but it took me a while to understand that it made me an outlier in the gay male community.

Many, though not most, encounters described in this book took place far away from my home. For most of my adult life I have been a professional touring musician. During those years, I was as likely to have a night off to go to a gay bar in Taipei, Lisbon, Yogyakarta, Beirut, or Mexico City as in my home town of San Francisco. Nights off on the road feel different. You have been working hard, playing a concert in a different city every night, and now you have one free night before the tour starts up again, so you make it count. And you are in a foreign place. You are not going to run into any friends. And most likely, you will not see the people you meet that night ever again. You are free: to find gold, to make mistakes.

This is a memoir of my encounters with men, not a work of investigative journalism. To the best of my ability, I have accurately recounted what men have told me they have seen, said, and done. As to whether those men were being accurate or honest in the stories they told me, I make no claim.

I have had the good fortune to meet a number of extraordinary men who do not appear in this book: Giovanni Arrighi (teacher), Dave Dellinger (pacifist), Anthony Braxton (who gave me my first professional music gig), Lou Harrison (composer), Delmas Howe (artist), and Jerry Kirby (musician and epic diva), all come immediately to mind, and there are many more. If I were to write a book titled "Great Men I Have Known," all these men would feature prominently. But that book would be about their stories, not mine.

I have a lover of six years with whom I share my home, my life, my everything. But my encounter with him is ongoing, and my perspective is forward-looking, planning and building and hoping for the future. I see the encounters in this book in the rearview mirror, often at great distances behind. I dedicate the book to him. Hopefully, reflecting on the experiences herein has taught me something about myself and my relationships with men, knowledge I can use to love him more and better. And hopefully, when he reads the book, he too will come to know me better.

There are many extraordinary women in my life with whom I have had profound relationships that shaped me deeply. If I were to write a book titled "The People I Have Loved and Who Made Me Who I Am," all these women would feature prominently. But this book is about men.

So, *Encounters with Men*. Like, *Encounters with Bears*, but with men.

PART 1

What a piece of work is a man.

– William Shakespeare (Hamlet)

DREAMS

The nightmares came every night, so vivid, so convincingly real in taste and smell and sound and touch, I often woke up screaming in a sweat. Or rather, trying to scream. But no sound would come out. All the required procedures for screaming were there. The terror enveloping my body like shrink wrap. The adrenaline. The sudden welling up from the diaphragm. The expansion of the chest. The opening of the mouth. And then, nothing. At the last possible moment, my scream would get lost finding its way to the outside world.

The dreams were full of blood and mayhem, mutilated bodies and psycho killers. Endless variations on one simple theme: I was being chased by a man who was trying to kill me. I never knew who he was. Never saw his face. Never looked in his eyes. Never knew his name or where he was from. Never knew why this was happening. Did I even know him? Had I done something to provoke this rampage? I couldn't remember anything that might qualify. Had I simply forgotten? Had I committed a heinous crime that had slipped my mind? Should I return to the places I had been in the last few days to see if there was some poor soul I had left crippled and bleeding in the streets and then expunged it all from memory? But how could I retrace my steps when it was straining all my physical and psychic resources to keep barely one step ahead of the man with the gun, or the ax, or whatever. I would wake up just as the assassin hurled the ax at my head, or fired the gun, or tossed the grenade. My dream self was quite inventive with weapons. The crack of the gunfire or the explosion of the grenade was so close I would wake up with my ears ringing. Wait. Were they really ringing? If they weren't, they should have been. I don't know, it was long ago. Considering the distance in time reminds me that I am actually getting old.

In other dreams I would stumble upon speechless boys who were the victims of horrible crimes. Boys whose voices had lost their mouths, just like mine. So no words or sound. All had been swallowed, maybe by those mouths we could not find. Just an exchanged glance, one to another, which opened out into a subterranean labyrinth we would never find our way back from if we fell in too deep, no matter how hard we looked.

I am on the deck of an old wooden sailing ship, gliding silently through glassy seas. Not a hint of wind, yet we move. The sky is painted orange with fire and black with smoke. Is this a sunset or the aftermath of a battle? Or perhaps we are sailing in the mouth of a volcano. The glassy water mirrors the burning sky, enveloping the scene in flame. In the distance another sailing ship appears, sails furled, adrift. I study the ship intently as the ship I am on draws nigh. There appears to be no one on board. Complete stillness. No sound. Not just quiet. A complete absence of sound. Now it is not just me – the whole world had lost its mouth. We come alongside and I see that the ship is not empty. A boy's naked body is hanging from the mast. He appears to be about ten or twelve years old, and his body has been mutilated. As my ship glides silently by, I see that this boy is not alone. More and more boys come into view: tied to masts or railings, or crumpled on deck. All are boys of the same age, and all have been cut. The sight is at once horrifying and beautiful. The ship glides off into the fire and smoke, until its silhouette is just one more black streak in the flames, leaving me in the silence of its wake.

I went to see a therapist, who thought the dreams might be the echo of my experiences in El Salvador during the civil war of the 1980s. Certainly I had seen enough blood and death there to give my imagination an ample supply of raw material to work with: friends blown up by assassins' bombs, the stinking corpses of combatants left behind by their comrades and bloating in the sun, macabre encounters with death squad leaders and intelligence spooks. But my younger sister was also plagued with nightmares about shadowy men who were coming for her, and she had never been to El Salvador.

It had been years since I had been with Bryan. I could hardly even remember his taste, or the touch of his wispy beard on my face. Gradually, the pain of losing him had eased. At long last I noticed that there were other men in the world one might love. As I began to act on that knowledge and seek emotional and sexual intimacy, the nightmares ended.

At my final meeting with the therapist, she asked if there was anything that she had said or done that had been especially helpful for me.

"When you asked me if I had ever considered that the nightmares might be related to me possibly being gay, it really hit me like a lightning bolt. I had never considered that."

"You're kidding"

"No, really. I was stunned."

"Well, I don't know who discovered water, but I can tell you it wasn't a fish."

It was a deeply weird time to try to get close to men. The year was 1993, among the worst of the AIDS epidemic in America. In San Francisco the epidemic was at its peak. Many traumatized gay men had stopped having any sex at all, even with condoms, even with their lovers. Sick and dying men were an unavoidable sight on the streets. Funerals were constant. The main gay newspaper kept reducing the maximum length of obituaries, so they could fit them all on the multiple pages counting the toll, week after week. The ninth international AIDS conference in Berlin had just announced that all AIDS medications available or in the research pipeline had failed. Community organizations were shifting gears from treatment advocacy to prevention, in recognition that those who already had the virus were lost.

My first new forays into male sexual intimacy were timid, anxious endeavors. Then one night in a bar I met a beautiful man with piercing eyes, sharp angular features, and a lean, muscular frame. He was wearing jeans, a leather jacket, and a pink triangle *Silence=Death* button. Which is to say that he had the full complement of signifiers of hip gay militancy during the ACTUP era. During the taxi ride back to his place we did not speak a word. I found this a little odd, but hey, I was new at this meeting-guys-at-bars thing. Bryan and I never set foot in a bar, gay or straight. We didn't even drink. Maybe this was what you did in the taxi going from the bar to someone's place. Or perhaps he was too timid to speak in the cab where the driver could listen.

By the time we got to his apartment I was floating. Not in any kind of normal state. Without exchanging a word it was determined that I was going to get fucked for the first time in my life. I produced a condom from my pocket, removed it from its package and handed it to him. He unrolled it over his cock, turned off the light, fussed with the condom a bit more, and penetrated me. I was flooded with millennia of sensation and emotion, floating, safe and free in a way I never imagined.

Phtttttt. Somewhere a fuse exploded. No, not a fuse. Wrong. Something was wrong. An undercurrent that shouldn't be there, sucking me down. Panic. Without really knowing what I was doing, I reached down and put my hand to his cock and all I could feel was flesh. No condom. I frantically kicked him off.

"Where is the condom?"

"Did that thing slip off? I am so sorry."

He was lying. The condom was on the floor next to us. He had taken it off after switching off the lights.

The dream feeling intensified, though the dream was now of a different sort, something I was much more familiar with. The soft glow of fantasy that had attached to everything in the room became menacing. The floor opened beneath me and I was dropping down a chute into a very dark place. I slipped into the familiar detachment I knew from my dreams, being an observer in one's own life. And here came the familiar sensation of not being able to scream, or speak, or even find my mouth. But this was no dream. Here he was, the assassin of my nightmares, in the flesh before me. Inside me.

A few days later I became violently ill and was terrified that my symptoms were a sign of the acute stage of HIV infection, when the virus first takes root in your body.

I called the man up, told him of my illness, and asked if he knew his HIV status. He assured me he was negative. Three days later he phoned me back.

"I got so worried after your call that I went and got tested and guess what? I'm positive. How does that make you feel?"

I struggled to answer. Where had my mouth gone? I managed
a whisper.

"It makes me afraid."

"Well how do you think *I* feel?" he sneered. "*I* was going to make
a *million dollars*, but I now I probably won't have enough time."

He was lying. Again. In those days there was no HIV test that
returned results in three days. The point of his call was to fuck with
me. He had fucked me, and fucked me over, and even now was fucking with me some more. But which was the lie? His initial assertion
that he was negative, or his second story of being positive? Or both?

*

Old film noir movies often employ a plot device in which the first
scene is actually the penultimate scene in the storyline. After the
opening scene, the film goes into an extended flashback that tells
the movie's story and finally leads back to the opening scene. But
after following the plot through the flashback, you have the context
to see that your initial understanding of the opening scene was all
wrong, that both you the viewer and the lead character had failed
to appreciate the significance of some small detail that made all the
difference, and which would lead to the protagonist's undoing in
the finale.

In the weeks that followed, I couldn't escape the feeling that I was
living such a movie. In this film, the opening scene is set at the therapist's office, where my "internalized homophobia" is revealed to
be the source of the nightmares that plague me. Then comes a long
flashback of my life leading up to that moment: Jerry is there, and

George, and Bryan of course. Many of the men who fill the pages of this book. All leading like an ocean current back to the triumphant moment of personal liberation where the movie began. But now the film continues on to its dénouement, and the plot goes nightmarishly askew. It is revealed that my nightmares were actually a warning, a premonition, of my own terrible end. My misreading of the clues they offered, packing them neatly into a clichéd Freudian narrative, was my fatal mistake. I had dropped my guard, allowed men too close. The nightmares were not a Freudian expression of repressed desire. They were urgent alarms alerting me to danger when men got too close. By ignoring them I had not achieved any sort of personal liberation. I had made the nightmares real. And now I was infected with their blood.

POETRY

When I was ten years old my parents loaded my sister and me into our little Triumph station wagon and drove from Colorado to San Francisco to meet some relatives us kids had never known. The year was 1967. San Francisco's Summer of Love, the high point of hippie culture. Years later, I would look back and wonder if visiting the relatives had been an excuse, and the real point of the trip had been my parents' desire to check out what was happening with the love generation. One day my father announced he was going to drive us to "see the hippies." I don't think I had ever heard of a hippie and had no idea what was in store. We loaded into the car. Destination: corner of Haight and Ashbury. The street scene was popping, so full of hippies and freaks and flower children with blossoms in their hair that traffic came to a complete standstill. A man with very long hair walked up to our car and asked my father if he could sit and read us poetry while we waited for the traffic to clear. My father readily agreed, and the hippie crowded in next to me in the back seat and read his poetry. I have no recollection of the poetry, but I sure do remember him. I had never seen long hair on a man before. I had never heard a man read poetry to me. He had such a gentle air about him, also new in my experience of adult men. I even remember his smell.

That did it for me. All I wanted to do was move to San Francisco and be a hippie and be with people like him. Sadly, I was ten years old, and by the time I was ready to leave home, even if I had run away at sixteen, the hippies were gone.

Thus began my lifelong love of slender men with long flowing hair and a gentle manner.

COACHES

In fourth grade I was the tallest kid in the class, and I loved using my body athletically. Pure joy. The kind of joy only a child can have. The fourth-grade basketball team could beat the sixth-grade team, mostly because I was on it. The sixth graders were unhappy about that, and one day after practice they set an ambush for me in the schoolyard. They knocked my books from my hands, threw some punches, kicked me, called me names. Being an athlete did not make me a fighter. I was shocked by the whole thing. I didn't respond at all, not physically and not vocally. My voice to mouth disconnect was already fully in place. After they had gone and I was limping out of the schoolyard, our coach passed by and stopped to see what was the matter. He knelt down on one knee and asked me what had happened. I just looked at the ground, but he quickly guessed what was up. "Did those sixth graders...?"

He didn't get angry. He didn't tell me he would punish them. He didn't even ask if I was OK. He just wiped my tears, held my shoulders gently in his hands, and stroked my hair once or twice. Even today I still remember the tenderness of his touch. My father never touched me like that. I think my father was frightened of that kind of physical tenderness with me, but that is another story. The coach had strong features and jet-black hair on both his head and face, sort of a more muscular version of Abraham Lincoln. I felt so comfortable in his caress. It made everything better. These days a coach could lose his job over touching a boy like that. What a pity.

*

I played Little League baseball. Different sport, different coach. I was one of two pitchers on the county's Little League all-star team. The other pitcher was the coach's son.

The day came for our big game with the all-stars of the neighboring county. Even my own father, who *never* came to my games, was in attendance. The coach started his son, who did well for a few innings but then tired, as kids our age did. Some of the "sports dads" in attendance started calling for the coach to sub me in. Soon the poor kid was crying out on the pitcher's mound, while the sports dads gathered around the dugout, yelling at the coach. The coach stood in the doorway, resolutely ignoring the dads and yelling at his son to start throwing strikes or he would beat him when he got home. I never got to play. We lost.

The next day we played the tournament's consolation game against another county team that had lost the previous day. My father did not attend. The coach had no choice but to start me. I was laser-focused. The entire world disappeared except the ball, the batter, and the catcher's glove. Time slowed. It was my first experience of what some call *flow*. I threw so hard the catcher had to keep adding more sponge inside his glove to protect his hand. I pitched a no-hitter. No one could remember that ever happening in a Little League all-star game.

In the dugout after the game, the coach refused to talk or even look at us. So the assistant coach gathered us together and said something about how sometimes in life you learn things too late, blah blah blah, but I didn't stick around to hear it. I was already walking home and out of baseball.

*

We got a new PE teacher in sixth grade, appropriately named Mr. Harms. Mr. Harms was a creep. Nobody liked him from day one. So many years later I cannot pinpoint why we all saw him this way, but we did. Mr. Harms was bad news.

One day Mr. Harms had us playing dodge ball in the gym. Unlike other gym teachers, Mr. Harms participated in the games he organized.

In dodge ball you divide up into two teams, which go to different sides of a center line. Then you take turns throwing a big rubber ball at the other team. Every kid who gets hit with the ball is "out," and the first team with all its players out loses.

When I got the ball, I threw it and hit Mr. Harms on the foot, but he insisted the ball had missed him. Every kid in the gym had clearly seen. It wasn't even close. The ball changed directions when it bounced off his foot. One of the things kids supposedly learn in childhood games is not to cheat, and we were incensed that the teacher himself was cheating right in front of us. Kids started pointing at him and yelling "Cheater!" Mr. Harms turned beet red and insisted over and over that the ball had missed him.

Bedlam ensued. Mr. Harms bellowed at us to line up single file at the door to the gym, then ordered us to spend the rest of the period standing quietly at attention until the bell rang and it was time to go back to our classroom. But the teacher's aura of authority had burst and there was no way a class of sixth graders was going to stand there for half an hour staring at the door just because a cheater told us we had to. We started chanting, "We wanna go, we wanna go," thrilled by our audacity and flush with the child's passion for fairness and knowing we were in the right.

Mr. Harms exploded.

"All right! Everyone can go except for big Mr. Ostertag!"

As the other kids filed out, Mr. Harms stomped over to where I stood, grabbed me by the throat with his left hand, and lifted me off my feet, pinning me to the wall by my neck. With the veins in his fat neck bulging and sweat dripping from his brow, he cocked his right hand into a fist and waved it menacingly in my face.

"One more word outa you and I'm gonna knock your block off."

Even if I had had a response, even if my voice had found my mouth, I could not have spoken because his hairy hand was crushing my windpipe. He stared at me for a few more seconds, then threw me out the door of the gym. I gingerly walked back to class and never told a soul what had happened.

*

In middle school I stayed away from sports entirely. My peers began to self-sort into teen social cliques. For a boy in a small agricultural town in Colorado at that time, the options were jock, farmer, or freak. (There were also the kids that would later be called nerds, but at that time and place they didn't carry enough weight on the social scale to even get a name.) I was certainly not a jock and was well on my way to becoming a freak. Music was the focus of my attention, especially after dropping my first acid and discovering Jimi

Hendrix. But during the summer between eighth and ninth grade, I got into some trouble, and as a result my parents made me play football. They didn't intend it as punishment exactly. Their idea was that I was hanging out with the wrong crowd, and being part of the football team would set me back on the right track.

Playing football was pretty much the last thing I wanted to do. But as soon as I got out on the football field, I rediscovered the joy in being athletic in my body. And I loved the physicality of football, loved crashing into the other boys with abandon. I was not the fastest or the strongest, but I was quite coordinated. The coach put me in the offensive and defensive line, and I thrived. In practice I would tackle and block so hard the players would complain to the coaches. I loved that: the only freak on the team played so hard that the jocks went crying to their daddies.

Our school had the best football program around and had not lost a game in three years. We won every game and it seemed the streak would go a fourth year, but we lost the last game. After nearly four years of wins, no one on our team knew how to lose, least of all the coaches. Fighting erupted between the teams at the final whistle. A fist fight between our coach and the referee was averted by our livid principal jumping between them.

I just walked off the field, found my parents, and asked them to never ever make me play sports again. On the way home they quietly admitted that maybe their insistence on football had been a mistake. Maybe my real friends had been a step up from the jocks.

The next year I entered high school, and when I did not show up for football practice, the coach sent the entire team in full uniform to my house to try to convince me to join the team. That was a happy moment for me: looking out the door of my house at all those jocks in their football gear and realizing that no one could stop me from saying, in plain English and broad daylight, that there was no way I was going to play football or any other sport. I was free of sports, and coaches.

FARMERS AND COWBOYS

I had loved basketball more than any sport, but that ended my first year of middle school at the preseason organizational meeting of the team. When the coach explained that only boys with military-style crew cuts would be allowed to play, I stood up and walked out. That would have been about 1968, and long hair on boys was the non-negotiable front line of the culture wars, often enforced by violence where I lived. I was considered a long-haired boy once my hair was long enough to cover the tops of my ears. American masculinity was evidently so fragile at the time that an inch of hair could bring the entire edifice crashing down. We didn't have that word *gender* back then, but tearing down or defending gender norms was what everyone on both sides thought they were doing. Pants on girls and long hair on boys. How would we know who was who? How would morality survive? When I walked out of the basketball meeting in front of the coaches and team, I wasn't quite "coming out" as gay the way we think of it now, but it was something close. And anyway, I couldn't come out as *gay* because we didn't have that word either. Instead, we fought about hair.

The freakiest kid in my middle school was Doug, a shy boy of small stature and slender frame whose hair ran halfway down his back. One day the boys from the "farmer" clique smuggled sheep shears into school and attempted to pin Doug down on the playground and cut his hair. Defending Doug that day was the closest thing to a real fight I have ever experienced. All the kids gathered around yelling. Me grabbing for the weapon. All of it. When teachers showed up and separated us, Doug still had his hair.

*

In the summers my family would load up into the station wagon and drive to my great grandfather's old house in southern New Mexico. Cowboy country. Real cowboys, who spent their lives on horseback punching cattle in relentless sun, chewing tobacco until their teeth rotted, drinking too much, and defending God, country, and the American way of life. My sisters (one older, two younger) had a great time dating cowboys on those trips. I did not date cowboys. In fact, I tried to keep my distance. I was young and naive about many things in life, and many things about myself, but I knew enough to know that cowboys were dangerous.

Once a month, everyone from all the ranches for miles around gathered for a dance at an abandoned schoolhouse in a ghost town called Lake Valley. I knew it would be a bad idea for me to go (my hair covered my ears) but my parents said I was being ridiculous. A teen-age boy trying to slink away from family activities. Once we got there, for some reason I ended up walking into the schoolhouse after the rest of my family was already inside. There was a group of guys lounging on the steps, chewing tobacco. They noticed me the moment I approached.

"Who-wee, look at her!"

"I get her!"

"No you don't. I saw her first."

I stared straight ahead and climbed the steps. A guy leaped out directly in front of me, and flipped open a switchblade.

"Jump up my ass, longhair."

I turned around and walked back to the car and locked myself in. Eventually my parents wondered where I was and came out to look for me. Again, they thought I was making a big deal over nothing. I would be completely safe inside. The deputy sheriff was even there, for goodness sake. They got me out of the car and walked me into the school house. I noticed the deputy sheriff immediately, because he gave me a sneer like he was a hyena and I was the adolescent zebra at the edge of the herd. Fifteen minutes later, my parents had concluded that the deputy sheriff was part of the problem not part of the solution, and they were grabbing me and my sisters.

"Come on. We are getting Bobby out of here. NOW."

Years later, I sat in a movie theater watching the credits of the film *Brokeback Mountain* roll through a wave of tears that had seemingly welled up from nowhere and would not stop. I was still sitting there crying when people began entering for the next screening.

TEACHERS

I took a summer job as a bellhop. The agricultural college in my town rented out its dorms and other facilities as a convention center during the summer, and working there as a bellhop was a good deal for adolescent boys like me: light work, consistent hours, good money, and lots of idle time hanging out in the office with the other bellhops.

One convention that came through that summer was the American Federation of Teachers, one of the two national teachers' unions. The first teacher whose bags I carried to his room had an air about him I had never experienced before. The way he carried his slender frame. The way he spoke. His limp wrists (really). It was all very effeminate, though I couldn't place it as such at the time. And he was very friendly in a way I also could not place. Not friendly like the few adult men I knew whom I thought were reasonably nice. And not friendly like my peers. A different friendly. I set down his bags and was on my way out of the room when he called me back in to give me a tip. I thanked him and started to go. He called me back again to offer me a Coke. Gee thanks, I told him, but I am working now.

"You sure you can't stay a while? I don't have anything to do."

I thanked him again but told him I really did have to get back to work and returned to the front desk a little puzzled, a little curious, but basically pleased. He had been very nice to me.

The next arrival was very different, a going-to-seed middle aged man with bad breath, a belt buckle he could no longer see, and a face that conveyed a sour disposition. Like the previous man, he gave me a big tip and kept searching for reasons for me not to leave his room after I had set down his suitcases. But this time, the extra attention I was receiving was not pleasant. This guy was a creep. That was a word that was actually in my vocabulary, and had anyone asked me about him back at the bellhop lounge, that is what I would have called him. I told him I had to get back to work. He asked what time I got off. I told him five pm. Why did I tell him that? I don't know. He insisted that I meet him in the bar downstairs after work. I headed out the door thinking there was no way in hell I would be meeting him in a bar downstairs or any other place. How could I get into a bar anyway? I wasn't old enough to drive.

When five rolled around and I punched out my time card in the bellhop lounge, I headed out the door to my bicycle but at some point my feet turned and began leading me to the bar. What was I thinking? I wasn't thinking. Some invisible pair of hands reached into my head, took out my own agency and placed it carefully in a box, sealed it tight, and set it high on a shelf where I couldn't reach it. Something else was in charge now. I don't know what.

I found him seated at a table with four or five other men. He invited me to sit down. I sat down. None of the other men at the table batted an eye. He offered to buy me a drink. I asked for a Coke. He ordered me one. I didn't want to be there. The whole thing was creepy. I didn't like him. I didn't like anything about him. But some invisible force field I was at loss to understand was pinning me down to my chair. What were the men talking about? I have no idea. How did I even get into the bar? No clue. A crack in the force field was somehow opened by the arrival of my Coke, and I mumbled that I had to go, jumped to my feet, and nearly ran out the door. He followed me.

In the hall outside the bar he called out, commanding me to stop. The force field was back, placing me on instant lock-down. I stood stock still while he continued at a leisurely pace until he was standing directly opposite me. The smell of his foul breath was overpowering me in the summer heat.

He reached out and rubbed his hand on my crotch.

"What's the matter, don't you like this?"

The force field closed in even tighter. Not only could I not run, I couldn't move my jaw or tongue. I couldn't even find my mouth. I resolutely stared at the floor.

"There's nothing wrong with this."

My eyes were drilling holes in the linoleum with a high-speed krypton bit. I would be hitting bedrock soon.

My penis sprung to life. I couldn't help it. I couldn't make my penis stay soft any more than I could make my feet run for the door.

"You see, you like it."

He smiled. A parched snake-bite of a crooked smile in a desert of icy hot panic. Once again I felt a tiny crack in the force field and lunged for it. I was out the door, running as fast as I could. I didn't stop running until I was back at the bellhop lounge.

I ran in and told my boss at least some of the details of the story, and the next thing I knew the other bellhops were looking at me in a funny way I had never been looked at before, and asking questions. Why had I gone there in the first place? Why hadn't I just run? The floor began to slip out from under me.

My boss, a young and attractive man I liked very much, rose to the occasion. Apparently, I was not the only bellhop who had reported such problems, though the others had the good sense not to tell their tales in front of their peers. He very calmly walked over and sat down in front of me, the very image of kindness and reassurance. His soft but firm tone that told me that he had the situation well in hand and I had nothing to fear.

"Now, if that guy or anyone else does anything like that to you again, I want you to kick him in the nuts as hard as you can, and then I want you to come straight to me and tell me what happened. In the meantime, I am going to the head of this whole convention and tell him that if his teachers can't keep their hands off my bellhops, I am personally going to see to it that his entire convention is shut down."

With those kind words, the clouds parted and all was right with the world again. The other bellhops shrugged and went back to their card game. I could have leapt into my boss's arms and hugged him tight. Thinking back on it now, I am struck at how closely his reassurance echoed the reassurance my grade school basketball coach had offered me when the older kids had ambushed me. At that moment too I would have been perfectly happy to snuggle into his lap for a long, cozy nap.

How did I get into the bar? The whole cultural obsession with keeping kids out of bars was already in full force. On several occasions my friends and I had tried to sneak into bars but always without success. But this was not a normal bar. It was the basement of a college-dorm-turned-convention-housing, made into a temporary bar for teachers from the union drinking liquor they had brought themselves. And in this makeshift barroom full of teachers who were respected enough by their peers to be elected union reps, a thirteen-year-old boy walked in and sat down at a table of pederasts without anyone batting an eye. One of whom followed the kid out of the bar.

I thank my lucky stars that these events occurred in 1970 and not today. Had they happened today, almost certainly the police would have been called, and in addition to having to deal with the creep in the bar for a few minutes, I would have to deal with big men with uniforms and badges and guns and nightsticks. Not for a few minutes but for a very long time. A legal process would have begun that I would have been a prisoner of for weeks, months, or even years. I would be sent to "experts" who would have explained that something terrible had happened to me, something that probably caused me lasting damage that would require professional help.

Instead, I got sixty seconds of kindness from a compassionate man who let me know I would be all right, that I had permission to fight off men like that, and that he had my back. The best remedy I can imagine.

MICHAEL

Michael was the son of friends of my parents, who had lived in Albuquerque when they were younger before they moved to northern
Colorado. Our family would pass through Albuquerque on our way
to ranch country on our summer car trips, and Michael and I would
be tossed together to play in a way that had nothing to do with the
choice of the child, and which children so often find unwanted. Still,
I wanted to play with Michael. Not at first. But after a while I did.
I even made up a story that he was my cousin. He came to visit me
unaccompanied by his parents when I was in sixth or seventh grade.

Michael was exceptionally beautiful. I could not have said that
about him at the time, but he was, and that drew me to him. A bud-
ding heartthrob for sure. But more than his beauty, there was a
sense of wildness about him that I found magnetic. Michael was
up for anything. One night we stayed up in my room folding the
newspapers for my newspaper delivery job in the morning. With
his let's-break-the-rules smile, Michael said, "Let's take our shirts
off and shoot rubber bands at our nipples." Such an idea would
have never occurred to me, and if, by some miracle it did, I would
most certainly not have voiced it. But once Michael said it, it was all
great. Off went our shirts, and we spent the rest of the night happily

shooting rubber bands at each other's nipples and laughing.

How I wished I had been like Michael. So open and adventurous and unconstrained and *sexy*. Ha! That was not me. There was a sexual bravado to Michael that is generally only granted to the exceptionally beautiful. Beauty is a kind of power. And Michael knew it. Maybe didn't know it in his head, but felt it right down to his bones. In his cock for sure. Michael and I grew apart because of all of that. He was on a fast track I could not keep up with.

How I wish I could talk with Michael now. Trade stories about rubber bands and nipples and the timidity and abandon of youth. Laugh and drink and sort out what was *really* going on in our young lives.

But I cannot. Michael moved out of his parents' house into the home of an older leather daddy and died of AIDS. Boom. Gone. Sorry about that. Leaving behind parents broken with grief.

Beauty is a power tool, but power tools cut both ways.

How lonely life can be.

His parents never recovered from the loss. Sadness was etched into their faces. Their postures became stooped under the weight which they carried the rest of their lives.

THE FREAK

Our little Colorado town was as white as the Colorado snow until you crossed the railroad tracks to where the Latino farmworkers lived. But one day while I was in high school an apparition appeared seemingly out of nowhere. His skin was black like black coal. With this ear-to-ear smile of perfectly white teeth. He was tall, maybe six foot five or more. And skinny. That alone would have made him one-of-a-kind where I lived, but there was so much more. He played electric guitar with a wah-wah pedal like Jimi Hendrix. He wore crazy clothes. He walked around town in a silver cape and purple goggles. Oh, and he was beautiful. I had never met a man who was beautiful like that. And he had a girlfriend, who was a black as he was, and as beautiful, and as tall, and spoke English with a French accent. Dazzling.

This was about the time that "hippies" turned into "freaks." Things that had recently been "cool" were now "freaky." Jimi Hendrix was singing a new song about waving his freak flag high.

If you don't think that a pair of towering black lovers in silver capes and purple goggles weren't waving a freak flag high on the streets of my little town, then you aren't paying attention to what I am saying.

I never knew how they arrived in such an unlikely place, had no idea what they had done or who they had been before they showed up in my life. And they never offered any details. They were just suddenly here. Maybe they had been living in a black community for which they had been too freaky and decided to see what living in some honky white town was like. Maybe they were running from something. Maybe it was all an art project. Maybe ... actually, I have no clue why they were there. But they were.

And here is the best part: they both really liked me. They liked having me around. And they had their own place. A parent-free zone! With them in it! And I was welcome there! I was a devoted electric guitar player back then. He and I were at about the same skill level. And we were both Jimi Hendrix devotees. So we worked on guitar licks together, and talked about this and that. Every time she would look at me and smile I would melt into a puddle. I had the feeling that she thought of me as a sort of pet, like a dog she really liked. Did she actually pet me once? I have an image of that dancing on the edge of memory. But him... Well, even though I didn't know what gay meant, didn't know that men sometimes kissed each other and sometimes did even more, I think I wasn't far from wanting to kiss him with every fiber of my being. In retrospect, he would have been the safest man to try to kiss I knew. Whether he would have wanted it or not I have no idea, but I am certain that neither he nor his lover would have been bothered by it, and it might have even made us closer friends. These were very freaky open-minded people. But I did nothing of the sort. He was just so *too much*. I mean, my sexy meter was only just being assembled, and it went from zero to a hundred. He would have rated in the thousands and blown every fuse, along with my mind.

Then one night the two of them had a party at their place for all the young friends they had been making. For some reason I cannot remember, I couldn't go. And the police burst in with guns drawn.

Now, to understand this moment requires a little context. Our little town had a sort of Andy of Mayberry vibe. We were in the Rocky Mountains, not in the south, and we were a bit bigger than Mayberry, but police in our town did not take out their guns much. I ran with kids who bought and sold drugs, and took more than our fair share, and we were always dodging the cops, and coming within an inch of getting busted, but there were never guns involved. Never.

These two beautiful people had done *nothing*, and the police busted into their party with guns drawn.

The next day they were gone for parts unknown.

And that was that.

THE CREEP

The creep is sitting across from me in a dimly lit room with his hands in front of his face, fingertips gently touching. In his creepy voice, he intones:

Now you are taking off her bra.

Now you are feeling her breasts.

Now you are taking off her panties.

The teenage me is sitting across from the creep. I have rubber cups like you would find on the end of spark plugs covering two fingertips. Wires run from the cups to an odd-looking electronic device which is buzzing and bleeping away, sounding like Robby the Robot from *Lost in Space*. I am sweating. Completely creeped out. Can I please be anywhere but here?

The creep is a psychiatrist or psychologist or some such thing. He works for the county health department in my little Colorado town. Good taxpayer money is paying him to do this.

What in the world...?

When I was a kid, I hung out with the kids that wanted to

experiment with sex and drugs as soon as possible. I think my first attempt at vaginal intercourse occurred at thirteen years of age. It went pretty much like one would expect. Of course, I was totally nervous and nearly overcome with anxiety. But over the next few years, that anxiety did not go away. I was as attracted to girls as I thought a boy should be, and sex between boys and girls in my crowd was not only expected but pretty much mandatory. But as much as I would think about it, and want it, and make arrangements for it to happen, come the moment I would be hit by debilitating anxiety.

Somehow I told an adult about my "problem." I think it was a priest. Not my father, certainly, but a sort of hippie priest my father knew. Anyway, he recommended I talk to someone, and so on, and eventually I ended up at the country health department with this creep. He instructed me to go to Radio Shack and buy their Science Fair Lie Detector. Then I was to bring it to appointments with him, hook myself up to the wires, he would turn the lights down low, and he would talk through a hypothetical encounter with a girl that would end in vaginal intercourse. The Radio Shack gizmo was supposed to measure my anxiety level. Every time its whining indicated an increase in anxiety, he would pause at that point in the narrative, lingering at one kind of foreplay or another while I tried to relax enough to quiet the machine. Then he would move on to the grand finale of vaginal penetration.

The whole thing was just so *weird* it is hard to take in the whole scene, even in memory. Who was this *weird* guy, telling me to go to Radio Shack and do all this *weird* stuff?

Of course, he didn't ask me if I might be *gay*. This would have been around 1970. As far as shrinks were concerned, homos were sick people. But in small town Colorado that question was not going to be asked, even to make a diagnosis of disease. But beyond that, why did this guy think that a teenage boy's anxiety about fucking pussy was a behavioral problem treatable with Radio Shack's home electronics version of a Skinner Box?

I am quite certain that this "problem" actually served me well, for without it I would have likely gotten one particular girl pregnant. And another guy I knew *did* get her pregnant, and it became an unbelievable mess, partly because she was a mess, and partly because the other guy was a criminal, but I didn't know that, and one day he wanted to buy some weed, so I took him to the house of some folks who lived just outside of town who dealt weed, but they weren't home. It seemed they were out of town, and that night he went back to their house and broke in and ripped off all their stuff, and those poor folks came back and found their house trashed, but they couldn't call the cops because they were weed dealers, and they threw everything they had left into their pickup and skipped town with no forwarding address, and somehow I got called in to the police station to make a witness statement to the effect that I had taken this guy out to that house to buy weed, but the guy had put out the word that if I ratted on him he would kill me, and I told that to the police, and they told me not to worry because he was going to be locked up for a long time, so I signed the witness paper, and then very shortly after that he was out of jail, allegedly because he had ratted on someone else, and now he was back in town saying he was going to kill me, and then his girl, who had been my girl, had a baby, and the only reason we knew it was not my baby was because of the "problem" I was trying to resolve with the Radio Shack thing, so the problem turned out to be quite the blessing.

But mostly what I remember about this strangest of chapters is how creepy it was, sitting in this guy's dimmed office, him sitting with his fingertips touching just in front of his face, and him talking me through his middle-aged man's fantasy of fucking a teenage girl while the machine I was wired to bleeped and blooped.

In hindsight, it strikes me as sexual abuse. Certainly, it left a bigger, uglier mark on me than the teacher who groped me.

As an adult, whenever I hear someone talk about how much better teenagers have it these days because they have so much better access to professional mental health care, I think, "Well, maybe."

BUSTER AND BUDDY

Buster and Buddy, the inseparable pair. "Look," people would say, "There goes Buster and Buddy." At least that was how whoever gave them their nicknames imagined it at the outset, when they were still too young for the outlines of who they would become to come into focus.

He was Buster, his older brother Buddy. Which was another joke, because Buster was not about to bust up anything or anybody. Buddy, the older one, was a bully and a braggart, with a mean streak a foot deep and a mile wide. Buster was quiet and introverted, more interested in the piano in the living room than in dominating the neighborhood. And the kid had an ear for it. On summer nights, when the west Texas desert sun seemed to have scorched the oxygen clean out of the sky in those years before air conditioning, Buster would rehearse his classical repertoire with the front door open, serenading the dusty neighborhood.

It was, or had been, a middle-class neighborhood but you would hardly have hardly known it because the Depression was in full swing. Their father somehow held on to his optometry practice and thus some income, but less fortunate neighbors were reduced to coming to houses like his to beg for food.

The household was run with all the austere formality one would expect of a conservative petty bourgeois German immigrant optometrist. At meals the children kept their elbows off the table and did not speak unless spoken to. They addressed their father as "Mr. Ostertag." Even the mother referred to her husband that way. "Just you wait until Mr. Ostertag gets home," she would admonish the boys when they misbehaved.

As for the mother, what can we say? She was as vindictive and manipulative as her eldest son was mean and bullying. One hundred years later a psychiatrist would have given her a learned diagnosis and a prescription, but El Paso had neither psychiatrists nor psychiatric medicine at the time.

Her punishments were unusual. A favorite was to lock Buster into the cramped crawl space just above the ceiling, to sort out his misdeeds in the dark with the spiders. And then there was the whole matter about his older sister who had died in childhood on the same date Buster was born. So every year on Buster's birthday, his mother covered all the furniture in black fabric and locked herself in her room where she would cry all day. There was never a cake, or a present, or any acknowledgement that the day marked two occasions and not one.

Buster tried to take it all in stride. He tolerated Buddy's bullying, his father's remoteness, his mother's sadism, the day of mourning that was his birthday. He sure did love that piano. He did his best to fit in with his peers. Even went drinking across the border in Juarez with the guys when he was old enough. But it took effort. Like acting. There was always this unspoken distance that went beyond the effect of the glasses he wore for his poor eyesight.

Hitler came to power, and life took a turn for the worse in the house with the austere German father and the crazy English mother.

Buddy's bullying now took the form of loudly celebrating each Nazi victory. He did this in part because he liked the Nazis, in part to aggravate his English mother, but mostly because he just loved to bully his younger brother Buster, who believed in FDR, the New Deal, and the essential goodness of American democracy. Then the US entered the war, Buddy joined the Navy and became a pilot, and Buster was drafted into the Army.

Buster became a medic and was assigned to a field hospital that followed General Eisenhower across Europe, moving just behind the front lines. A battle would begin and a river of wounded men would flow into the tent. Quick decisions were made over who was salvageable and who would die. Living go over here, dying over there. Corpses over that way. Arms in this pile, legs in that one. He almost never spoke about any of this for the rest of his life. He didn't stay in touch with war buddies. No clubs. No parades. No reminiscences over drinks. He developed a lifelong phobia of all things German and a passion for all things English and Russian, his country's two principal war allies.

He returned home from the war to find his mother fawning over his swashbuckling fighter pilot brother, whose earlier support of the Nazis was now forgotten. Everyone loves a winner. He looked in the drawer where he kept his precious piano scores but the drawer was empty. "Oh, I didn't realize you wanted all that," his mother explained. "I burned it all."

Buddy liked the Navy – the violence, machismo, the rigid hierarchy, and the money. He became a career pilot.

Buster had made it through the war under the mentorship of an Episcopal chaplain assigned to the field hospital, and had decided that if and when he made it home he would become an Episcopal priest too. And he did.

Each married and had children.

Their mother made some half-hearted attempts at suicide, then checked herself into a nursing home. She was actually in fine physical health, but confining herself to a nursing home provided daily confirmation of her psychotic belief that no one in her family cared about her.

Buddy had a career in the Navy, becoming the commanding officer on the flight deck of the USS Enterprise, the Navy's first nuclear-powered aircraft carrier. He left the Navy for work as a military contractor specializing in "nuclear security" all the while becoming meaner and more erratic.

He carried laminated placards in his sports car that said things like USE YOUR BLINKER ASSHOLE, which he would flash at those whose driving he disapproved of. When the placards proved insufficient he would jump out of his car in the middle of traffic and beat the crap out other drivers.

When Buster's son hit his teenage years, Buddy sat him down for a man-to-man talk about the facts of the world. "You know what the problem with this country is, young man? The problem is that people like you and me, white men, have nobody representing them in Washington. The women, the niggers, the spics, they all got their people. Who do we got? Nobody!"

This would have been around 1970, when the President and Vice President, the Cabinet, the Senate and House, the Joint Chiefs of Staff, and the members of every corporate board in the country were almost entirely white men.

Buddy's wife divorced him. His children stopped talking to him. But not Buster. Buster's children, now grown and well-aware of the emotional toll paid by Buster for dealing with his brother, urged him to break off communication. Buster would not hear of it. Family first, he said. You always reach out your hand. That is the part you control. Whether they take it or not is up to them.

Buster grew old and moved into assisted living. One night the phone rang and Buddy was on the line. "Ed," he began (they had long stopped using their childhood nicknames), "I'm dying. There is something I have always wanted to tell you, and I must say it now."

"Say it then."

"I hate you, and I have always hated you."

BUSTER AND HIS FAMILY

Buster married a pretty girl from Albuquerque, of English heritage of course. On his wedding night, he woke up to a tower of coffins falling onto the bed. In the nick of time, he threw his bride out of one side of the bed while he leaped out of the other. The newlyweds stood on either side of the bed, staring at each other. He panting and sweating, grateful that the coffins had not hurt her. She in confusion. Only then did he realize he had been dreaming.

They landed in a small church in a small Rocky Mountain town. Being a parish priest suited him. "For those who never felt like they found their place in the world, being a minister gives you that ready-made," he once explained. "You show up as the new priest, everyone loves you, welcomes you, invites you to dinner and to weddings and baptisms, seeks your counsel, and tells you their secrets." He was good at it, and his bride embraced the role of minister's wife. She tried to fashion herself after the tough Western gals she had looked up to as a child: family first, best foot forward, keep a sunny disposition and a stiff upper lip, don't ask for much, no whining, play the hand you are dealt, and never, ever talk about your own feelings.

His church grew. His family grew, three girls and a boy. He was a good dad, if sometimes a bit aloof and removed. Until he would suddenly fly into a rage and beat his son in a manner that seemed incomprehensible for a man like him. One time he burst into the bathroom where the boy was peeing, screaming, "I am going to paddle your bare bottom!"

As the boy grew into adolescence, paddling his bare bottom evolved into straight up beatings with fists. It didn't happen often, and in that part of the country, well, the boy had a friend whose father beat him when he got home from work as a matter of course, to go with the man's beer. The boys would hightail it out the back door, or even out the bedroom window, if the father showed up unexpectedly. But the fact that Buster's beatings didn't happen often made them that much harder for the boy to understand. That, and the way Buster would suddenly explode out of his usual self in a way he clearly could not control. The boy never fought back, though he did run away after one such episode. After a week away he returned home. "You're just in time for dinner," his mother told him without looking up from her cooking. "Would you please set the table." The boy's absence of a week was never spoken of or acknowledged in any way.

Outside the home, the man's New Deal idealism found an easy home in the relatively liberal Episcopal Church of the time and the cultural shifts of the 1960s. He became the public face of sixties liberalism in the town. He supported civil rights, women's libera-tion, bitterly opposed the Vietnam war, and worked to improve race relations between the lily white farm town and the migrant worker ghetto just on the other side of the railroad tracks. He made national news in 1980 marrying a gay male couple in his church. The most conservative members of his congregation fled. Most of the flock adored him.

But all was not well. He began to cry every now then. Then more often. Then he was crying a lot.

One day he told his wife what it had taken him more than fifty years to say aloud, that he thought he might be gay. She replied, "We will never speak of this again."

A few months later his head exploded.

It happened on a Sunday morning. He just walked out of the church sanctuary in the middle of mass. His wife found him in his office, hiding under his desk, crying uncontrollably, unable to breathe. The drive down the highway to the mental hospital in Denver was terrible. Buster in hysterics, trying to open the door and jump out to his death. His wife trying to drive, keep the door locked, and calm him down all at the same time. He ended up in a padded cell under 24-hour suicide watch for three months, then another three months in a regular unit, then many months of intensive outpatient care and disability.

In the mental hospital, he told his psychiatrist that he might be gay. The psychiatrist assured both him and his wife that this man was not actually gay, he just had some issues with his crazy mother that needed to be worked out. It would take some work, but they could do it.

As far as both he and his wife were concerned, they had promised God they would remain together until death did they part, and that was that. Gay or straight, sane or sick, they could not go back on God. She sold the house in their town, got a small apartment near the mental hospital in Denver for her and the two daughters still living at home, and a job at a travel agency.

Over the ensuing years, he carved out a sort of liberated zone in the family's increasingly bizarre existence which both his wife and his

only child left at home were determined not to notice. At first just a
few very small things. There was a bodybuilder calendar in his closet.
Not "in the closet" like gay people say, but literally in his closet.
Actually, in the closet he shared with his wife. He had given it to his
wife as a present, though it was obviously meant for him and not her.
She said thank you very much and hung it in the closet. Best foot
forward, stiff upper lip, no whining, and no emotions.

He took aerobics classes at a gay leather bar. ("Well, you know
I really wanted to get in shape, and I looked around for an aerobics
class, and there weren't any at times and places that worked for me,
and then finally I found this one at the gay bar, and I thought, 'Well,
I don't mind if they don't mind.'")

His wife came down with an extraordinarily rare disease in which
the body attacks and destroys itself. Her immune system went after
her own organs as if they were foreign invaders. It was going to be a
bumpy ride, but the disease progression would be rapid. He would
care for her and love her, and then she would gone and he would
begin the gay life he dreamed of. And then she outlived her diagnosis by years, as if she were holding him to their marriage by holding
on to life. His patience grew thin.

Her kidneys went first, leaving her dependent on dialysis. As they
had moved to a ghost town in the desert at his insistence to try to
calm his nerves, dialysis was not simple. Or rather, it could have been
simple. In-home dialysis was by far the easiest option, but he would
have to be trained to administer it, and he refused. The alternative
was the hospital in the nearest real town, a two hour drive over a
mountain pass from their ghost town in the desert. So he drove her,
hours of driving, week in week out, complaining about it all the way.
The no whining part had been his wife's commitment, not his.

Finally, a day came when they were preparing for the dialysis drive and he was whining away and she announced, "I'm not going."

They both knew that refusing dialysis meant certain death within seventy-two hours.

She called her children, told them of her decision, and told them not to come.

The two sat on the sofa. "If there is anything we have to say to each other, now is the time to say it," he began. "I would like to say that if I have done anything to hurt you over the years, I apologize. Is there anything you would like to say?"

"I can't imagine my life without you," she replied. And then she was gone.

He waited a year from her passing, then told his children (who by then had known for years) that he "might be bisexual." Gee Dad, no kidding? Wow. We never would have guessed. But by then he was seventy years old and living in a ghost town, so his options for exploring a gay lifestyle were limited. Even after coming out to his children, he could not approach the subject except through an elaborate maze of detours and u-turns. The following story must have meant a lot to him, because he told it to both his daughter and closest friend in exactly the same words.

> I had to go into Albuquerque to sign some papers a few weeks ago, and I didn't want to impose on the same old friends and relatives so I thought maybe I would stay in a bed and breakfast. And then I thought well, why not a gay bed and breakfast? So I asked around to see what might be available and found a *nude* gay bed and breakfast. So off I went, and I checked in. And when it was time to go to bed I found I couldn't get to sleep so

I went to the front desk and asked if they had any reading material.

And they said, "Why yes we do. What sort of reading material might you be interested in?"

And I said, "Well I think I might be interested in S&M."

So they gave me a copy of *Drummer* magazine [a gay porn magazine from the seventies and eighties that fetishized the most conventionally macho of men]. And I took it back to my room and opened it up and there was a picture of my son!

Both people who later recounted his telling of the story then asked him, "Umm, are you sure it was your son?"

"Oh yes," he replied. "It was the back of his left shoulder. I would recognize it anywhere."

It had taken him more than seventy years to speak aloud of his sadism. He was handed a porn magazine and opened it up and what do you know, there was his son.

Me.

More specifically, the back of my left shoulder, which he would recognize anywhere.

I have never appeared in any pornography anywhere.

Unless you were to ask my father.

*

My father was not a bad man. Looking around the world at the scale of such things, he was a good man. He certainly tried very hard to be a good man. And many remember him as such. I still have the eagle feathers and chief regalia given him by the Lakota of South Dakota when they made him an honorary Lakota chief for what they considered to be his exceptional service to the tribe. I am proud of them. My father at his best. But my father was very, very complicated. Like me. Like you. Like all of us. Running into his complexities could be like running into a buzzsaw. You never knew if you were going to get the beloved community leader known for his compassion and empathy, or the man disfigured with anger bellowing how he was going to beat your bare ass. Like reaching into a magic hat and not knowing if you were going to pull out a rabbit or snarling lion. And at the end of the day, I don't think it is accurate to say that he killed my mother, but the truth of her death includes something of that. I think he understood that, and it became one more stone in the massive pile of guilt he carried through his life.

Like he was the son of his parents, like all of us are the children of our parents, I am his son. As much in what I am not as in what I am. I detest religion. I am allergic to ritual. I don't hang my attraction to men in my closet. I don't dance around it, don't pray about it, don't ask forgiveness for it, don't explain it away, don't save it for later. I put it front and center. I want to see men clearly and completely: sadists, masochists, all of it. No flinching, and no quarter.

JERRY AND GEORGE

Jerry and George were my closest friends in high school. We grew our hair long, took lots of LSD, wore the kind of clothes that wannabe hippie kids stuck in a small Colorado town in the early 1970s wore, and pretty much lived in each other's pockets.

We came from very different families. My family was, at least from outside appearances, the picture of middle class stability, with a preacher dad, the minister's wife, four kids, a cat and a dog. Jerry lived outside of town with his redneck parents, a younger brother who was as emotionally expressive as yesterday's mashed potatoes, and a redneck littlest brother who tried too hard to be the mean macho man Jerry was not. His mother was an obese woman who never stopped yapping but had nothing to say. His smaller and quieter father basically sulked around the house while his wife carried on, until he exploded and did stuff like throw hammers at his kids.

I never met George's parents. George never talked about them. All I knew about them was that at some point George had decided things between him and his parents just weren't working out and he put himself up for adoption. He got taken in as a foster child by a very kind married couple who were born again Christians before that was even a thing to be. This was a very confusing situation for

George, who listened to Frank Zappa, grew his hair down to his butt, and was pretty much the freakiest kid in town. He basically owed his life to his foster parents, even though he had nothing to say to them or their God.

George was sad a lot.

George played bass, Jerry played drums, and I played guitar. Jerry and I played in various bands around town. George always wanted to join, but that never worked out because George could never focus long enough to practice much. The time that Jerry or I would spend in our bedrooms practicing our instruments, George would spend lying on his bed and staring at the ceiling, or, frankly, doing I don't know what.

George and Jerry were always up for doing crazy shit, the freakier the better. We didn't know we could be gay but we could be weird. We watched freaky movies like *One Flew Over the Cuckoo's Nest* and the psychedelic western *Zachariah* (our options were limited, as neither video tape or for that matter "independent cinema" had been invented, and foreign films never came to our little town), listened to freaky music like Miles Davis's electric period (which was actually possible, thank goodness for records and FM radio), and wore freaky clothes. We threw ourselves into making our own weird movies, music, and clothes. My last year in high school we made a movie as a class assignment. It was called *Cleetus Allreetus Allrightus: A Legend in His Own Thyme*, which was just a series of scenes featuring George and Jerry doing the craziest stuff our small-town adolescent minds could think of: Jerry dressed like a television set dancing through our school study hall; George in a toga diving into a swimming pool; Jerry taking a bath of food we took from the fridge. More than anything else, we listened to music, played music, and dropped acid, tripping our way through high school.

We were always up for flaunting freaky behavior because we were dancing all around – but never confronting – the freakiest part of us. It is hard to convey to people in the twenty-first century how unavailable the whole idea of being gay was in a small town in Colorado in the early 1970s. The Stonewall riot had happened a short time before, but that was in New York City. The Castro was emerging as a gay Mecca, but that was in San Francisco. A few years after I left my home town, a gay student group formed on the local college campus. Some time after that, one bookstore started carrying gay-themed titles. Some time after that, a small gay bar appeared in a trailer on the outskirts of town. But when George and Jerry and I were growing up there was nothing. No group, no book, no bar, no dirty magazine hidden under the cash register available only by request, no internet, no YouTube, no people, no words. Nothing. Not that, as high school students, we would have found the men or books or bars if they had been there. For us, the possibility of being boys who loved boys was simply not part of the known universe.

We didn't even have language for it. Certainly I had never heard the term "gay," and I am uncertain whether I had even heard the term "homosexual." As kids we had played a rough all-on-one game on the playground called "Smear the Queer," but I had no idea what queer referred to. The one term I was familiar with was "corn-holing," which I knew meant to butt fuck, but with animals, and I didn't think anyone actually did that. I thought it was just part of the trash talking the farmer kids engaged in to make themselves sound more sexually confident than they were. It seemed incomprehensible that any of them had actually fucked a sheep in the butt.

Looking back now, I am not so sure they didn't.

Around about 1970, I was in the first class in my school to receive "sex education." It happened during middle school gym class, which was run by the wrestling coach. There were always vague sexual rumors and innuendo that followed this coach and his wrestling team around. In retrospect, I suspect all kinds of shenanigans went on with that team, but none of us eventually-to-be-gay kids went near the wrestlers. (Later, I read a book about gay American men in the Second World War, and how often times they hid on the side for fear of being found out, while the straight guys engaged in all kinds of sexual experimentation.)

The coach, a squat bulldog of a man, had a habit of walking around PE class in his gym shorts scratching his balls. "Coach" came to journalism class one day to talk about sports journalism, and it was revealed that he could not spell at middle school level. He reveled in it though, standing in front of the class, scratching his balls, and admitting with a smile, "Spelling never was one of my gooder sports."

But Coach did not do the sex education himself. He retreated to his office at the far end of the locker room, leaving us boys assembled on the locker room benches before a somewhat odd, tall, and very thin specialist who came in from somewhere to lead us through three lectures on the ins and outs of sex education. The last session covered venereal disease, or "VD." The tall thin man went through the basics of syphilis and gonorrhea, and then opened the floor for questions. He emphasized that even though this was an embarrassing subject for teenagers, this was our big chance to ask any question at all, without fear of ridicule or punishment. Nothing was off limits. Don Dunn raised his hand, smirked, and asked, "Can you get VD from corn-holing?" Coach's voice shot out of his office and silenced the laughter. "Dunn! Get in here! I am going to beat your butt!" Coach made Don Dunn bend over and grab his ankles while Coach beat his ass with a board.

Less than a decade after Don Dunn "got the board" for asking if you could contract disease from corn-holing, gay men started dying by the thousands from a disease they contracted from corn-holing. The then-President of the United States could not bring himself to say the name of the disease aloud. Maybe he was afraid of getting his ass beaten with a board.

LSD was like an instant jailbreak from the confines of life in a farm town just becoming suburban. This was true for many young people at the time. It is impossible to understand the sixties and early seventies in our country without taking LSD into account. The fact is that many, many members of a generation, from rich to poor, rural to urban, student council presidents to dropouts, future soldiers and future farmers, swallowed a tiny dose of a chemical and woke up the next day thinking that the values they had grown up on were phony, and the world their parents lived in was a façade.

But Jerry's trips started going bad, each one worse than the last. He spent one trip crying, his hands covering his face. "My soul! My soul!" We held his hand and tried to talk him through it.

To us at the time, that was just LSD. It could take you on all kinds of unexpected journeys. Who knew what lay in wait once you dropped? That was both the risk and the adventure. It was all deep, and all meaningful, the ritual of freaky teenage culture. Some kind of truth would be forged on the journey.

Except for Jerry. We started counseling Jerry that perhaps he should give LSD a rest. But Jerry did not stop going back to that well, looking for that trip that would at last free his mind.

LSD, it turned out, was not addictive, and thank goodness for that, because we probably would have taken it one way or the other. It was not addiction that kept Jerry coming back, but the promise of freedom.

Finally, there came a day when Jerry and his next younger brother dropped acid and went for a drive to the lake west of town. By this time all of Jerry's friends would have strongly advised him against doing any more acid, but his brother had no opinions about much of anything, and for that matter rarely spoke at all. A strangely emotionally vacant kid. They ran out of gas coming home and decided to turn off the car and coast, not knowing that killing the engine would lock the steering wheel, and they ran the car off the road. They ended up at our friend Stuart's house. Stuart felt the situation was over his head and asked me to come help. Jerry's parents and aunt arrived shortly after I did.

From the moment his parents burst through the door, it was clear that this was not going to end at all well. His mother *ran* into the house with his aunt close behind, and scurried back and forth between Stuart and me, bending over and putting her fat face inappropriately close to ours while cooing in an unsettling imitation of the tone one might use to address a three-year-old, "Honey, what did they take? What did they take?" Meanwhile, Jerry's father went back and forth between Jerry and his brother, admonishing them to pull themselves together and act like men. Jerry just sat in his chair and cried. His brother stared at the wall and tried very hard to be somewhere else. Somehow in the chaos it was decided that they would all go to Burger King, which would make everything better. (Jerry was vegetarian.) Parents and aunt whisked the brothers out the door and for a moment Stuart and I sat there feeling the sudden calm left in the wake of a tornado, and then we heard a scream. We ran to the window to see Jerry lying face down on the front lawn while his father kicked him in the head. Then his father yelled, "Where's Ostertag, I'm going to get Ostertag," and ran back towards the house, which sent me out the back window, across the yard, over the backyard fence, and then running with no particular destination in mind.

I did not understand why, but Jerry's parents were certain that I was responsible for anything in Jerry to which they objected. So from Stuart's house they went to my house. My eleven-year-old sister was home alone watching TV when three unhinged adults she had never laid eyes on burst in and ran through every room in the house shouting for my parents. They grabbed my sister and screamed, "Little girl, where are your parents? Where are your parents?" then rushed back out of the house as abruptly was they had entered. A while later my parents came home to find my sister cowering in the dark with all the doors locked.

When Burger King failed to make anything better, Jerry's parents headed to the emergency room. My father happened to be at the hospital too, visiting sick people, as clergy often do. Somehow he crossed paths with Jerry and his panicked parents. Jerry grabbed my father and asked if they could talk. Seeing my father's clerical collar, his parents consented, and my father took Jerry for a drive so they could talk in private.

I knew this because my father called home to say that he was going for a drive with Jerry and would be home later than planned. I was full of trepidation at what was going to happen when he got home. Certainly, he was going to know that Jerry was tripping, and that his parents somehow thought I was to blame for all his problems. There was going to be hell to pay.

When he arrived, I had never seen him in such a state, shaking with rage.

"*SIT DOWN.*"

Done.

"I only have two things to say. First, your friend Jerry is a fine young man. A little confused, but a fine young man. He is welcome at our house any time. Second, I *never EVER* want you around his parents. You are not to go to his house, not to ride in a car with them, not to be around them at any time. *DO YOU UNDERSTAND ME?*"

Outside my head I said, "I understand."

Inside my head I thought, Wow, Dad. Really? What? I might have really loved my father at that moment, or perhaps felt proud of him, but mostly I felt a relief that I did not want to examine too closely.

Back at Jerry's house things were not going nearly so well. Jerry had been acid tripping through a car crash, an assault, a hamburger, and a hospital, all with parents who had driven my father (who was not doing acid) berserk in just a few minutes. By the time his parents got him home, Jerry had stopped talking or doing basically anything at all. His parents took him to his bedroom and laid him on his bed on his back with his hands crossed over his chest, as if he was a corpse they were arranging in a casket. Then, finally, they left him alone.

Jerry laid there for a time, wondering if he was actually dead. Then he got up, walked out of the house, across the back yard, and into the river that ran past his house. It was January in northern Colorado. The ground was covered with snow and the river bank was icy. Jerry was wearing jeans and nothing else, but Jerry was beyond feeling cold. He just walked into river and disappeared into the night. Maybe that was where the freedom he was looking for could be found.

A sheriff's deputy picked him out of the river when he was spotted approaching a bridge. His frostbitten feet were in such critical condition that the hospital nearly amputated them. In the end Jerry got to keep his feet, though he could not walk on them for some time. He did not speak for even longer.

Weeks went by. Jerry had to quit school. He never spoke, and barely even moved. He was trapped in his parents' house. My friends and I would go to visit him. (I didn't tell my father.) It was spooky, like visiting someone dying of a dread disease. Jerry would just sit, and my friends would sit with him. But whenever Jerry would see me he would begin to cry, and he wouldn't stop until I left.

Soon I stopped going. What was the point? He wouldn't talk to me, and my mere presence triggered an endless stream of tears. I waited and hoped for things to change. Finally, I broke up the band that Jerry and I had formed, which had been the center of our lives. We had worked so hard on that group. But I couldn't imagine continuing the group with another drummer. I was not yet eighteen, and this was all beyond me. I tried to focus on what to do next.

George, meanwhile, wasn't doing much better. All that time staring at the walls of his room didn't help his grades or his friendships. Somewhere in all of that I graduated from high school. I can't remember if George or Jerry ever did. I hung around town for a while, working as a night watchman in an old hotel at which I took a room. The last time I saw George, he came by that room. I think there were four of us sitting in the room, smoking weed and listening to music, as we did.

Out of nowhere George blurted out, "Do you guys think I am a woman?"

After an awkward silence, our friend Stuart, whose heterosexual inclinations were never in doubt, and in whose front yard Jerry's father had stomped on his son's head, said, "George, I don't think I know what you mean?"

"Just that," George replied. "Do you think I'm a woman?"

"Well, no George," replied Stuart somewhat dryly, "seems to me you are a guy. Anyone want another hit off this joint?"

That was the last time I saw George. I escaped that town for college, an option unavailable to George both due to his grades and his financial situation as a kid in foster care. A few months later, George hung himself.

I completely lost touch with Jerry. Years went by.

I moved to San Francisco in 1988. One day I was riding a bus when who should sit down across from me but Jerry.

He was the same person but different. The flamboyant, ready-for-anything freak boy I had known had completely vanished, and in his place was a timid, unsure of himself ne'er-do-well who taught word processing classes for a school that advertised on removable cards on buses and subways. Though by now he had a male lover, he was still uncomfortable talking about his sexuality directly, even with me, even after learning that I was "out," which he couldn't quite bring himself to believe. "You can't be gay. You had hair on your chest when you were sixteen."

And he was dying of AIDS.

Before he died, Jerry told me what had happened that night years ago when he grabbed my father in the hall of the hospital and asked if they could talk. They went for a drive and Jerry, tripping on acid, finally away from his parents and the hospital and with tears flowing, came out to my Dad. It was the first time in his life he had told anyone he was gay. (Since that word had not yet arrived in high school circles in our little town, I don't know what words he said to my father, but he got the point across.) Not only that, Jerry told my father that he was in love with me.

And then, as his life was being sucked out of him, Jerry told me he had been in love with me all through high school, but he was certain that I, the former football star with the sauciest girlfriend in the school, was straight and that he could never tell me of his love. He explained that when he took LSD he became convinced that everyone could see through his façade, see this terrible stain on his soul, and this was the cause of his bad acid trips.

To be honest, had he confessed his love back then I cannot say how I would have reacted. I like to think I would have welcomed it, that I would have reciprocated, that we could have shared the sweetest of puppy loves. But the truth is I have no idea what I would have done. I loved Jerry very much, and looking back, I can see that I thought of him as very sexy, though I couldn't have really put that together. Perhaps I would have recoiled from feelings I was not ready to feel, that it all could have blown up in a horrible way, and that Jerry's intuition was accurate when it told him to hide his love at all costs.

The convoluted layers of hiding, ignorance, shame, and suffering in this story take my breath away even now.

Jerry hiding his love for me, refusing to talk at all if he couldn't speak this love, trading words for tears, and when the tears were not enough, an icy river.

Jerry and my father driving in the night, Jerry bawling his head off and telling my father that he loved me, unaware that my father himself was hard at work hiding his own attraction to men, a struggle which would land him in a mental hospital in a few years' time, and unaware also that soon I would find myself in bed with a man I loved, wildly happy.

My closeted best friend telling my closeted father of his love for my closeted self.

The Jerry I met in San Francisco was seriously damaged, not at all the Jerry I had known, the Jerry I wish I had loved in a more intimate way. But I did manage a certain intimacy with the later Jerry nonetheless. I helped his lover care for him as he died of AIDS.

Young gays today know the history of the AIDS epidemic in terms of how many men died. What is not well known is how horrendous AIDS deaths were. Maybe that's fine. Who wants to know that?

Jerry's death was as horrible as all the others. First lesions appeared all over his body, then he went blind, then lost control of his bowels. Lying in bed, diapers soiled, eyes wide open but seeing nothing, his entire body convulsed in pain.

At the last moment his parents arrived. They too were changed: Colorado rednecks in San Francisco to say goodbye to their dying gay son. Totally at a loss. Tears in abundance. When death finally came, they asked me to go to Colorado and give the eulogy at Jerry's funeral. I was the preacher's kid after all. But then I saw the obituary they wrote for my hometown paper. There was no mention of the cause of death, nor the fact that he was survived by a male lover of many years who had cared for him through a long and horrible illness while his parents did not. I considered telling his parents, yes, I will give a eulogy. I will speak of a beautiful young man who had been destroyed by the homophobia of the culture he grew up in, whose memory was dishonored by his parents even now, whose one stroke of luck had been to find a man he loved who would care for him through his illness and death, but now that man was shut out of the memorial. I would talk about how I would give anything to go back in time and have just one night naked in bed with the beautiful boy who loved me. I imagined what it would be like to speak all of this aloud at the funeral.

In the end I just told his parents I was sorry but I could not attend the funeral.

I never got to say goodbye to George. It was my parents who told me of his suicide. I think they read it in the paper. I never met his real parents, and I had no idea where his foster parents were. As far as I know there was no memorial, no funeral, no gathering of loved ones, no reminiscences to share. George was just gone. What? Hung himself, that's what.

Didn't even live long enough to die of AIDS.

The story I told myself for years was that George and Jerry and I were too closeted, too embedded in an impossible place and time, to have acted on our loves and attractions. But the fact is: I have no idea what George and Jerry did when they were not with me. Was I the only one who was missing the plot? Who says that George and Jerry weren't intimate? Or, I don't know, on a dark road at the edge of town trading blow jobs for beer with middle aged men? The thing about secret lives is that they're secret.

I never even knew why George left his birth family. Teenagers have a way of being here now. You don't want to talk about your family? Or about what you did last week when you missed our rock band practice? Or about pretty much anything except what is right in front of us right now? Ok, that's cool.

I also wonder how I grew up so unaware that I would find my way through life loving men. How I went through high school completely unaware that my best friend was in love me. Never once thought about kissing Michael or Jerry or George or any other guy. Never once fantasized about gay sex. I am not even sure I was aware that men had sex with men at all.

Not that my experience requires explanation. I do not subscribe to the belief that the lives of gay men unfold as journey of overcoming social repression and self-hatred, all leading to the moment of coming out and discovering your true self. To the contrary, I am persuaded more by the Buddhist belief that the self is an illusion.

But looking back, what stands out is how carefully I kept my distance from my father. The less he knew about my life and what I was really up to, the better. The other side of that coin was him keeping his life separate from mine. I now know that the other Episcopal priests around him were also closet homosexuals, as were his closest friends. Late in his life, I asked him what portion of Episcopal priests were secretly gay. Eighty percent, he replied. Maybe eighty-five.

I tried hard to know nothing about these men. Not their desires. Not their shame. Not their cover stories. Didn't want to confess my sins to them. Didn't want to put on a dress and eat the body of Jesus, nor drink his blood. Most definitely did not want to be an adolescent acolyte alone with one of them in the sacristy, most of all with my own father.

But for a brief time, that was unavoidable. I was the preacher's kid. Kids in the church who were my age were supposed to be acolytes. Thus I was to be an acolyte. I would be able to finagle my way out of it later, but I had to at least try. Acolytes are the boys who dress in robes and carry the cross and the candles and bring the priest the bread and wine. One of the jobs of an acolyte is to help the priest undress from all the frilly ritual clothing backstage after the show. One by one he peels off the layers and hands them to you, mumbling a bunch of religious mumbo jumbo. Magic incantations. You wait attentively at his side, as he hands you what are effectively his shawl, his dress, his petticoat, and his ritual undergarments. I had to do this several times for my own father. We did it exactly the way the rituals of the Episcopal Church specified. There was no touching or nudity, but if I were to single out an experience from my youth that would qualify as "sexual abuse," that would be it: a boy and a man absolutely alone, no one else can see or hear, the crossdressing, and that somehow we are supposed to be "united in the body of Christ," that revolting, bleeding, tortured, nearly naked horror.

As my father grew old, I did become close to him in a way. Once he needed me and I no longer needed him, an easier familiarity became possible. He passed many years in assisted living, needing ever greater assistance, so the tables were turned, in the way that life's rhythm dictates for parents and their children. But in a fundamental way I kept my distance. For one thing, he had been in and out of mental hospitals with depression so bad he became dissociative. So you never knew if having a real conversation with him about difficult topics would set off another crisis.

One day the phone rang and it was him, calling from a hospital where he was recovering from surgery.

"Bob, I have had a lot of time to think and reflect on my life while lying in this bed, and I think I owe you an apology."

"Really? For what?"

"There was a time I spanked you too hard. It has been weighing on my mind. It was too hard."

"Oh, come on Dad, don't worry about it." That's not your problem anymore, I thought. It's mine.

BRYAN

I arrived at college in a small town in central Ohio pretty unsure whether the whole college thing was going to be for me and even more dubious about living in a dorm with a roommate. But when I walked into my dorm room and met Bryan, I knew instantly that my roommate problem, at least, had been solved.

Bryan was a wiry little guy with wild brown hair, a Billy-goat beard, an angular jaw, a pleasant face, and a joint in his hand. Things were looking up. His most pronounced feature was his warmth: he always had a smile; he looked you in the eye; he listened, and made friends easily. He was as passionate about music and as joyous in sharing it as I.

Bryan and I were so different. Bryan was from a working class Russian Jewish immigrant family in Detroit. I was a middle-class WASP from Colorado. I had an athletic six-foot frame. Bryan was a little guy, a bully magnet. Bryan was a very talented composer and had been admitted into the Oberlin Conservatory composition program. The same program had rejected me, and thus I was enrolled in the College.

Our friendship quickly began to deepen beyond anything either of us had known. We went everywhere together, made music together, got stoned together, and negotiated the rocky emotional terrain of college freshman life together. When either of us would meet a new friend, the first thing we would do was show off our roommate. Bryan's high school girlfriend, Ilene, came to visit and Bryan showed me off like I was a new composition he had just completed. I don't think I have ever smiled and laughed as much as I did during this time.

Friends noticed it too. One blurted out, "I can't believe the college put you two guys together as roommates. It's like you guys are in *love* or something." If that statement was made on a campus today, it would be followed with an inevitable, "Are you *gay?*" But this was before that was a question.

I started noticing things about Bryan that I had never noticed about a boy. The spring in his step. He had a sort of pointed-toe walk that made him literally spring from one foot to another as if he was about to take flight, making his scrawny frame seem even lighter than it was, as if he was walking in less gravity that everyone else. Or the way his eyes would sparkle when he was happy, which was most of the time. Maybe no one else's eyes sparkled like that, or maybe I had just never noticed anyone's eyes before. But I sure noticed Bryan's. His sharp features, sparkling eyes, and light step gave him a bird-like quality: a beautiful, rare bird.

Bryan's creative process was the opposite of mine. I lacked Bryan's musical ear and talent, so my musical method was to start making noise and then just work longer and harder than everyone else until I finally had something I liked. Bryan's ideas seemed to arrive fully elaborated, and at the oddest times, like he was plucking ripe fruit from trees no one else could see.

He had an ability to roll things around in his mind just to see them go. Often times we would be together and some unusual sequence of words would just pop into his head out of nowhere, and rather than trying to develop them into a narrative or poem, or impose some kind of meaning on them, or write them down for later, or forget about them, he would just go around mumbling them to himself in odd situations and giggling.

Bryan:

> I wrote a rhyme upon a ring
>
> I rolled it round and round
>
> just to see it go its own way
>
> just to hear the sound

I was a little jealous of that creative spark, but mostly I wanted to be around it and marvel at it. One evening we were walking across the campus square. I think Bryan was acid tripping. At the time we were enrolled in the same electronic music class. All of a sudden Bryan let out an exclamation and excitedly described to me an idea that had just occurred to him for stringing two modified tape recorders together to make an odd sort of instrument. Before he could finish his sentence, he let out another exclamation, and began to explain that, no, it would take three tape decks. But before he could finish *that* thought, his eyes widened and he started cackling and explaining that actually what would be required was three tape decks, some grommets, and some helium balloons. That was it, Bryan had invented a musical "instrument" that four years later I would use to record my first LP, and today, thirty years later, remains unique in electronic music. It was simple yet complex. It worked. It was funny. And it had occurred to him in three rapid bursts which outpaced his ability to verbalize them, arriving out of the blue, while we were walking along discussing something else entirely.

Bryan loved people in a way that made it hard for him to fit into the mold of a conservatory composition student or any formal school for that matter. For his big freshman opus, he wrote a "composition" that involved every student on our freshman dorm floor. It wasn't music in any conventional sense, but it had detailed parts for everyone, calling on them to open their doors, or stick their heads out, or run down the hall, or fall down, or shout out inanities, or sing as best they could, in specific sequences. He actually got the stuffed shirts of the composition faculty out to the dorm for the one and only performance of *All in Prall Hall.*

One day Bryan and I went to the forest at the edge of town, dropped acid and climbed trees. At the peak of the day, we stood in a clearing about two feet apart and just stared into each other's eyes. I had no idea how long we stood there, holding each other in our eyes, while layer upon layer of defensiveness, insecurity, armor, general bullshit, and even our very skin seemed to peel away. I started crying. And without words, we started making these odd hand signals to each other in unison motions.

Those hand signals became our secret code with which we communicated our mutual understanding of the world. At parties, boring lectures, amazing concerts, and awkward social gatherings, we would sign our secret language. The message conveyed was that we understood the situation the same way, and we were in this together.

I had grown up in Colorado and the Rocky Mountains were my spiritual home. I couldn't wait until summer to share them with Bryan, so I invited him home for Christmas. A friend drove and Bryan and I shared the back seat. Sitting next to Bryan and watching America go by, I felt like my life's horizons were as limitless as the Kansas sunset that painted the sky a million shades of flame.

For everyone whose soul feeds on mountain wilderness, the joy of climbing into the alpine tundra is like no other experience on earth. As you approach that ethereal boundary where the trees fade away, your feet become light despite the steep pitch of the terrain and the weariness of your muscles. You begin to float. Then the trees fall away and you are in another world, covered with wildflowers and moss, crystal clear springs and animals that exist nowhere else. This is what I wanted to share with Bryan, and I understood that he would immediately *know* what this meant to me. The air would get thin, the light would get white, the oxygen would come rushing into our lungs, the sights would fill our souls, and there we would be, Bryan and I, alone in the world, making our sign language that only we knew.

I had never been camping in the winter and really hadn't the faintest idea how to go about it. And this was before all the high-tech lightweight camping gear people use these days was available. But we piled into a car and headed up into the Rocky Mountains without the proper clothing, boots, skills, or even a weather forecast, but with all the recklessness of youth and a couple of tabs of acid.

The day unfolded just like I imagined and hoped and knew it would. Bryan and I nearly ran up the mountain, no matter the steep grade, our heavy packs, or the thigh-deep snow. Everything I saw and heard, I knew Bryan saw and heard the same way. All the beauty that embraced me embraced Bryan with the same touch. At sunset we sat on a tree that had been felled by the snow and said nothing, just losing ourselves in the silence of the mountain. There is no silence in the world like the silence of a snow-covered mountain when there is little wind. All the mountain sounds of the other three seasons get swallowed by the snow. The rustling of leaves, say. But the leaves were gone anyway. The quiet is so complete you can hear your own heart beat if you listen closely, and I was listening. Eventually I turned to Bryan and whispered, "It never plays a wrong note." Bryan smiled and replied with our secret hand signals. Perfect.

Bryan returned to Detroit to visit his family before school resumed. It was the first time we had been apart since we had met, and for once I couldn't wait to get back to school. Soon after we returned we spent an evening out, and arrived back at our rooms late and happy. I got into bed, and for the first time it occurred to me that maybe Bryan and I should get into bed together. I didn't wonder if I was gay or what kissing a man would be like, or what we would do once in bed, didn't consider what the world or our friends or families would say – which may seem preposterous in light of everything else in this book, but it is the truth. I only thought about Bryan, that boy in the next room, him, without category or identity.

And just as the idea of getting into bed with Bryan started to take shape in my mind, Bryan's figure appeared in the dark next to my bed. "Bob, can I get into bed with you?" "Sure." I pulled the covers back and Bryan hopped in and the world changed. We laid motion-less in each other's arms, unsure of what to do, overwhelmed by the newness of the feel and smell of our bodies. Soon our lips found each other, then our tongues, finally our cocks, and yet another new world opened before us. His body felt so new and strange yet so familiar, wave after wave of happiness washed over us until our beards were full of each other's cum.

Then we laid together, basking in the glow, telling each other, "I love you," marveling at the novelty of professing love to a man, or a boy becoming a man. Bryan said the words in just the same way he would play with other crazy words that popped into his head. "I love you Bob, I love you, Bob." Then he would pause to let the words roll around and come to a stop, and then he would cackle with delight, and then say them again.

After a while of letting the feelings and words lead where they would, we arrived at the inevitable, "Does this mean we're gay?" We considered the question, without any sense of panic or anxiety or fear, but rather in the delight of shared discovery. We had several close gay friends. Were we like them? We thought about them one by one. We didn't think so. What did we know about gay people? They liked disco. We HATED disco. They liked campy old movie stars. We liked Luis Buñuel. They seemed very urban. We liked the mountains. Should we go to meetings of the Gay Student Union which had recently formed on our campus? Or were we just in love? Very much in love.

In the morning, I awoke to find that it was all still there. I had not dreamed it up. Coincidentally, the Gay Student Union had distributed fliers calling on all gay students to wear jeans that day. It was a joke intended to raise the visibility of the organization, since almost everyone on campus wore jeans every day. We discussed whether we should put on jeans. I decided yes, Bryan no.

I do not remember a thing that happened that day. But that night is as clear in my mind as if it was yesterday. All day I counted the hours and minutes until I could be back in bed with Bryan. And finally there we were, naked in each other's arms. But in the midst of the celebration, our friend Peter walked in unannounced as he often did. "I, I, I can't handle this," he stammered, and ran out of the room in a panic.

Until that moment, Bryan and I had been in a cocoon. Some invisible veil had shut the rest of the world out, allowing us to find each other on our own terms. When Peter walked in, the rest of the world came crashing in behind him.

Oh.

Right.

People don't like this.

People hate people like this.

Queers. Faggots.

Right.

Uh oh.

There was no way to reconcile the world Bryan and I had created with the world that Peter brought in. The universe simply could not encompass such a discrepancy. I decided I had to find Peter. If I could just find him, talk to him, explain to him that this was the most beautiful amazing thing, all would be right. It would be all right because it had to be.

I jumped out of bed, pulled on my jeans and t-shirt, and headed off into the night to find Peter. I wandered through the entire campus but no trace of Peter. My emotions grew increasingly out of control, tears running down my face.

Finally, I found a mutual friend who said Peter was at a party. I got to the party but there was no Peter. I gave up the search. I was lost at sea, a storm was moving in and my compass had fallen overboard. I desperately needed to orient myself, get my bow turned into the wind and drop anchor. I did two things I had never done before. First, I got drunk. (I had always viewed alcohol as a drug that fucked up old people took to dull their senses – I took drugs to sharpen my senses.) And then, I went home with a girl. I had had girlfriends, and plenty of sex with girls, but I had never met a girl at a party and had "casual sex." It took a lot of dating for me to get confident and comfortable enough with a girl for sex. But now off I went with a girl who was more drunk than I.

I woke up in the morning feeling great. I had scored. Casual sex with a girl. Proved my manhood. Asserted my masculinity. And the sex had actually been fun. It had only put a slight damper on the evening when she had to get up from the bed to vomit all that alcohol into the toilet. Like I always did whenever I had a new experience, good or bad, I rushed off to tell Bryan, my true love, about what had happened.

I barged into the dorm room and blurted out the story of my accomplishment to Bryan. I will never forget the look on his face, how it fell, how he struggled to hold back his emotions, how he turned and walked away.

A teenager's ability to fail to consider how others will see them and their actions is a wonder. Until I saw his face fall, it had not entered my head that Bryan's experience of the night might have been less positive than mine. Forgot how he had been in bed with his new lover, only the second time the two of them had lain together, how a friend had surprised them in bed and freaked out, how his new lover had run off almost without a word and not come back. Left him waiting up all night. Then finally showed up in the morning all full of himself for fucking a girl.

When Bryan turned away, I could feel a door slam shut. The tendons tore from the bone. The fingers clinging to the ledge let go. I had blown it.

*

That was it. Bryan and I were over. I tried and tried to steer us back to where we had been, while Bryan just as steadily refused to go there. "I'm not into that anymore," he would say. Bryan reconnected with his high school girlfriend Ilene. Still, I tried to get back into the cocoon with Bryan. I was heartbroken. Finally, I had to drop out of school. If I could not be in Bryan's arms, I couldn't be in the same school, not in the same town.

I hung on to my dream of winning Bryan back for years. I visited him in Detroit. I went camping with Bryan and Ilene. In the meantime, I went back to dating women. I wasn't gay. I was simply deeply, passionately in love with Bryan. No other man interested me. If I could not have Bryan, then I would not have a man at all.

As time went by the dream of Bryan began to fade. I partnered with a woman who I was happy with. I wasn't in any closet. I told my new partner all about Bryan and would tell anyone else about him if the subject came up, though it rarely did. But I carried in my heart a deep melancholy about Bryan. It was not so much that I wanted Bryan back; it was more that I could not imagine how I could ever get that close to another man.

By this time it was the late 1970s and I was living in lower Manhattan. Just a few blocks from my place, gay New York was having its heyday. Yet it never once occurred to me to go check it out. Anonymous sex? Bryan and I had the most emotionally-connected sex I could imagine. Bars? I hated bars, I didn't even drink. Disco? I was in the musical avant garde. Cocaine? Rich snobs snorted that stuff. While the gays partied their way out of the era of gay liberation and into the hedonism of clone culture, I started hanging out with refugees from El Salvador, and eventually went to work for the revolution seeking to overthrow the regime that had driven them from their homes. Where in my life would the space appear to get close to a man, so very close, to fall in love personally, politically, artistically? To fall in love without slogans or gyms or flags? To fall in love without once asking if he was my "type" – the right size, the right body, the right sexual proclivities, the right face, the right cock?

*

In the end, Bryan and I each succumbed to the heavy weight of cultural expectations and adapted to the social roles expected of us. Bryan became straight. To my knowledge, I am the only man he ever slept with. I became gay. I go to gay bars now. I enjoy them. The bars I frequent cater to others like me, men who do not fit into the gay mainstream: the misfits, drag queens and bikers, the fringe. I feel at home there. I have loved many men. I care for them deeply. I have passionate, meaningful sex with them. We keep in touch. They are family. I will know them until I die. But I miss the love I had with Bryan, before I was gay. And I miss Bryan.

*

Years rolled by. Eventually I decided that it was time to get back in touch with Bryan. There had been a time when I needed to break off. The emotional space that Bryan occupied in me had become so convoluted that distance was necessary in order to move on with life. But now that distance had lost its purpose. It just continued out of emotional inertia.

By this time Bryan and Ilene had been settled for quite some time on a leftist kibbutz in Israel. They were raising organic dates and three children. Bryan had done time in prison for refusing to serve in the Israeli army. I was a touring musician, and I set about trying to arrange concerts in Israel and Beirut to pay my way over so I could visit Bryan and his family. To begin to grow back the connections which had torn. I did not contact him to tell him of my plans. I wanted to wait until I had the concert confirmed.

I got a phone call from Israel. It was Ilene. Bryan had been killed in a car crash.

He had been driving on a two-way highway when his car suddenly swerved into the wrong lane, head on into a truck. Ilene was never sure if it was an accident or a suicide. Had the catastrophe of the Israeli-Palestinian conflict driven him out of this world? Had he been rolling thoughts about it around in his head, to see where they would go, and he followed them into the opposing lane of traffic?

Ilene and I have become very close. We talk on the phone and exchange emails. She brought the kids to the US for a visit and I managed to spend time with all of them. We give each other advice on parenting, politics, and our romantic endeavors.

Ilene sent me a picture of Bryan in our room at college which I put up on the wall. I remember everything. I remember the shirt he was wearing, and what it smelled like, and what Bryan smelled like, and exactly the way he would close his eyes and smile like in the photo. It is so vivid. She also sent me a picture of her and the three kids. I have that up on the wall too. They are part of my family, even even though they don't know me, and the are on the other side of the world.

Once I wrote to Ilene that I wished she and I were in bed together; not anything sexual, just dressed up in pajamas all cozy and reading. She wrote back that she knew exactly what I meant.

On the scale of what actually happens in life lived by real people, this is not a such a sad story. Yes, there are elements of tragedy but there is much, much more. As far as I am aware, I have never met another gay man whose first homosexual experience was with a man he deeply loved. Back in that time, most young men had their first time in a dirty bookstore, or public bathroom, or a truck stop, or an alley. Or in an abusive situation imposed on them by an older man. More recently most guys set up their first time over their smart phone. When I tell them my story of Bryan, they are incredulous and envious.

It seems that with every year that goes by, the meaning of being gay becomes yet more rigid. Boys "come out" and declare their "identity" at an ever more tender age. A few years ago a twenty-five-year-old man sheepishly confessed to me that he had come out "late" – at the embarrassingly ancient age of twenty-one. What an impoverished notion of his own life path, I thought. Where did this idea come from that the good stuff of life begins when we arrive at one of a handful of available sexual identities, while the journey we took to get there is meaningless, something one just must endure and hopefully get done with as quickly as possible? If only humans were actually so simple.

At the close of my first letter to Ilene after learning of Bryan's death, I wrote, "How will I ever fill this hole in my side where Bryan was?" I waited years for it to heal. And the holes where Michael and Jerry and George had been. The full complement of my early loves, all gone before I reached middle age. Over time I learned we are all full of holes. And that's OK. We make peace with these holes. They become not just sad but also beautiful. You can feel the breezes move through, and the rain, even the sunshine. Every now and then you can catch a glimpse of the one who was once there.

The following years would lead me first through the civil war in El Salvador and then through the AIDS epidemic in San Francisco. Talk about holes where people had been. I had no idea what was coming.

There is a layer of irony here too. I moved to New York in 1978, exactly when the very first bits of the HIV virus began to pass from one gay man to another, though no one knew it at the time. If I had jumped into the gay culture of Manhattan, I would almost surely not be here now to write these words. I would now be a hole in someone else's side. I dodged a bullet on that one. Just as I would dodge several more over the coming years in El Salvador.

*

Bryan again:

He was an arrow

Not shot straight enough

To hit a target so far away.

PART 2

War is a man's game ... the killing machine
has a gender and it is male.

– Virginia Woolf

THE SOLDIERS, THE COLONEL, AND THE PSYCHOKILLER

Why did I go to El Salvador? To find some truth, I suppose. About myself, about people, about men, about the world. El Salvador was, as they say, a good place to be from. A tiny, overpopulated, environmentally ransacked country operated as a private plantation by fourteen rich families. Like all plantation economies everywhere and at all times, the only thing that held it together was violence. There is simply no way to compel millions of people to labor in the sun on land that is allegedly not theirs, for profits that are not theirs either, other than through constant, relentless violence, by threat or deed. In the 1980s the poor of El Salvador were engaged in one of their periodic uprisings against this brutal state of affairs. In response, the military rampaged through the countryside, murdering unarmed *campesinos* as if they were legitimate military targets. *Salvadoreños* by the thousands fled north to the US. By return mail, Washington, which could not imagine that starving plantation laborers could have any agency of their own and saw the whole thing as a Cold War Soviet plot, sent bullets, guns, planes, helicopters, and military advisors to the fourteen families.

My little part of the story began with assisting refugees arriving in New York City where I was living, then playing a lead role in the solidarity movement that formed as the war moved to the front pages of the world's newspapers. I ended up getting chewed up and spit out by the ugly politics of the Salvadoran diaspora. Rather than leave the movement for greener pastures, which would have been the obvious and sensible thing, I resolved to up the ante and go into the center of the storm in El Salvador. Surely a revolutionary movement that was successfully resisting the combined violence of the fourteen families and the US military must have more going for it than what I had encountered in the diaspora. I decided to work as a freelance journalist at first, then look for a more substantive way to make whatever contribution to the cause I could. I never found that deeper role I had imagined for myself. I found the center of the revolutionary movement just as ugly and messy as its outer reaches, and discovered that writing about the revolution suited me more than being a militant in a revolutionary organization.

With the assistance of a million dollars of US military aid every day – to the government of a country of just five million people – and a wave of mass political murder by murky "death squads" (*escuadrones de muerte*), the war was turning in favor of the regime. It was easy to find fear and death in El Salvador. It was everywhere. Unavoidable. The violence became so extreme that the Catholic Archbishop in this very Catholic country declared on national radio that the law of God was *thou shall not kill*, and called on the soldiers to disobey their orders. He was assassinated the next day while saying mass. The killing went on, didn't miss a beat. I wanted to meet the men at the apex of all this. Those at the controls. What kind of monsters were they? Or were they not monsters but something else? How did they command that kind of loyalty? What secret truth about men did they know?

So I started at the bottom of the food chain and worked my way up. At the bottom I found the soldiers of Yanqui Company, Atlacatl Battalion, Army of the Armed Forces of El Salvador. I had been air dropped by one of the many Vietnam-era helicopters my country had provided the regime into their camp in guerrilla country. All I had was my backpack and press pass from the High Command. I spent the next week with them, clambering around the volcanoes of the Central American isthmus in a fruitless search for revolutionaries who were known to be in the area but succeeded in keeping their exact whereabouts to themselves.

The soldiers of Yanqui Company were kids, really. I would guess, for the most part, between sixteen and nineteen years of age. By this time an entire generation of fighters had been killed on both sides. In order to sustain the war, the regime had instituted a universal draft, but the draft didn't work the way it does in richer countries. You didn't "get called up" to report for duty at an induction center. You didn't get an envelope in the mail with your draft number. What happened was this: a truckload of soldiers would suddenly appear at a bus stop and grab any young males who didn't run fast enough. You're in the army now son, no matter your age.

The boys of Yanqui Company were the sort of brash, boastful, goofy, shy, curious, and awkward kids one would expect to find among teenagers anywhere, but also scared. And, like teenage boys everywhere, they did their best to hide their fear. What was remarkable was how they had been transformed from kids rounded up at a bus stop into a reasonably disciplined and motivated military unit. Yanqui Company was part of the Atlacatl Battalion, an elite force which had actually been flown to the US Army base at Fort Bragg in North Carolina for training, surely a mind-blowing experience for a teenage *campesino* who had until then lived on a dirt floor and cooked over an open fire. They enjoyed their male camaraderie, worked at impressing each other with bravery and feats of strength, and maintained an intense pace scouring the mountains for an enemy that not so long ago could have been their playmates but who they had now learned to hate. Their understanding of the ideological underpinnings of the war seemed to come almost entirely from the schlock movie *Rambo*, in which Sylvester Stallone plays a Vietnam vet, angry at how his government had supposedly "sold out" the soldiers it had sent to Vietnam. He returns to Southeast Asia to fight the Vietnamese Communists single-handedly. The movie was a staple of barracks life. Everyone in the company had seen it eleven times. Some many more. None seemed to be aware that their American patrons had lost the war in Vietnam. I tried to break it to them gently.

*

As part of the effort to justify continued American support for one of the most murderous regimes in the world, the Reagan Administration made a big deal about how a big part of the Atlacatl Battalion's training in the US focused on "respecting human rights." They graduated, returned home, and carried out the most documented massacre of the war, in which more than seven hundred *campesinos* – men, women, children, and babes in arms – were rounded up and executed in cold blood. An entire village. The army made it difficult for journalists to access war zones, but the *New York Times* correspondent managed to get to the scene and reported it in detail. The Reagan Administration was not pleased, and leaned so hard on the *New York Times* that the correspondent was pulled from El Salvador and reassigned to the city desk.

The colonel in command at that notorious massacre was later killed by a bomb the guerrillas planted in his helicopter, which left Colonel Sigifredo Ochoa Perez as the most prominent leader of the army defending the fourteen families which owned the country from Communism, whatever that might be. (The families themselves produced no war heroes. They spent the war in Miami, their children enrolled in private schools. They did, however, fund the death squads, and some family members may have actually dirtied their hands in the thousands of murders these squads executed.) Ochoa had commanded a massacre of his own, but managed to keep pesky journalists away from the carnage. I resolved to get to know the Colonel.

Leaders of the far right in El Salvador did not talk to the press. They had learned that the more hidden they remained, the more likely the flow of US military aid they depended on would continue without disruption. If I was going to meet Colonel Ochoa, I was going to have to ingratiate myself in some way, appear to be something I was not. I suppose I was learning how to be a spy.

I had two rules. First, never tell a lie unless you absolutely cannot avoid it. Be honest. Just pick and choose carefully what you will talk about. If you find yourself having to lie, you screwed up. Second, find things you can actually agree on. No matter who you are talking to, there will be something on which you can agree.

Thus I found myself sitting in living room of Colonel Sigifredo Ochoa Perez. Not so long before, the colonel was being touted by his American military advisors as the Salvadoran military's most effective combat officer and great hope for the future. But then he declared his garrison in insurrection against his own General Command and its American military advisors. Instead of following the advice of the Americans, Sigifredo advocated for what he called the "nuclear solution" to the civil war. Of course, El Salvador didn't have a nuclear bomb, and anyway the guerrillas were tightly interwoven among the population, so there would be nowhere to drop one even if they had one. What Sigifredo had in mind was a wave of mass murder on an even larger scale than the one that had left fifty thousand out of five million dead and about a third of the population displaced. A sort of national catharsis that would kill on a scale comparable to what would happen if a nuclear weapon was actually used.

Yes, he explained to me, many people would die. But it would also end the war, which costs new lives every day. Less than fifty years ago you Americans were in a similar situation. World War Two was going on and on, and people were dying every day. So what did you Americans do? *You dropped a nuclear bomb and ended the war. Two of them, in fact.*

I could honestly agree with the colonel on this point. It was, in fact, an obvious hypocrisy in the American position. And the Americans did indeed drop two nuclear bombs to save American lives, without regard to the lives of the Japanese.

The colonel was delighted to finally find an American journalist who was willing to look his own country's hypocrisy in the face, and "who really understands our thinking." I became his good friend. I asked if he would introduce me to others who shared his understanding of this truth, and that was how I came to be invited to the fortieth birthday party of one of the great mass murderers of the late twentieth century.

*

Roberto D'Aubuisson is cracking jokes for my benefit but I don't understand them. First, his Spanish is all slang and puns. Second, he speaks with a lisp. Third, he is drunk. My Spanish can't keep up, but it must be funny because the guys around us explode with laughter.

Of course, Roberto is the not the kind of guy that one would dare to not laugh at his jokes, but this laughter seems genuine.

And why not? These men have a lot to celebrate. Their boss here is big man in the country now. Just a few years ago a coalition of students, labor unions, *campesino* coops, and radical Catholic priests was poised to overthrow the military dictatorship that had ruled this country for decades, and Roberto D'Aubuisson was a minor figure in the army of a collapsing regime. He was pushed out of the army by a movement of young reformist officers trying to rein in the "death squads" secretly run by certain sectors of the military, for whom D'Aubuisson was the public face. He was publicly denounced by the American ambassador. He was too much even for Ronald Reagan, whose State Department refused to allow him into the US. In response he ratcheted up the death squad activity even higher and founded an explicitly fascist political party. Fifty thousand dead later and he is the biggest fish in this very small pond of five million souls, crowded together on a small piece of the Central American isthmus that is nearly completely deforested and poisoned with pesticides. Those students and labor organizers who managed to escape the reach of his death squads have mostly fled to the mountains. His political party is about to take power. True, he cannot be president himself, as that would make the country even more of an international pariah than it already is, but everyone knows that he is the real power behind the front man who is poised to win the coming election.

All of that, and he is only forty years old as of today. So why not party? That is why we are all here, the death squad goons and I, to party down and toast the big man. Except that he is actually rather small. What a cut-up he is, holding the room like an obscene stand-up comic. The last laugh is his. He killed the country's Catholic Archbishop as the man was consecrating the host while saying mass. Ha ha. The opposition leadership called a press conference to denounce the killings and were kidnapped before the very noses of the international press and turned up a short time later face down in a ditch, horribly disfigured. What a joke! At one point residents of the capital were waking up to more than a hundred bodies a day adorning their streets, hanging from lamp posts, breasts cut off, testicles stuffed in their mouths. Hee hee! It got so bad that the only way the Reagan administration could get Congress to continue signing off on the millions of dollars of military aid to this tiny backwater was for the Assistant Secretary of State for Latin America to go before a subcommittee every few months to "certify" that the "human rights situation" in the country was "improving." Which the functionary in question, Elliot Abrams, did with a straight face. What a punch line! I'm telling ya, ya can't put one over on Roberto D'Aubuisson. Let's drink to that! Happy birthday *Señor Esquadrone de la Muerte.*

The fact that I am here at all is remarkable. D'Aubuisson *never* gives interviews or talks to the press in any way, much less invites a journalist to his private birthday party. But I have been brought to the party by Colonel Sigifredo Ochoa Perez, the guy who declared his entire military base in rebellion against the US military advisors and their pesky talk of human rights. Anyone the Colonel vouches for is welcome. In fact, I am almost a guest of honor, and thus the object of D'Aubuisson's humor. Any American journalist trusted this much by Colonel Ochoa must be quite a friend indeed.

Hanging out with D'Aubuisson is unnerving. I knew that the ladies of the fascist right found him irresistible. I had seen them line up in the hot sun after his speeches just to have a giddy hello. But I didn't get it. He's a slimy guy and not much of a looker. What's the appeal? Up close, I get it: when a man throws all morality into the trash and becomes, say, a mass murderer, he acquires a magnetism and sex appeal that is impossible to deny. You feel it when someone like

that walks into a room. Everyone knows he is a killer. *Their* killer,
but a killer just the same. There are others in this room who have
killed, probably many times, but he is the alpha dog. Watch a pack of
wild dogs for a while and you will get the idea. Everyone else here is
effectively on their backs with all fours in the air. And he is not just
a killer, he is also a torturer. He hurts people in unspeakable ways.
Everyone knows that too. This weird sexual energy he exudes, does
he bring it into the torture chamber? Does he get off on it? Do his
victims sense it? These questions are here, hovering just out of reach.
An amorphous swarm which could suddenly coalesce into night-
marish clarity at any moment but somehow never does. The swarm
enters the room with him. That's how you know he's here.

We are in a hacienda in the central part of the country, and we need
to leave before nightfall. The roads are dangerous at night. If it's
not the highway robbers it's the guerrillas, and I came in a car with
Colonel Ochoa and the fascist candidate soon-to-become-president
of the country. As we say our good-byes, D'Aubuisson cracks another
joke I cannot quite follow and tells me that to prove his point he
is going to give me a present, a pistol from Ilobasco, a tiny village
down the road. This line is his *coup de grace*. The entire room busts
up in laughter. I don't get the joke, but I am relieved beyond words
to be leaving this gathering of murderers. Yes, I wanted to look evil
in the eye, but on this one I might have punched heavier than my
weight. I want outta here and fast. What if these thugs figure out
who I am? Nope, this is not the time to think about that. The right
time to think about that might be never.

Colonel Ochoa and the soon-to-be president ride in the front and the
candidate's wife and I take our places in the back. We come around
a bend in the highway and there, in the middle of the road, stands
a lone man flagging us down. We come to a stop. It is D'Aubuisson's
driver. D'Aubuisson, we learn, jumped into his sports car and raced

down the highway in front of us, then took the turn to the village of Ilobasco to get me the pistols he promised. He left his driver in the road to flag us down. We are to wait here for his return.

The situation is strange beyond words. I am standing on a highway in El Salvador, with the renegade Colonel and the fascist first family. This part of the country sees regular confrontations between the army and guerrilla units which pass through this rugged terrain on the way to the capital city, where they are trying to rebuild their urban movement that D'Aubuisson and the crowd back at the party has slaughtered. The sun is going down.

Time flies when you are having fun, and now time slows to crawl. Finally, we see D'Aubuisson's car speeding up the dusty side road, followed by a beat up old van. As they approach, I see that the van is overflowing with *campesinos*. Every spy and death squad goon from the village and his wife and cousin come piling out of the van and form a large circle on the highway with me in the center. Is this really happening? I remind myself to breathe. One breath, two breaths...

And then he is in front of me, and with a flourish, the butcher of El Salvador hands me a box that contains my pistols from Ilobasco. The circle of people around me watch intently with eager eyes and bright smiles. It is Christmas in August on the sweltering equatorial asphalt.

I open the box and inside are two ceramic models of pistols. The grips are fashioned to look like real pistols, while the barrels are life-size replicas of large erect penises, in a hideous fleshy pink, replete with veins, big mushroom heads, and urethras. The crowd is falling over themselves laughing. D'Aubuisson is standing before me, watching me intently through beady eyes.

Clearly I'm expected to say something.

"Muchas gracias major. Have you killed a lot of *subversivos* with these?"

"No," he replies, keeping his gaze steady on my face. "But I have killed a lot of *subversivas* with them. They like it! They go ooh aah ooh ahh." The Major did a little dance on the highway. The crowd howled.

PART 3

Ari: How many guys you reckon you fucked?

Johnny: I don't know. Hundreds I suppose.

Ari: Have you ever been in love?

Johnny: Every time, sugar.

– Christos Tsiolkas[1]

---

1   From the movie *Head On* (1998), based on the novel *Loaded* by Christos Tsiolkas.

DON'T BE SAD,
LIFE IS SHORT.

He is dancing. He is dancing by himself. He is like a dream, and perhaps he too is dreaming. Dream within dream. He is wearing jeans and no shirt. He is small, a man with nearly child-like proportions, neither buff nor thin. His body is lithe and tight in a way I do not know. His rich skin tone and delicate features are likewise hard to place. And the dancing. What are these dance moves? His head seems to float above his torso, while his arms float independently at his sides. His moves have a grace and elegance that I can somehow imagine in the far away court of an ancient king. But we are in a leather bar in Amsterdam at the tail end of the twentieth century.

I cannot take my eyes off him, yet he is blurry and hard to see through my tears. I have hidden myself in the darkest corner of the room. Who wants to be seen crying in a leather bar? But the accumulation of tears has proven more than the dam can handle. The spillway has overflowed and a river of tears is pouring down. Exactly three weeks of tears, though it feels as if they have been flowing for a lifetime.

I am three weeks in to a five-week concert tour in Europe. I left the day after my birthday. Not long before I had become sexually active with men for this first time since falling in love with Bryan more than a decade previous. It was the peak of the AIDS epidemic, so my timing was off in the worst way. But I was cautious and careful, to the point that those whom I considered my mentors in the whole strange endeavor would joke about it and try to get me to loosen up. And then there had been one... one what? Event? Episode? Rape? One moment that went wrong. A completely fucked-up, non-consensual, frightening moment. It was just a moment, but I couldn't put it out of my mind. I fretted about it, obsessed about it, to the point that those closest to me felt my panic as a burden. "Come on, Bob. You don't get HIV in one moment of one sexual act that doesn't involve ejaculation or any other bodily fluid. Get over yourself. You are surrounded by people who actually have AIDS. Some are dying. You are new to this, but stop acting like a baby." So I decided I would discreetly give myself the birthday present of a negative HIV test to finally put this whole mess behind me. I wouldn't tell anyone. I would just do it. This would be part of my gay growing up. On the morning of my birthday I got the results. Positive. Even the phone call was wrong. AIDS was an incurable terminal disease at the time, and test results were only to be shared in person, with emotional support people on hand. The nurse somehow thought I had already been told so she just blurted out the result.

What an unforgivable dumb shit I was. Who could possibly be so stupid? The worst kind of stupid. Stupid doesn't even get it. I had let everyone down. And now there would be hell to pay. For me and those closest to me.

The next day I was supposed to leave on a five-week concert tour with an ensemble in which I was the only gay member. If it had been a solo tour, or even a tour of my own ensemble, I would have cancelled it. But this tour was the big career break for the band leader. If I had played, say, saxophone, he could have found a last-minute replacement. But the project had been built around my particular use of a unique electronic instrument, and without me the entire tour for a nine-member ensemble would be scrapped. So I loaded up with Valium and went. Didn't tell a single band mate what was up. Just sat off to the side, took Valium, and tried to hold it together. After three weeks of back-to-back shows in one city after another we would have a few days off and I could go stay with my dear friend Joel in Amsterdam.

Joel had recently lost his lover of many years to AIDS. It was a horrendous, messy death. Gregory had been quite the intellectual young man, then completely lost his marbles with AIDS dementia. Joel had administered the morphine shot that finally ended it all.

Joel would understand. Joel and I would cry together, hug each other. Maybe we would sleep together. Somehow we would make each other whole. For three weeks my single goal was to hold it together until I could get to Amsterdam and be with Joel. But when I finally arrived at his door there was a note informing me that he had been called to another city for work on short notice, along with instructions as to where to find the key.

I began to walk. Walking to nowhere. Walking just to walk. The goal was to put one foot in front of the other. Left then right. Walk. Walk through a city that was not mine, listening to a language that was not mine, in a world that was no longer mine. If I walked long enough maybe I could walk myself right out of this world. Just detach. Fade away. Fading away would be so much preferable to dying of AIDS. Could one turn oneself into a ghost by walking far enough?

After twelve hours of walking, I found that my feet had led me to the door of a leather bar. I walked in. Or was it my ghost? I headed straight for the darkest corner, wedged myself in, and started to cry and watch this dreamy man dance. The beauty of his movement seemed to be the exact opposite of the ugliness I had made of my life. Maybe, if I hadn't ruined everything, I would have been able to touch a man like this. To kiss him. To love him. But not now. Who would want to touch me now? All I could do was cry cry cry for what might have been.

Suddenly, he is in front of me. How? I had not seen him walk over. He had been dreamily dancing in his dream, and now he is here. Some strange magic, that.

He is looking at me very intently. A deep long drink of a look.

"Why are you crying?"

I tell him.

"I thought it was something like that. Don't be sad. Life is short."

He gently takes my hand and leads me across the room. Maybe I really have become a ghost, or maybe this is a dream. This cannot possibly be real.

The very small, very beautiful dancer in jeans and no shirt with the delicate features and glowing skin leads me by the hand into a bathroom stall and lovingly gives me a blow job.

And then, just as suddenly as he appeared, he is gone.

Beautiful dancer! Where did you go? Come back! Can't we do this forever? Fall in love for more than fifteen minutes? You could teach me to dance like that. We could fall asleep in each other's arms. Heal our wounds. Repair all of our broken parts. Right every wrong. Perfect every fault.

Whoa! Wait! What did you just do? Did you just commit suicide on my behalf? To teach me that life is short and I should not be sad? Or did you already have HIV? Or are you trusting that all will be fine since I did not ejaculate in your mouth? Or are you truly a magical creature, not of this world but of another world I have been trying to walk myself into?

*

Thinking it over later, I sorted out that he must have been Indonesian. Holland had been Indonesia's imperial overlord for hundreds of years, and there is a substantial Indonesian population in Amsterdam. This would be the beginning of a life-long love affair with all things Indonesian.

Years later, effective AIDS drugs appeared, and the AIDS death I had been looking down the gun barrel at faded away into memory, fainter and fainter, eventually haunting me as a dream, just like the beautiful dancer.

THEY DON'T UNDERSTAND WHAT AN ORDER IS.

His smile lights up his face in such a beautiful way. Our glances connect and he lights up like a carnival attraction, like when you hit the bullseye and the clown's happy face is suddenly illuminated. But this time, instead of winning a stuffed animal, I win him. The effect is completed by the way the glow of his smile connects with the sparkle in his eyes. The eyes sparkle and the smile glows, and the connection between the two closes a circuit and his radiance shines forth, sending a high voltage arcing across the room and enveloping me in warm light. I am aware that a circuit has closed in me also, an equally charged energy of opposite polarity enveloping him. When circuits close, energy flows, and I can feel it all over: the flow.

What is this circuit closing in me? I can see it so clearly in him. It's extended beyond his face now, lighting him up like an educational mannequin in an anatomy class: the light goes on and you can suddenly see the precise layout of the blood vessels, the intricate connections of muscles to tendons to bone, the delicate branching of the nerves, the soft organs floating each in their appointed place. But you can't see this in yourself. That's just how it is. My energy is arcing out across the room, not spiraling inward. I am revealing myself to him, not me. For the circuit between us to close, I must let go of myself. Which is fine by me.

So here we are, locked in, yet suddenly more free, separated by a few feet of floor and twenty-eight years of time but nevertheless flowing into each other. Big smiles. Just smile. Take your time. Fully inhabit the smile. Nothing so sweet.

He says he is twenty-one. He is Vietnamese. Born in Germany to refugee parents who ended up in Palo Alto. Until recently, a college student. Images of him in one of my classes flash by. Warning signs. I take my time examining them. Yes, he could be one of my students. But he is not. I don't even teach in this city. A student is not all he is, and a professor is not all I am. These are very small pieces of us, actually. I let them go. Yes, this age difference between us is shot through with power, but the power is not flowing in just one direction. It is circulating. That is how circuits work.

He tells me he is in the Army Reserve and he has been called up for duty in Iraq. He ships out in a few months. He has withdrawn from school and is working full time with his unit preparing for deployment. I take it all in, allowing this stunning piece of news to wash over me.

Iraq. He is going to Iraq.

More lights switch on: the intersections between his path and mine light up like the Parisian subway maps illuminating the route between two stations.

Departure: his parents were refugees from the Vietnam
War that so deeply shaped my own coming of age.

Change trains: he was born and raised in Germany, the country my own father fought in the Second World War.

Second transfer: here he is, not even a US citizen, but shipping out to fight for George Bush and Dick Cheney and the Haliburton Corporation in Iraq.

End of the line: a war whose outlines we even now cannot fully grasp but which will likely continue to color the world for the rest of my days and probably his.

Mind the gap and make sure you have all of your personal belongings as you exit the train.

There is nothing I can change about this hugely twisted journey. I cannot change history. I cannot will George Bush and Dick Cheney away. The whole world can see the horrors unfolding in Iraq, but no one can stop them. The gears of history are engaged and the engine is too big, sweeping up millions into its fire box. The spark between us, illuminating this whole room and our whole beings, would not even be visible in the furnace powering the engine of war downhill at breakneck speed. I cannot stop it. I cannot even stop this beautiful man with the radiant smile standing right in front of me from going into it. Lying naked with him, loving him, being tender with him, seems like the next best plan. Standing here by the pool table with our clothes on we have already made the bar disappear. Naked we can make war and terrorism and religion and hate disappear, at least at one place and time. We can make love not war.

I ask him about his impending deployment. No judgment. Just listen. Just keep the circuit open. There must be some truth here.

He is not afraid of going to Iraq, he says. To the contrary, he is looking forward to it. "It will be an adventure for me." He likes the army.

He likes his sergeant. He enjoys following orders. The whole package agrees with him.

He is not going to be a frontline soldier. He is a dental technician. He enjoys this job. "Soldiers get to Iraq and they stop taking care of themselves because they are too busy with everything else." His job will be to make sure that a soldier's teeth look great when they are blown from his mouth.

A strangely detailed image flashes into my mind unwanted: the smoking wreckage of a Humvee after an IED explosion. The driver is still there, strapped in by his seat belt, ready to step on the gas and speed away. One hand on the wheel, the other on the stick. The shrapnel has cut a hole in the Humvee's floor, which is now the ceiling of the overturned vehicle. Slanted rays of sunlight slither through the haze of the dark interior to catch a sparkling row of pearly whites that were blown up through the driver's skull and embedded in an exploded smile across the ceiling of the cab, which is now the floor. A skeleton smile across a dark expanse of charred metal and fabric, the teeth perfectly manicured by a twenty-one-year young Vietnamese kid who is not even an American citizen, is not even "out" yet to his parents, who enjoys following orders.

He says, "My friends think I'm crazy. They ask if I really think I can shoot someone, kill someone. I say, 'If I am ordered to I will have to.' They don't understand what an order is. They don't understand that if you don't do what your boss tells you to do you get fired, but if you don't follow orders you go to jail."

He is smiling. He is happy. He likes talking about his most excellent adventure which is about to begin. He has absolutely no idea what's coming. He understands what the army wants him to understand, no more and no less: this will be an adventure; all he has to do is follow orders; it is an opportunity to *serve*.

I shudder at the catastrophe I imagine awaits him. Maybe the mangled body in the vehicle will be his. Or maybe he will come home and sink into his own private PTSD in a rented room above a hardware store. Maybe not. I recently spoke to a career military man who told me that one of the biggest problems confronting the US military in Iraq is obesity. The majority of personnel in Iraq are support personnel, not combat troops. Many never leave their base. The perfect physical specimens that emerge from boot camp ship out to Iraq and get stuck on bases with Burger Kings and Baskin Robbins and not a whole lot to do and it is dangerous to leave the base so they play video games, eat junk food, and get fat. Perhaps he will have his most excellent adventure and go to Iraq and be a soldier and clean teeth and learn a skill and Be All He Can Be and come home an accomplished dental technician. Maybe he will leave a boy and come home a man. Is that what he wants?

What does he want from me? To get next to a man like the one he thinks he wants to become? I can offer him that, at a cost far below the price he will pay for his Iraq experience. Free, actually. Here, take it. You're impressed by this manliness thing? Take it. I don't want it. Never did, never will.

So many gay men seem haunted by insecurity about manhood. They are enveloped in masculinity that is somehow in another dimension they cannot access. How did I escape that? Me, the Little League baseball star, elementary school basketball star, middle school football star, expedition skier, open ocean kayaker, war correspondent, blah blah blah. No, I don't lack the masculinity of which so many gay men seem to feel a deficit. My problem is that my masculinity doesn't fit. It clings to me like a too-small button-up shirt and tie on a hot, muggy day. I have spent years trying to shed it. Go away. Stop following me around. Knock it off. Get out of here. Go play on the freeway.

If this kid wants some, I have some I am dying to get rid of. Is that the energy running through the circuit that connects us? OK. Deal. He wants to lie naked with his ear to the heart of a man who is older and bigger and stronger, and I want to lie naked with my head resting on the heart of a man who is untouched by the whole violent, abusive, manipulative fucked up world of men. Not a boy, but not yet a man. Twenty-one. Old enough to drive, and drink, and vote, and kill and die. Old enough to choose his sexual partners. Old enough to be ordered to Iraq. But not old enough to know what lies ahead.

On the way home, he tells me that the only men he has ever had sex with were men he met on the Internet. He goes to gay bars a lot, but has never connected for sexual intimacy with anyone there, or any other place he has been physically present. To him, cruising has nothing to do with a sly glance, a coy smile, an amazing dance move, a movie and a drink, or a friendship that grows until it suggests something deeper. It is all about transistors and information packet switching and internet service providers. No wonder he is searching for something more real. Iraq will be real. Is that one of the fundamental male needs that war serves? To make the alienated lives of men finally real? Is that the root of PTSD? That after the real experience of war men cannot stand the loss of that connection to a real life? Well, I am real. I can give him that too.

He tells me that the only older person he is "out" to is, of all people, his sergeant. Two vectors cross in my mind: one represents the army's increasingly desperate search for willing canon fodder for the war in Iraq; the other is the gay male subculture's fracture into internet hook-ups. The two lines intersect in this young man who has access to the whole gay Mecca of San Francisco, yet the only mentor he can spill his guts to about sexuality is his army sergeant. Don't Ask Don't Tell. Gimme a fucking break.

His lips are the sweetest thing imaginable. His skin is a field of...
I have no metaphor. Maybe his skin is just his skin. Maybe if I take
a bite I will discover he is made of flan, the most delicious and
creamy flan the world has ever known, but in fact the world will
still not know, because with the first bite I will begin to dissolve,
my flan-man melting me from the inside out, and who knows what
would happen then?

We kiss and touch and caress in every possible way. I feel so peaceful. There is no rush to get to "sex." Every movement and touch is
sufficient unto itself.

At some point, far down the road, he has unbuttoned my pants
and wants to blow me, and I remember HIV. In the gay world of
San Francisco now, oral sex without cumming is considered "safe."
There is a small chance of infection but everyone acts as if this
were not so. It is a choice the community seems to have made. As
someone with HIV, I generally accept this decision, but then again
I mostly have sex with my peers. My peers have been living in this
epidemic for years. They have watched friends die, in some cases
lots of them. The ones who are still negative have gone through it
all, periods in which they limited their partners to other men they
thought were negative, periods in which they shut down and had no
sex at all, and periods in which they took risks they regretted later.
They have emerged with personal sets of rules about sex and safety
that they have lived and made their peace with. I don't try to second
guess these men.

But this young man is something else. His understanding of HIV
and risk is shallow, like his understanding of war. There is no experience to go with it, no pain, no dirt under the fingernails, or over
the coffin lid. No way I am not going to use a condom with this innocent one who doesn't know better, whose radiance is overflowing

my bed and filling my room. I need to protect him and keep him safe. Send him off to George Bush's war in one piece.

NUKE IRAQ

He is six foot ten with glistening black skin and a lean muscled body. (Did I mention I am a basketball fan?) He tosses me into bed and jumps on me. The sex is all fireworks and bullseyes. For his every desire, I have a reciprocal desire. On and on it goes. Connect connect connect, until no dot is left alone and the full picture has been revealed. And then we are lying naked together staring at the ceiling. He is soft-spoken and polite. He is way into me. I think: this has got to be too good to be true. Something has got to give, but what?

Given recent events in the world outside, the pillow talk inevitably turns to politics, and the US invasion of Iraq. We agree that this invasion should never have happened, Bush is a mad man, the whole thing is a tragedy. Then he offers his solution. "I think we should give the situation there three more months to work itself out, and then if it is still a mess we should just nuke the place."

The place. As in: Iraq?

Yes.

Nuke, as in nuclear bomb?

Yes.

Not joking?

Not joking.

LUSTY LADY

He calls and says he wants to go on a date. He has the whole evening planned but doesn't want to tell me what. He wants me to just go along with it. Wonderful. He arrives on his bike a short time later wearing a bright orange leg warmer on one leg and a lime green leg warmer on the other, a sort of frumpy housewife dress a la 1950s, combat boots, a black leather jacket, a pink feather boa, and too much mascara, which, along with his dyed jet black hair, gives his pale ivory skin a ghostly shine. We ride through town on our bikes, the apparition and I, and come to a stop in front of the Lusty Lady, a local strip joint. The plan, he announces, is to make out in a peep show booth. And off we go.

It's Monday, and The Lusty Lady is a sad and lonely place. The man who takes our money at the door is so bored that, just to break the tedium, he goes on the house speaker system every now and says things like, "Message to all employees: work harder!" The peep show booth is slimy with the splooge of the night's previous customers, or the week's, or the year's. Come to think of it, do they *ever* clean these walls? We put our quarter in the slot and when the window cover goes up, we start kissing.

The window reveals two ladies on a round stage ringed by windows identical to ours. The ladies are naked, but nowhere close to lusty. They look bored out of their minds. They make the most minimal gestures intended to reference dancing but seem to actually function just to keep them awake. But then they see us and their frowns are replaced by broad smiles. They move across the stage to our window to get a better look. Soon we are getting our own VIP show, as the girls take turns squatting down and thrusting their pussies in our window. We keep making out. I notice the Japanese businessmen, the only other patrons, craning their heads from their windows trying to see who is getting all the action, wondering if their tips were not high enough.

The boy, the drag, the girls, his skin, the sleaze, the ridiculous loudspeaker, his lips, the businessmen, the scent of his hair which I can somehow drink in over the stank – all coalesce into an unexpected beauty. Can I just be here forever? No, really. Isn't there some high-tech way to freeze us on the spot, and Martians, landing on Earth in a million years on an archeological expedition to determine what catastrophe ended life on this forsaken planet, will find us just like this and say, "Oooooooooooo."

That was so much fun we decide to stop by the gay strip theater on the way home. Gay strippers never really caught on in San Francisco, and anyway it's midnight on Monday, and the tired old man who took our money at the door is the only soul in the place. No stripper, no nobody. Just canned porn sequences flickering larger than life on a lifeless screen. We take our seats, watch for a minute, and then he and I are making our own damn porn movie, performing for no one but ourselves. Step right up. Cheap at half the price.

JERUSALEM'S PARKS

He is visiting San Francisco from Jerusalem. I tell him my first lover moved to Israel. I ask him about gay life in Jerusalem. He explains that Western sexual ideology has completely pervaded Jewish culture there, so to Jewish men in Jerusalem, "gay" means the same thing it means to men in San Francisco. But Palestinian men in Jerusalem still hold to the idea, commonly believed in many parts of the world not long ago and still common in Muslim lands, that as long as you are the one performing the "male role" in sex, your manhood is intact. As long as you do the penetrating, you are not gay. He also explains that in Tel Aviv there is a vibrant gay scene, but in Jerusalem where the religious authorities hold sway, everything must be hidden, so men cruise the city's parks for late night encounters.

Thus, every night the parks of Jerusalem are full of Palestinians fucking Jews.

KING LEER IN THE MEN'S ROOM

My father comes to San Francisco from his ghost town in south-ern New Mexico for a visit. He is elderly and frail, and getting him around is a production involving a wheelchair and adult diapers. But he didn't "come out" until he was seventy years old and isolated in a ghost town, and I know he wants to see something of gay San Francisco, so I take him to gay country western dancing. Will this be fun or melancholy, seeing the life he might have had if he had been born a few decades later, and felt several degrees less guilt-rid-den and conflicted? I put a cowboy hat on him and off we go, and he just loves it. Can't get enough. It takes some maneuvering to get him into a spot where he can watch the dancing from his wheelchair, and we are graciously assisted by a perfectly costumed gay cowboy. Like most of the men here. Urban gay men have an idealized notion of cowboys that is pure Hollywood, which is absurd to those like my father and I, who grew up around the pot-bellied working stiffs of the real world. Except this guy's costume appears to be actually worn. Could this be a real cowboy?

We chat, and it turns that yes, he is a real working cowboy, from southern New Mexico not far from where my father lives. How is that possible, that in this crowd of urban gays, the one working cowboy is the one helping my father, eventually going above and beyond what might be seen as properly chivalrous, and I begin to wonder: is this guy *cruising* my elderly father?

Soon my father has reached his limit and it is time to leave, but first he needs to pee. I wheel him into the men's room and the guy follows us in. He strikes a macho pose leaning against the bathroom wall and watches me help my father out of his wheelchair and to the urinal, making not the least effort to hide his interest in watching my father piss. My father then asks to be wheeled to the sink to wash his hands. The man watches the hand washing as intently as he watched the urinating. And then, in a deep, manly voice which booms through the men's room with Shakespearean flair, he declaims:

YOU GOTTA WONDER ABOUT A MAN WHO WASHES HIS HANDS AFTER HE GOES PEE. I MEAN, WHERE'S THAT DICK BEEN THAT IT'S SO *GAD DAMN DIRTY.*

STARTING FROM ZERO

"It's been five years but it's still hard for me to talk about," he says, gently touching the ring on his slender finger. "But it is good for me to talk about it so I will." My eyes follow from his slender finger up his slender arm to his slender shoulder. Everything about him is slender. Except for his smile, which is a mile wide and slightly goofy. Utterly charming. Jet black eyes like marbles. He only sees out of one of them thanks to childhood glaucoma. He weighs all of a hundred and five pounds, thanks to childhood intestinal cancer. If a strong wind came up, would he blow away if I didn't hold him down? Sometimes when I touch him, I worry I will break him. But here he is, telling me his story, so he's got staying power.

It all started when he was fourteen years old. He was going to school in a small village. It was still a world before smartphones, but the village had an internet cafe, where he found a gay chat site. Soon he was trading messages with a particular guy, and eventually the guy invited him to come to the capital to meet. The bus ride took two hours. "I was so scared. I had never been to the capital. I had never been to a city, any city." He arrived in one of the world's densest, smokiest urban jungles, found his way to the McDonald's to which he had been directed, and ordered a hamburger. "I had never had a hamburger. Now I was *really* scared." But who among the customers was his mystery date? They had not exchanged pictures, nor even said much about their appearance. "And then I realized it was a *foreigner*. He had chatted with me in my own language, so I had no idea he was a foreigner! But he had no idea I was so young, because I had said nothing about my age."

So the adult foreigner and the fourteen-year-old village boy faced each other across a table at McDonald's.

"I'm so scared," he blurted out. "I have never met a foreigner before."

"I'm so scared, I think this might be criminal," the man answered.

But neither one bolted, and they went for a walk, and he learned that the man was twenty-four years old and from Switzerland. They eventually ended up back at the man's apartment, where the boy from the village spent the night on the couch. There had been no sex or even touching. In the morning after breakfast he took the bus home. The next week he returned and again slept on the couch. And then again. Soon the village kid was visiting the urban foreigner two or three times a month. School on weekdays, then the hours on the bus, walks and a meal together, then hours on the bus home.

"After six months, he told me he was falling in love with me. I said I was falling in love with him too. We decided to finally have sex. Now I was fifteen. I had never had sex. I was so scared. He asked, 'Do you want me to fuck you, or you fuck me?' I looked at his cock. It was so big. I was so small. I was so scared. I said, 'Better I fuck you.' So I did. Four times that day!"

I try to imagine this willowy figure in front of me at fifteen years old, topping a man ten years his senior. It's hard to picture.

It occurs to me that he and I are the only gay men I know who were in love with the first man we had sex with. A curious bond, but real. We talk about that, acknowledge it. But my first love quickly decided he was straight and left me. The village kid and the urban foreigner became passionate lovers. "I was always the top. I tried to bottom a few times but it was too uncomfortable." Not surprising, given the childhood cancer. "But he wanted that, so after seven years we decided to have an open relationship so he could have that experience."

The man got to know the kid's entire family. "We told my family he was my English teacher. He visited often."

Years went by and the kid was not a kid anymore. After eight years they began discussing adopting a child. After nine years they began planning to marry. Then came the motor bike accident.

"When I regained consciousness, I was in a hospital. They told me he was dead."

We take a moment to let that statement breathe. It starts small, just a wisp of mist from his mouth, then spreads out to cover the entire bed, a cloud comforter of sadness. But that isn't all.

"His extended family in Switzerland were so distraught they were not thinking clearly, and they raised the question of whether he had been *murdered*. So I had to answer a lot of questions, we had to get CCTV video of the accident. It was terrible. He owned the apartment we lived in, but we owned the furniture together. Finally, it was too much. I gave everything away to charity, moved to this new place, and decided to *start again from zero*."

He moved, got a place to live, a good job, and new friends, and then

Covid arrived. His new home happened to be one of the worst places in the world to be during Covid, because nearly the entire labor force worked in tourism. People with years of experience in good jobs were suddenly reduced to fishing as their only source of food. He had some money saved and tried opening a small cafe which failed, then another which failed, then a photo studio which is working better. It seems his one seeing eye is a good one, and he has a knack for putting people at ease and making instagrammable pictures for young people in love or married couples with babies. Cuter than they could have made for themselves. But the money is just enough. Or almost enough. He has hungry days.

Right now he has a hunger for something else. It has been five years since the accident. He might be ready to make a new love. Might that be me?

You love deeply, beautiful friend. Your sincerity seems naive in this cynical world: a gay boy who fell in love at fourteen and touched none but his true love for ten years. You have an unusual heart, and if you were anyone else I would be worried for how it would be trampled. But you are special; somehow, I can picture you finding someone offering the kind of love you are ready to give. For now, we have a few nights, let's make of them everything we can.

*

We stayed in touch from opposite sides of the world. Though we were in the same place for only a short time I became his closest confidant. This is not unusual where he lives. The culture is so repressive for gay men that it is safer to share intimate thoughts and feelings with men far away than with those close by.

Life has not been kind to him. He contracted HIV. He interpreted that as karma. He decided that his karma demanded that he must no longer hide part of his life from mother, that he return to his home village and tell her that he is gay and has HIV.

The trip did not go well. He told his mother, who told his grandmother, who told the entire family. There was a family council. It was decided that he was not welcome in the family or the village for two years, after which they would reevaluate. Unless he got rich, in which case he would be welcome again.

That way of thinking about money is common in village culture in his country.

It's uncertain whether he will stick around this world long enough to go back in two years. He is not responding well to the HIV meds. His immune system is weak and the intestinal cancer has returned. His doctors say he requires urgent surgery. But where would he go to recover, if not to his family home? He has no savings and must work every day to pay for food and rent. He has yet to tell his boss about the cancer for fear of losing his job.

I thought I was done burying friends with AIDS years ago, but it is looking like that is not the case. Perhaps that is my karma.

FATHERS

He stands about six foot two, a solid big-boned chunk of a man with a thick mane of dark hair, a densely forested face when he doesn't shave, and piercing eyes. He radiates an anxiousness that undermines his hippie persona. He channels his nervous energy into chain smoking, chain talking, and various arts and crafts projects, at which he excels.

When he was very young, first grade maybe, his father left him pretty much alone in a mobile home for a year while dad worked construction and fucked a girl in the next town over. He lived on TV dinners, watched television, and taught himself to sew. By his late teens he was sewing extraordinary clothing: period-correct Victorian dresses for the theater and the costume balls of the one percent, one-off wedding dresses, unbelievable get-ups for drag queens, and so forth, all of which he sold for far less than he should have, for he had absolutely no sense about money.

He should have become a fashion designer, *could* have become a fashion designer, but every time he got a leg up he made sure to shoot himself in the foot. He is now (almost) making a living from wedding dresses. The women who commission the dresses start out thinking they're getting the deal of a lifetime, gorgeous things that should have cost several times what he charges. But the poor brides-to-be invariably end up camped out in his apartment in the last days before their betrothal, having learned that unless they sit by his side and watch, their dress will never be done. They bring him food and cigarettes, chat, remind him again and again exactly how little time is left before the big day, and simply refuse to leave.

He got his big break when a fashion magazine invited him to do a photo spread. Another guy would have thrown himself into a frenzy of work to create the perfect collection for his initial shoot. This guy did pretty much nothing. On the day of the shoot, he showed up with a beautiful man and a roll of butcher paper. Right there in the studio, one at a time, he made a paper dress right on the model. Once it was photographed, he ripped it off and tossed it in the garbage, then made another. Again and again. It was brilliant. But you can't sell pieces of paper out of the trash.

Twice he took all extant photos of himself, put them in a pile, and burned them. All he needs is some stability, I thought. I offered him my basement as a studio. He took weeks designing his dream studio, complete with a large work table with intricate drawers and cubbies for all his supplies. I bought him all lumber he would need to build it, as well as the necessary tools and hardware. At long last he would be able to realize his enormous potential. He worked and worked building the table. The day it was done and the studio was all ready to go was the day he left.

*

Jerry's father beat him violently, and George's father did something I never learned the details of, but resulted in young George fleeing the home and putting himself up for adoption.

N___'s father never even acknowledged paternity of his son. But he did blow his head off with a shotgun when N___ was around ten years old.

M___'s father was a drifter who got a job driving a quadriplegic across the country from the west coast to the man's new home in New York City. Somewhere along the way he pulled off on a county road, pushed the man out of the car, and drove off with all his things. For which he was serving a long term in jail.

S___'s father beat his mother. Either S___ or the neighbors called the cops so regularly that the cops stopped knocking at the front door and would just let themselves right on in. Sometimes S___ would intervene, in which case the father's violence was re-directed at him. Things came to a head one night when S___ grabbed a knife to defend himself and threatened to kill his father. That sort of settled things down until his birthday. He opened a birthday card from someone he had never heard of and five dollars fell out. He looked to his mom for explanation, who in turn looked at his dad and asked, "Honey, do you think it's time to tell him who his real father is?" Eventually he met his real father, once. Real dad came by the house one day and took him for a drive. Told him he was going to make him a man. Took him to a dirty bookstore outside the city limits and introduced him to jerking off in video booths.

P___ was a bookworm when he was young. He won the New York State spelling bee, and came in third at the nationals. But dad thought his boy should be out playing and roughhousing like other boys, so he locked his son out of the house after school until dinner time. P___ would go buy novels at the drug store, then go sit by the railroad track and read until dinner time. He figured that by the time he left for college he had stashed a small library of books in the bushes by the tracks. The spelling bee got him a scholarship to Yale.

Quite the accomplishment for a white trash kid who remembers
having oatmeal for Christmas dinner because that was all there was
in the house. He had his first sexual experience during his freshman
year, and with redneck naïveté marched into the campus mental
health clinic the next day and said "I think I might be a homosexual. What can you tell me about this?" He spent the next two years
in a mental hospital, signed in by the clinic and his father. Twice
he escaped, and twice he was brought back in a straight jacket. He
walked out of the place on his twenty-first birthday, the moment he
could legally sign himself out. By then he had received thirty-six
electric shocks. He was still in love with writing, but absolutely
phobic of Yale and elite culture, so he made a career writing soap
operas for television. At night he would tie his lovers up and give
them electric shocks and stuff like that.

I don't walk into a bar with a sign on my forehead indicating a
preference for men with disaster dads, but these are the men I have
found. Maybe I have a sort of sense for them, or they for me. Or
maybe this is just who fathers are, and if you get close to numerous
men over the years, these are the father stories you will collect.

GUMMY WORMS

He's muscled up, sandy haired, and corn-fed. Not my usual flavor, yet I am captivated. He props his elbow on the pillow and coyly lets out that he used to hustle, though not anymore. If he was looking to shock he came to the wrong place. Do tell.

This was before the internet, when male hustlers ran "escort" ads in the back pages of the local gay paper. An ad came with a voicemail number supplied by the newspaper. Interested clients would call and leave you a voice message with their number, and you decided whether to call back. He was uncomfortable putting his picture in the paper like the other hustlers did, so he used an image of a stick figure under the headline "Mr. Stick: So Strong, Yet So Flexible."

What sort of guy responded to an ad like that, I wonder?

"Well, there was this one guy. I walk in and he hands me $125 and says, 'You don't have to take your clothes off or touch me or anything. I just want you to watch something.' Then the guy jerks off, and when he cums, it shoots across the room and splats against the wall, and there is a worm in it that goes slithering down the wall. Then he turns to me and whispers, 'Do you wanna see how I do it?' And he leads me to the freezer where he kept a supply of ...

frozen gummy worms. Somehow he had figured out that when you freeze gummy worms they not only get hard, they also straighten out. Then you can insert them through your urethra and up into the shaft of your cock, and masturbate until you fire them across the room."

The client was so pleased at this discovery that he paid the man in bed next to me $125 just to watch him do it. I wonder how many things he had inserted into his cock before settling on frozen gummy worms. Rome was not built in a day.

PSYCHEDELIC

I am walking through the Museum of Anthropology in Mexico City and discover that one of the oldest items in the museum is identified as an ancient "psychedelic enema."

I wonder how many things the ancients put up their butts before they hit on the psychedelic.

FREE LOVE

He is one of my favorite old school gay hippies. He got so annoyed at how many of his friends were making ends meet by putting hustler ads in the back pages of the gay paper that he bought his own ad. No photo, no image. Just a few words in bold type: *Sex should be free.*

THE CHAMPION

He is pure Grade A cowboy. The hat. The plaid shirt. The right cut of jeans. Flashy boots. Spurs. The smell of horse hair and cow shit. Even his posture: one foot up on the lower bar of the corral fence. The perfect picture of cowboy macho. Yet when he opens his mouth, out comes the voice of the ditziest drag queen serving up endless dish.

We are at the rodeo, the *gay* rodeo, and he has just won the bull riding event. Bull riding is the butchest event in this butchest of sports. Angry bulls are no joke. Trying to ride on the back of an angry bull is not a right-minded thing to do. Even the rides of experts are typically counted in seconds. Riding an angry bull hurts, and falling off hurts even more, and then you gotta run. High up on my list of no-not-ever.

"Gay bull rider" would strike many as a non sequitur, so I just had to go say hi to check him out. Turns out he is the national gay rodeo bull riding champion. (Yes, there is a national gay rodeo circuit.)

I briefly attempt to hide just how funny I find the clash between his appearance and mannerisms, but it quickly becomes apparent that he doesn't mind. Welcomes that response. Thrives on it. The more I laugh, the more he dials it up. I ask him about bull riding and he explains some of the finer points. I ask about his life growing up cowboy and gay, and his story fits the mold of the poorly-educated working-stiff white-trash cowboys I grew up around, with the addition of his Big Secret. I notice he has enormous matching scars on his forearms: a single continuous line from wrist to elbow, with rows of what look like nail or staple holes on each side.

"Whoa! Did you get those from bull riding?"

"These? Nah, I got these when my boyfriend threw me off a highway overpass."

WHATEVER YOU WANT DARLING

He is only eighteen, yet he carries all the confidence, even arrogance of his class. A rich kid in a poor country. Not looking for money or a sugar daddy or a visa. He has all the money he needs. He can go anywhere he wants. His accent is aristocratic British, the native tongue of the global boarding school elite.

The fantasy we are playing out is his, not mine. He sought me out. Went to considerable effort. Had it all planned out, had a clear vision of it in his head. The first thing he said to me: "OK, I am going to call you Papa Bear."

"What am I going to call you?"

"I don't know. It's not important."

And he is going to stop by on his way to school to give me pastries. That is also part of the plan. Then he will text me from school, which he will find fun and deliciously transgressive.

When we get into bed, he takes off his clothes, lies down on his back, opens his arms, smiles, and coos, "Whatever you want, darling."

This was also, I am sure, part of the plan. He had played it all through in his mind, many times.

THE STRIPPER

This bar doesn't typically have strippers, but there he is, dancing on a tiny stage and working each piece of clothing like a precious work of fine art. Speaking of fine art, his body is amazing. A Greek statue brought to life in onyx rather than bronze. Each muscle exquisitely carved by the hand of a master. Breathtaking, the way those ancient Greeks manifested their love of the male form.

Strippers are not generally my thing. I often find them silly. But for some reason this one has my rapt attention. I cannot look away. Probably making a fool of myself, the only one in the bar so obviously taken in by the show. I probably have my mouth hanging open but who knows, because my attention is all on him. His shoulder, bicep, forearm, wrist, hand, finger, nail. Every inch. Every gesture. Every slinky dance move. I drink him in. Every drop.

One day, I say to myself, one day before I die, I would like to have sex with a man with a body like this.

The last of his clothes come off and he is done with his routine. He picks up his things and, butt naked, lightly leaps from his perch and makes his way across the room directly to me. "Hi, how are you?"

And I remember: I did have sex with him.

How could I have possibly forgotten that? Then I remember. He was so completely self-obsessed he hardly noticed I was there. Or rather, he acknowledged my presence, but not as a sexual partner. The sex that was happening was between him and him. An orgy of self-adulation. I was there as the supporting cast. My job was to confirm that he was worthy of adulation. And to make known that if he would be so generous as to take a break from worshipping himself long enough to allow me to worship him for a moment, I would leap at the chance. In the meantime I should be content to watch.

THE
ANESTHESIOLOGIST

It's hard to know just what kind of condition you are in lying on a gurney in the back of an ambulance, but I noted that we had set out on our journey to the ER with only the light flashing, and then the siren went on. I figured things weren't looking so good when the ambulance driver suddenly hit the gas and we accelerated to a different speed entirely.

I had been at home convalescing from surgery when an artery in my throat burst. By the time the ambulance arrived I had blood coming out of both ends, and my bedroom and bathroom looked like a horror movie set.

As the gurney was lifted from the ambulance, someone handed me a bowl to vomit blood into. An orderly grabbed the gurney and ran me through the ER and down a hallway. As we careened around a corner, the bowl flew from my hands, sending HIV+ blood everywhere. "That was *awesome*," the orderly whispered, but he didn't slow down.

Alarms were going off like cyborg blackbirds signaling the approach of a predator. People shouting "No Pulse! No Pulse!" People rushing to and fro with one device or another.

I discovered an amazing thing that happens when a body swallows that much blood: the blood goes down as liquid but congeals in the stomach, so the body must produce an otherworldly convulsion to expel it. The back arches, the legs kick, the vocal cords emit a sound with no human reference, and a blood jellyfish comes flying out of the mouth and sails across the room. In a previous century, someone would have put a stake through my heart.

I learned this because I was watching it all from the ceiling. I observed my body doing these amazing things, but I did not feel them. Man, that must have hurt, but I felt no pain. I observed this team of highly trained professionals, the special forces of medicine, executing a high precision series of maneuvers, correctly and in the least possible amount of time, but I wasn't on that team. They were going to do what needed to be done in time for me to continue living or they weren't. I had no say in that matter.

I didn't see a white light at the end of a tunnel, yet it was very peaceful up there on the ceiling. If this was going to be my last experience of life, I wanted to notice everything. The energy crackling through the room as everyone applied brain cell and muscle to the task at hand. The tension in the curt commands and reports shouted back and forth, complete economy of syllables. My body doing all these things I had no idea it was capable of, and all without me.

I didn't see a movie of my life play fast forward in my head, but I had time to contemplate my life. I thought lovingly of my child who was becoming a young adult and was ready to find her way in the world without me. It occurred to me that my life had been a good one and had been enough.

From their actions and words, I learned that I would have to
undergo surgery to repair the wound, and they could not put me
under general anesthesia unless they could get some blood into me,
which was not so easy precisely because I had run out of it. I had lost
so much blood that my veins had collapsed and they couldn't get a
needle into one to pump blood back in. So that was the race: were
they going to get enough blood into a vein to get me into surgery
before I expired?

Eventually they must have found a vein because I was suddenly
whisked from the ER into an operating room, which brought me
down off the ceiling and back home into my body, with the strange
taste of liquid blood in my mouth and dried blood caked on my face.
A new team of differently trained professionals were rushing into
place with a different collection of high tech instruments. I was
aware that someone had sat down next to me and was intently
focused on the display of medical device nearby: the anesthesiologist. For the first time since I entered the ambulance, I was aware
of someone not as a medical action figure but as a human being.
A man. With sandy hair, a kind face, and a calm that was immensely
soothing to me at that moment. I smiled. He smiled back.

"Are you gay?" I was startled to discover I had a voice, and a sense of
humor.

He gave a start, and his smile widened.

"Why, yes, I am."

"Can I have your phone number?"

We both burst out laughing. Everyone in the operating room looked
at us in surprise. What could these two possibly be laughing about?

"I'll tell you what," he answered, holding that mask just above my face. "If you live through this, yes, you can have my phone number."

And everything went black.

*

I didn't call him, and he hadn't *really* given me his number. But I did take chocolates to the ER staff when I was well enough to do so. I was so grateful to all of them. I figured that at that point in the AIDS epidemic, a man spewing HIV+ blood all over everything in sight was not exactly their dream patient. I wondered what sort of care I would have received in, say, Dallas, instead of San Francisco.

THE PANTS

When he comes on to me in the bar I am reluctant. I have no fetish for the leather he is wearing, but life is short and I am feeling good and why not. We walk to his place and he goes directly to a trunk and starts pulling out more leather. And then more leather. Here, try this on. And this. And this. Oh this will be perfect. He strips off his clothes and puts on more leather, which gets him so excited that he spends awhile preening before a mirror before noticing that I have not followed suit. I explain that I generally prefer to have my clothes off when having sex, but he is having none of it. On go the leather plants. The pants for some reason seem to be the centerpiece. Everything else revolves around the pants. Leather pants with a stripe down the side. I realize that we are not going to have sex as I understand it. Or if we are, that is going to be way down the road, a dessert and not the main course. What we are doing is playing dress-up. He doesn't want a sexual partner as much as a mannequin. I excuse myself. He doesn't walk me to the door. In fact, he hardly notices I am leaving. He is completely absorbed in admiring himself in the mirror, in the leather pants with the stripe down the side.

On the way out, some light goes on in my mind, and I ask him what he does for a living. He's a motorcycle cop.

HI, I AM IN THE LOBBY.

I am trying my best to flirt, but he is completely indifferent to my efforts. Which is not surprising. He doesn't know me. Speaks only a little English. It is too loud in the club to talk anyway. And I am a good bit older.

So what am I doing? He is not even my type, or rather, one of my many types. But I am thirsty for anything gay, and he has a pleasant way about him. I have been on a long concert tour, a city a night. And my music world is nearly completely straight. It used to bother me that my music was not popular in gay culture but I made my peace with that long ago. Nevertheless, after a certain amount of time on the road I just want to go to a gay bar and be around gay people. Straight people often find it arrogant or off-putting when I say things like that, but gay people understand just what I mean. And today, I landed at the airport, went to the venue, and it turned out that the concert curator at the art center I am playing at is gay. And that, as far as I know, is a first.

So after the show I ask him if we can go out to gay bar before he drops me off at the hotel, and he readily agrees. When we get there he runs into some friends, and it is one of those with whom I am fruitlessly attempting to flirt.

After a while I tell myself I need to knock it off. It is late. I have traveled and flown and sound checked and played a concert, I have another flight and concert tomorrow, I need to sleep, I probably have had too many beers, and I am hitting on the concert organizer's best friend who is showing no interest in me at all.

I return to the hotel a bit forlorn, shower and brush my teeth, check the schedule for the morning, set the alarm, and am turning off the light when the phone by the bedside rings.

"Hello?"

It's the man with whom I was trying to flirt.

"Hi Bob. It's me. I am in the lobby. Can I come up to your room and sleep with you tonight?"

Sometimes gay sex and gay cruising can feel like the grimmest thing in the world, completely devoid of joy. And sometimes the stars align, and you suddenly find yourself in the sweetest physical and emotional intimacy with a man you don't know and will most likely never see again. And on this night, this man and I have a beautiful romance of a few hours that is so deep, so touching, that years, decades later, I cannot think of it without a smile. I hope he feels the same about his memories of that night. I am pretty sure he does.

UNCLE SAM WANTS YOU

He is hard to miss in the bar. A sort of black superman. Impossibly chiseled muscles. Pecs for days. Biceps for weeks. Abs for months. Thighs for years. Shoulders for decades. A back for eons. How much time do you have to spend pumping iron to look like this? Is he training for Mr. Universe? I am not drawn to big muscles, but wow, who is this person?

I sort of sidle on up and say hello. He responds with a smile as big and broad as the rest of him. I learn that beneath all this muscle is a very warm and gentle man, an easy person to be with. Kind. Modest (despite all appearances). Just lovely, really. Nothing not to like.

Eventually we go back to my place, and do the do, and it's lovely, just fine, but when it comes down to it I am just not enthralled by muscles the way many men are. It is the talk afterwards that leaves a deep impression.

He is in the Air Force.

Some backstory: When the whole gays-in-the-military

don't-ask-don't-tell drama played out under Bill Clinton, I could not
have cared less. Fight for the right to be canon fodder in the Imperial Army? Travel to beautiful places with beautiful people and kill
them? Really? I watched with a smirk as the clamor for gay people's
right to "serve" suddenly got very quiet when the US invaded Iraq.
Oh right. Soldiers kill people. And get killed. Forgot about that part.
Dumb asses. But then I learned how many black gay men use the
armed forces as a ticket out of wherever they are from. And I remem-
bered that life is always more complicated than we think.

There was, for example, the stunningly beautiful black Marine grac-
ing my bed, who worked for the Obamas in the White House, all spit
and polish. Yeah, if I was going to have a Marine in dress uniform
around all the time, I would pick him too.

Or another man who told me how his older brother had used the
Marines as his ticket out of their redneck Texas town and it seemed
to have worked out pretty well, so he had considered doing the same.
But the older brother was straight and butch, while the man in my
bed had been an effeminate, obviously gay kid. So, the older brother
came home on leave, and the gay kid told his big brother of his intention to follow him into the Marines. The older brother thought for a
moment, then picked up the family cat and threw it at his gay little
brother. Claws and teeth and fur and screeching, right in his face.

"What you do that for?"

"If you liked that, join the Marines." The older brother turned and
walked out of the room.

In my book, that is a good older brother to have.

Gays and war. War and gays. Supposedly, during the Vietnam war,
gay liberation activists hung around outside the Army induction

center in Oakland where eighteen-year-olds who were drafted reported for duty, their first step on the way to Vietnam. The activists had polaroid cameras and would offer to take the inductees into a nearby ally and photograph them in fellatio with a man to get them out of the draft. The story may be apocryphal, but I find it beautiful whether true or not.

In Istanbul, a man told me that gay men were not allowed in the Turkish military, but to avoid obligatory service you couldn't just say you were gay. You had to present a photo of yourself being sexually penetrated. (Like many Muslim cultures, in Turkey the taboo is not so much against having male sexual partners as allowing yourself to be penetrated.) Thus, before the internet began drowning us all in sexual images, the Turkish military had one of the largest gay porn collections in the world. This too is a story I have not verified, but is beautiful to contemplate as fact or fantasy.

But I digress.

Back to the Adonis in the bar on leave from his duties in the Air Force.

Turns out that he is stationed in a nuclear missile silo. Lives underground. Turns out there is not much to do in a nuclear missile silo. The missile just sits there being a missile that will hopefully never be fired. But just in case, someone needs to be there ready to push the button, so to speak. And to ensure that whoever is there is truly ready to do that, there are occasional drills. But you don't know if it's a drill or not. You swing into action, do everything that needs to be done. Then you learn if it was a drill. The purpose of the drill is to test not only the readiness of the missile but the readiness of those on site to incinerate whatever the missile is aimed at. So that's the job for which you are paid: to demonstrate, over and over, your willingness to fire.

Other than that, there is not much to do in your underground life. So you lift weights. All day. Day in. Day out. And count the days until your next leave, when you can go to San Francisco, walk into a gay bar, and dazzle everyone there with your muscles.

CLASH OF CLANS

The Southeast Asian moon shines down on our naked bodies, which glisten so differently in their different shadings. The Southeast Asian surf caresses the beach just outside our open door. It is quiet in the village. The nearest city is several islands away. We make beautiful, passionate love. The moment the fireworks explode, he whips out his smartphone in flashlight mode to make a close examination of what white–people–cum looks like. His curiosity satisfied, he rolls over and disappears into his phone.

Time passes.

I am flummoxed. Eventually I take out the iPad I use to write my journal, and write about him and his phone. Here we are, side by side, naked in bed, each at our screen. We could have been anywhere. New Jersey, say.

Finally he becomes curious about what is on my screen. I show him. He is embarrassed to find I am writing about him and his phone. He puts his phone away and, for the first time, we talk. About his phone.

He had been playing Clash of Clans. He is part of a "clan" of real people scattered across the real world who play together virtually.

Since they live in an assortment of time zones their clan is always playing 24/7. The sun is always shining somewhere.

He got his first smartphone just three months ago, when he left his home village to work at this humble hotel. Since then, his social life has existed entirely on his phone. Sleeps in an earthen house with a dirt floor and a smart phone. He got a Grindr account right away, but I am his first Grindr date. In fact, he says I am the first person he has had sex with. There is not a lot of Grindr action in this village. Clash of Clans, however, is always there.

He rolls over and resumes his game.

THE BEACH

It is a beautiful day on the northern Pacific Ocean, sunlit diamonds dance on blue water as I move my kayak along. I decide to take a break on a particularly beautiful beach, well-known to gay men, but difficult to land on in a kayak. The grade of the beach under the water is steep, so the waves break directly onto the sand. You have to time your landing just right or the wave will flip you over and slam you into the sand, and then as soon as you are through the surf you have to grab your boat and run up the beach before the next wave washes up and pulls you or your boat back out. My timing is good. I come barreling through, jump out and run my kayak up the beach, and find myself standing next to a naked man, lying on his back, with his eyes closed and his cock erect.

So I give him a blow job. His cum tastes like the ocean, and I remember that salt water in the face cures a multitude of evil: the sea, tears, or cum.

I jump back in my kayak, wait for the window between waves, and paddle as hard as I can to punch out through the surf. Soon I am back in the blue, watching the diamonds dance, and asking myself if that really happened. It makes me so happy to know that he too must be lying on the beach asking himself if a man in a kayak just burst through the surf, blew him, and then disappeared from whence he came.

Not a word was spoken.

WHAT DO YOU WANT, A DOLLAR?

He stands out, which is saying something. Not so easy to stand out at a Radical Faerie winter solstice orgy. The room, or rooms, are full of naked men of every age, size, and description, feasting on a long menu of sexual activities that anyone who has not been at such a party would have a hard time imagining.

He is dressed in leather, which is saying something. Nearly everyone else is naked. I have never had a fetish for leather, not even a hint, but somehow the black leather on his slender frame and his pale white skin, with long blond hair running down the animal hide covering his back, makes a package I find riveting.

And then there is the whip he is holding. I have never been whipped. Never even thought about it. Not even close.

Finally, he is leaning suggestively against a pillory. What is a pillory even doing at an orgy organized by the Radical Faeries? Well, this place we are in is used in turns by the full range of sex clubs in this city, and one of those clubs hosts parties where whips and pillories are the order of the day. But this is not one of those parties. Tonight is free love night for gay hippies. His long hair fits the faerie mold just fine. The rest of it, not so much.

True to form, I find myself drawn to the outlier, and I wander over.

"So, how about I put you in that pillory?"

"Umm, it's not really that kind of party."

"I know, I know, don't worry. We're not going to do anything serious, just play around."

"Hmmmm. It's an intriguing proposition. I have never done anything like that, but, really this doesn't seem to be the night for it."

"I know. This is a faerie party, I get it."

"What will happen after I get in the pillory?"

"We will play around."

I look at the whip.

"No marks, OK?"

"Listen, don't worry. I won't do anything even close to leaving a mark. We'll just play around."

I look over this blond angel in black, and the pillory and the whip, take a deep breath, and say OK. He locks my head and hands in the pillory. I feel quite electric. All the circuits are live.

Whack.

"Stop!"

"What's wrong?" He sounds a little annoyed.

"That was way too hard."

"Oh OK."

WHACK.

"STOP!"

He walks around to the front of the pillory.

"What's wrong now?" He makes no effort to disguise his annoyance.

We both turn our gaze to my arm. The whip missed my back entirely, and opened a large gash in my arm instead. Blood is seeping out.

"I thought you weren't going to leave any marks?"

"Oh. I'm sorry. What do you want, a dollar?"

I pass out.

Sometime later I am telling the organizers of the party what happened. They offer no sympathy. Instead they offer this: "Well, now would be a good time for you to sit and think about why you let someone you didn't know put you in a pillory and whip you."

If something like that happened today, the man would have been immediately bounced from the party. There would have been a long discussion about consent. I know of at least one party in San Francisco where a serious discussion of whether to call the police would ensue. But this was not the age of consent. This was the age of learning to look out for yourself.

BOY WITH
SCISSORS

"I don't know what voice got into my head and told me to do this," he
says sheepishly.

"How old were you?"

"Oh gee, maybe eight or nine? I don't know."

"And what happened exactly?"

"I found my father's porn magazines, and I took some scissors and cut
out all the penises. I mean, I very carefully cut around the outline of
them. Again, I have no idea why I did that. I didn't know anything
about sex or anything."

"And then?"

"And then I hid them all in the back of a drawer."

"What did your father say when he found out that all the penises
were missing from his magazines?"

"He didn't say anything. But a few weeks later I noticed all the penises were gone from the drawer."

"I guess he needed them back."

"Ha ha."

BOY WITH FLOWER

The flat was full of hustle and bustle. It was Saturday night, and four handsome and horny gay twenty-somethings were getting ready to go out on the town. Happiness and excitement for what might come next.

It was the early nineties. There were still no effective AIDS drugs, but a new generation of impatient young gay men had decided not to wait. They were not like the previous generation, who had learned too late that a strange retrovirus was spreading, who were told to use condoms when most of them already had the virus in their blood, who buried their friends by the dozens or the hundreds, and who in their shock and grief pretty much just stopped having sex altogether. Celibacy was for old men. Meaning, everyone over forty who was still alive. The new generation were getting their looks together and mapping out their route for the night. Some were getting their drugs in order.

It was the early nineties, before websites and smartphones and finally Grindr had fractured the vibrant community of young gay men on the hunt into isolated homebodies glued to their phones swiping right. The new generation would soon be leaving the flat for places that would be full of other young men like them, everyone hoping to score, to find another new-generation mate for sex. They were going *cruising*.

It was the early nineties, and all the frantic campaigns to educate gay men about safer sex and condoms had sunk in, and the rate of new HIV infections was going down down down. But it was before the community learned that there was a limit, that there was no amount of education that would push that rate below a certain floor. That because of mistakes and drugs and stupidity and bad luck, AIDS would not leave the community until effective drugs would arrive some years later.

The new generation preparing for their evening adventure were not thinking about that. Frankly, they were bored of it. They had thought about it from the first moment it occurred to them they might be gay. They were over it. They were going to use condoms. Safe sex wasn't that complicated, really. They were truly sorry that all those older men had died, but it wasn't their fault, there wasn't anything they could do about it, and they had their own lives to live. So lighten up, take a hit off this joint, and let's go.

All the boys in the flat were on the same page but one. Smaller than the others, the outlier wandered through all the getting ready as though he was invisible. Like a giraffe wandering through a herd of buffalo. Same savannah, different worlds. The small one was not preparing for a night out. He was in his pajamas. He had AIDS. He was likely going to die soon. His presence in the flat was awkward, but the boys managed it as best they could. No one could change the fact that the small one had AIDS. And no one could change the fact that the others were going out to have fun. It was what it was. They shared that understanding.

I was the other outlier. Not a roommate, a bit older, a little less excited by gay nightlife, watching the scene in the flat unfold at a certain remove.

The small one in the pajamas was carrying around a dead potted plant that the boys in their fast-paced twenty-something new-generation lives had forgotten to water. He walked up to me and held it out as if he was giving me a gift. "Like me," he said softly. "It never got a chance to flower."

PEDAL TO THE METAL

He is thin and small and beautiful and young dumb and full of cum and the cockiness that comes with knowing that he is the latest hot young gay thing, and he is going to work that for everything it's got, no apologies and no looking back. Until a short time ago he might have been a bullied and timid kid in some nowhere home town, unsure of everything, most of all himself. But not now. He has discovered his sexiness. He has his dream job working in the theater making costumes, in his dream city of San Francisco. He is having *fun*. And right now he is very *stoned*, as such gay boys often are. And we *fuck*, pedal to the metal. And then, laughing his sexy little head off, he recounts a barely coherent but hilarious story about tricking at some guy's place, and the guy has all this amazingly strong weed, and the guy does something that really pisses this boy off, so to get even he decides to go back and steal the weed, and somehow the police get involved, and one thing leads to another and he finds himself in a room in the police station, high as a kite, being interrogated by two cops, and somehow they let him go, because now he is here, still high as a kite, hasn't gone home yet, and he recounts his interrogation which he remembers as uproariously funny, and there was an older cop and a much younger "sort of rookie" cop, and "they were trying to play good cop bad cop with me, and I cracked up and turned to the young cop and said, "*Dude*, are you an *understudy?*"

And I so much want him to do well.

And I think he is only stoned on lots and lots of weed and nothing else, so that's a plus. And he's holding a steady job, another plus.

But he thinks he's bulletproof. They all do right about now.

One thing for sure: he is going to do what he is going to do. Nothing I or anyone is going to tell him is going to matter a whit.

I will be so happy if I run across him in a few years and he is still working in the theater, or still following his dreams, or at least still in one piece.

THE NAIL

They walk into the bar carrying a large board about the size of a door and dressed head to toe in standard issue "leather man" uniform. We are in a crowded cruise bar in Montreal in the early 1990s. There is sawdust on the floor and oil drums here and there being used as tables. The overall vibe is quite masculine, and there is stand-up sex going on in the dark corners, but these two immediately stand out in their leather outfits and their... what *is* that board for?

They go to the middle of the bar and shoo the men away from two oil drums, upon which they lay their board. The board has metal straps screwed to it here and there, the kind that you would use to strap your hot water heater in place in case of earthquake, and a wooden dowel protruding a foot or so from the surface.

The smaller of the two men strips down to a leather jock strap. (Man, that was a lot a layers of expensive leather to put on just to take off.) The larger man produces a gas mask into which he places the smaller man's head, and the smaller man climbs onto the board and lies down on his back.

All of this is happening in a crowded bar on a Friday night. They do not appear to be part of a planned show. They are just two more bar patrons, who happen to be doing this.

The larger man now fastens the smaller man to the board with all the metal straps, legs, feet, arms, legs, neck. It's Dr. Frankenstein, locking down the monster on the slab before throwing the switch which will bring it life.

The wooden dowel sticking up from the board is nestled up against the guy's crotch. The leather jock strap he is wearing has a zipper, which the larger man now unzips. He pulls out the man's cock, which has a large nail through it. Not down the urethra but crossways through the entire shaft. He then produces a hammer and nails the guy's cock to the dowel. And then he departs, leaving the smaller guy alone in a crowded bar, in a gas mask he cannot see out of, strapped to a board with his cock nailed in place.

Is he just going to lie there for the night, or are there more surprises in store? I cannot say, because at this point I flee.

STORM TROOPERS

We are in Los Angeles at the fiftieth birthday party of the oldest gay motorcycle club in America. All the gay motorcycle clubs in the western states are here. When I got the invitation I imagined a night of debauchery, but what I find is a formal sit-down dinner at a posh supper club. When I arrive, the guests are milling about having before-dinner drinks and conversing in hushed tones, almost whispers. Everyone seems oddly nervous. I notice that many of the men have soft drink cocktails. Well, hooray for them for being clean and sober, but a little snifter of something might go a long way toward livening up the atmosphere.

I mill about with the others, and try to look like I am having fun, though not trying as hard as everyone else. The one ready conversation piece, and thus the only thing anyone talks about, is the impending "presentation of colors."

"The presentation of colors should be really something."

"Yeah."

"Are you going to be presenting colors?"

"Nah. I have done that before, I thought it should be someone else's turn."

"Say, have you seen Joe?"

"He's here somewhere, but I think he's really nervous. He is going to be presenting colors for his club."

Though I am now genuinely curious to see what this presentation of colors might involve, there is only so much of this sort of thing a guy can take, and I am grateful to be rescued by the call to dinner.

We are ushered to a room full of round tables facing a stage, one motorcycle club to a table. We eat in near silence as no one seems to have anything to say to each other. I make a feeble attempt at breaking the ice with the man to my left, which ends abruptly when he remarks on how Latinos are ruining the great state of California. My Latino date, who owns a chopper and is a club member, is seated to my right. Did the guy not notice? Or did he not care?

A photographer circulates through the room. His arrival at each table signals a sudden break from the melancholy of staring at taste-less food, so that everyone can perform happiness for the camera.

It is when my table is going through this ritual that I notice the table just behind me populated entirely by men dressed as Nazi storm troopers. All of them. Identical. Down to the last detail. We could be in Munich in 1931.

Now, it's one thing to be at a leather bar or a gay street fair and see one guy playing out his sexual fetish by dressing up like a storm trooper. But, as I am suddenly aware, it is another thing altogether to see a whole table of men dressed like storm troopers out to dinner.

My first take is amazement that men can be so obsessed with want-ing to look tough and masculine, so desperate to dress in the mantle of authority, that they can abstract the actual history right out of these clothes. Or maybe they are ignorant enough to not even know the history. But no, they couldn't be that dim. Impossible. More likely they want to wear those clothes *because* of the history. They don't simply want to look like cops, they specifically want to look like Nazi cops. This is not a pleasant thought.

And then it hits me: *What if the Nazi storm troopers were in it for the clothes?* What if the original storm troopers fetishized their outfits just as much as these guys at the next table, and beating up gypsies and commies and Jews and yes even faggots was just a means to an end, and the end was wearing the outfit?

I can see just how it would unfold. You start a club, and you build it the way men's clubs are built. You have initiations in which people are required to do any old random thing. Doesn't matter what. All that matters is that it is required. Men who are unsure of what they have to do to be real men will be so relieved that you have provided them with a specific task. Do this and you will be a man. Why will that make you a man? Because this club is for men, that's why. And you can't be a member unless you do precisely this stupid thing. And then you demand that they do more, to prove they are truly worthy. You invite them into an extremely codified male camaraderie through which they can bond with other men according to an easy-to-follow set of rules, so that men who are perplexed and paralyzed by the ambiguous and conflicting demands of manhood feel more properly male than they ever would otherwise. What matters is not the rules themselves but the rigidity with which the rules are enforced. And what you dangle in front of them, the big prize for following the rules, is the outfit. As long as they do what you say, for the glory of the club, they get to wear the outfit. The outfit has a certain kind of magic, because many men who are unsure how to perform manhood are at a loss as to *what to wear.*

What if your sexual desires were mapped so that you didn't want to kiss or cuddle or fuck, you didn't want to touch or caress, all that you wanted to do was wear that outfit? What if there was only one way to get to wear it, and if you didn't get it that way you would never get it at all? Would you join a motorcycle club?

What if the motorcycle club was not one of the ones present at this ridiculous dinner, but a different club led by a guy who has this very same fetish for leather and geeky uniforms, but also has enough guts, charisma and stupidity to take his fetish out of the closet and put it on full display, to transform it from a weird little secret to a symbol of power acknowledged by hundreds, thousands, millions? What would happen is this: the closet uniform fetishists would go absolutely crazy. They would stop wearing their outfits in hidden clubs of like-minded fetishists and start wearing them in parades.

What if the men at the top, whose masculinity everyone looks up to and envies and craves, start to hint that their power trip fantasies might be acted out for real. Are you in or out? And real blood starts to flow, and the first person dies, and the line between who is in and out hardens. And being in is still the way, the only way, to get to wear the clothes...

Someone appears at the podium and announces the Presentation of Colors. "Representing the blah-blah club from Sacramento, Mr. John Johnson," he intones, and a man carrying a small banner with the logo of the blah-blah club marches to the front of the room and turns to face the diners. "Representing the bleep-bleep club from Oakland, Mr. Sam Samson." Another man carrying a small banner with the logo of the bleep-bleep club walks to the front of the room and takes his place by the first man. This continues, on and on and on, until we are confronted by a line of fifteen or so men facing us with little banners. I try to guess what comes next. What is the

activity or performance that had the participants on pins and nee-
dles before dinner? What happens is this: the MC proclaims, "There
you have it, the Presentation of Colors. Let's give these men a big
round of applause!" The diners offer polite applause and a relieved
bunch of men carrying little banners returns to their tables.

But the show is not over. Nope. A chubby drag queen in a red, white,
and blue dress appears, and the MC asks that we all rise and join
him in the singing of our national anthem. Everyone rises and
places their right hand over their heart, while a drag queen vaguely
reminiscent of Ethel Merman belts out the Star-Spangled Banner.
I glance over my shoulder and there they are, the storm troopers,
hands placed patriotically over their hearts, dutifully mumbling along.

IN THE DARK

We meet in the dark. Pitch black. No shading. No hint of a shadow. The dark is absolute. The shuffle and breath of random masculinity all around. Suddenly a passionate embrace. That random passion that transcends its own randomness. Everything disappears. How can darkness disappear? I don't know, but it does. The sound disappears. I disappear. The part that was just me is gone. It is only him and me now.

Finally, I whisper in his ear, "Do you want to get a beer?" We emerge into the club, my eyes adjust to the light, and I lose my breath for just a moment when I see who I have been with. He looks to be about sixteen. Was I just having sex with a teenager? A warning shot is fired across the bow and duly noted. This is new and unexpected terrain. Hmmm. At previous times in my life I might have turned away in fear and fled. But I am more confident in uncertain terrain than I used to be. So yes, let's have a beer.

We get our beers and he leads me out of the bar to a small grassy place across the street where we can sit. Well, he knows his way around these parts. Enough to know that we can take our beers outside, and that two people of our age difference can sit and talk and sip beer without problem. But he can't be here in this bar legally.

Or can he? Do I know what the drinking age in this country is? Do I know the age of consent? More importantly, do I know his age? People keep telling me people here look younger than they are. Anyway, he is adorable. And not on drugs. And delightfully emotionally present, if extremely timid. But beautifully so. I decide to forget about age. I will not ask his, nor volunteer mine.

We have a lovely talk. We go back to my room. We fuck. It is beautiful. I am so happy. He is so happy. His happiness seems to even exceed mine. He leaves for home. His mother will be wondering where he is.

He comes back the next day and we fuck for three hours. I have never wanted to fuck someone in this way. I want to penetrate him so bad.

Then he takes me to his mountain, his special place in the city he wants to share with me. It is a park on a very steep hillside in the city. It is night. There are wisps of clouds and a light rain. We climb very steep stairs carved into the hillside until we are soaked in rain and sweat, until we reach the top. We sit slightly sheltered from the rain under a boulder and watch the city lights. Our umbrella gives us just enough privacy from passersby, who see that there is something romantic going on under the umbrella but not what or who.

He tells me about his life. How he loves poetry from the Tang dynasty. How at one time he wanted to teach Chinese literature but there are no more jobs in that anymore. "So now I just lost." He doesn't seem panicked by being just lost. That's just his life right now.

He is waiting for his notice to report for a year of obligatory military service. This sounds to me like impending doom. There is not a single martial cell in his body. He is the gayest thing ever. His step is so light, his movements so delicate. He floats through the world. I cannot take my eyes off him because of it. He shrugs off my concern. "I will get to be around lots of guys. And anyway I don't know what else to do. Just lost." The words float out of his floating mouth. His floating eyes are eager. Again, "lost" does not seem to trouble him. It is what it is.

He tells me of how much he loves this place, his refuge from the city, within the city. The quiet and the calm. He has no money or car, so "this is as close to nature as I can get." Or sometimes he goes to visit his grandmother is the countryside. He loves doing this, but he can only go for one day at a time. There is no cell phone or internet service there, and if he goes without those for more than a day the anxiety becomes too much. I ask if this troubles him, but it seems not, as he cannot imagine being a different way. He is intensely curious about life before smartphones and wifi, however, and he spends many hours watching old movies searching for clues. Not because he wants that life for himself. Out of curiosity. Watches them on the internet, of course.

I tell him how much I like to go camping for days and even weeks at a time, without phone or internet or even people. He simply cannot compute the idea. It is an idea from a foreign language for which there is no translation. As curious as he is, he cannot even see how to be curious about this. So let's talk about something else that makes sense.

We meet the next morning and fuck again. So much passion. Fire, actually. It's cliché to say but true. I finally ask him his age. Twenty-two. He never asks about mine. Doesn't need that number. Just me. Then it is time for me to take the train to the next concert in the next town.

In the morning there he is, in the next town, at my hotel. He came all this way and we have almost no time, for now I must take a flight to the next concert in the next country. Our love making is brief and even fiercer than before. I drink his cum for the first time. I am on my back and he is straddling me, and he starts to cry. Softly at first, then deeply. I drink his tears. More and more tears come. His face is directly over mine and the tears fall into my eyes, become mine. I am old and jaded and it is hard for me to cry. So he is sharing his tears.

He rides the train partway to the airport with me. For the first time he is tentatively affectionate with me in public. He apologizes for crying. "I thought I got rid of all my tears last night." He was crying last night? The tears start again during our parting embrace. I go through the airport. I fly. I disembark and collect my bags. I check into the hotel and go to sleep. In the morning I find this email waiting for me.

Dear dear very beloved Bob,

"Beautiful." Probably one of the very first words learned when one starts learning English language, but not until we met did I know how this word can be so frequently and gracefully used, by someone just like you.

So how do things turn out to be this "beautiful"?

Friday night at the bar. People know it is a (gay) bar; it is just somewhere for groups of (gay) friends to hang out, or oppositely, for some really lonely souls with their horny bodies wandering to get simple pure physical excitements and pleasure. Alone, I was one of the latter and completely aware of that. Please just alcohol and sex and bodies; no more boring talks, top/bottom questions, mind games or any other human complex which I had been disappointed with.

With that clearly in mind, I just got in the room for an "orgasm." Before I had never got out of the dark room with somebody or left any contact information.

But then as I touched this person, that felt like a magnet. After a short while of hugging and dicks jerked off I tried to get away to another person, just as I always would do. There was, however, this strong power pulling me back again, and somehow I got drowned in this hairy chest and strong powerful arms, thinking "this is the one" I would stick to until he left for somebody else.

And it was this unexpected whisper in my ears inviting me to have a beer. And it turned out I said yes. When we got to see each other, I was surprised it was you – this tall strong sexy tattooed man.

Never thought it could be you.

Then there followed things really enjoyable: breaths of fresh midnight air, really-get-to-know-each-other talks, and the very first crazy fierce f*ck. And another afternoon sex (can't believe we were in bed for almost 3 hours), the walk and mountain hike in the rain, the great view we shared on the mountain, delicacies at the night market. The very knowledgeable queer talk at the bar by the Red House and another midnight sex. AND another "urgent" morning sex just hours later.

(Though it seems most of the time we were having sex) I see something within you really friendly and passion- ate and gentle and, just "beautiful." That makes me so comfortable being with you. I've never been this happy for a long time. And I kinda feel the sense of love too. Really, I like you so so much. You are just a gift!

This morning it was just wonderful that we got to meet. The last f*ck was just as wild and beautiful as the former ones. After the orgasm I enjoyed hugging with you so much. I tried so hard to remember your moderate body temperature, every touch of your hands on me, the dick that f*cked so hard inside me, and the arms that held me so tightly that would made me feel so safe and secure. I knew later I cried maybe because of the so-called "post coitum animal triste;" this would probably be the last sex that we could have in the recent future, and all I could do was nothing but just feel and then let go. I knew these would end anyway, but I was just not that strong to face that yet so I bursted out tears.

But when at Starbucks you said "I seldom see men cry, and I seldom cry myself; but when you cried your tears fell into my eyes, and that was very beautiful. Very beautiful tears." That was a very artistic observation of your own and made me so much better. And I liked what you did to my tears in the hotel, since it was "for the first time someone wiped out my tears with his tongue, and that was romantic."

The last train ride was also so beautiful. I wished it would never end: leaning on you, feeling the heat, with two hands holding tight. Never would I forget the last hug and kiss by the ticket gate. I looked at your back until you disappeared from the sight, with eyes filled with tears again. Thank you, Bob. Thank you for so generously giving me so much.

If I get to miss you in the future, I will definitely listen to your music, hold that yellow beanie you gave me, and think of our five-day romance.

And if you ever think of me, please also remember there was once this boy, who had cried so hard and filled your eyes with tears, so that made you "cry" as well. :-)

So I guess that's all...

Bob, thank you again for all your love and passion! May your trip and concerts go well!

PS. If I am ever in San Francisco, I am so going to visit you! Please pick me up then!

I promise I will send you emails every now and then. You do too please.

Love

THE ARTIST

We meet in a dive bar full of bikers with long-beards and big bellies, aging leather daddies, drag queens out of drag, and hustlers waiting for their beepers to go off. (Yeah, back in the age of beepers.) But he is none of that, this small, wiry guy in overalls. He has just dropped half a tab of acid, which makes me curious as it has been decades since I have done LSD. We engage in a lovely, airy conversation about I-don't-know-what that is quite out of place in this room full of men looking so hard to get laid.

We opt for a change of scene and go out for a walk. The evening air is cool and fresh. We walk and walk and walk and walk. It is so easy to talk to him, this charming half Irish and half Pueblo Indian man. He tells me about his art. I'm intrigued and ask if I can see it. Eventually we end up in front of his place and he agrees to invite me in to show me his art. I have a certain amount of dread, because this is San Francisco, and if you meet a guy in a bar who claims to make art, the chances are good that the art will be so bad that you would prefer he had worked in real estate. But his art is wonderful. He makes Kachina dolls that are beautifully situated halfway between the desert Indian culture he is from and the urban gay culture to which he has come. A lovely man who makes lovely art.

We lie on the bed and talk, our bodies touching in a relaxed, un-needy way. It is a beautiful time, and I feel very alive. After a while I am toying with the buttons of his shirt and kissing him gently on the lips. Sweet. And then his shirt is open and I look down to take in his fine torso and am confronted with a ghastly mass of lesions. Neither of us can move or speak. The lesions are horrendous, festering things. Kaposi sarcoma. We stay frozen in place as the angry rush of the AIDS epidemic comes pouring into a room that just a moment ago was light and airy. After a while he slowly begins to button up his shirt, and I lie back down next to him. We hold hands. We stare at the ceiling. After a while he softly speaks.

"I'm sorry. I really didn't go out looking for sex tonight. I just went out with friends and dropped a half a tab of acid, and it was nice meeting you and talking with you and showing you my art. I really didn't mean for this to happen."

He was right, it was I who wanted to see the art, I who ever so gently nudged things to the point that his torso was bare.

I am so, so sorry my beautiful friend. Truly I am. I wish there was something I could do. But at that time, there was nothing anyone could do.

I feel I could have loved you. It is so easy to go down a rabbit hole of "what ifs." But there is nothing down there. Not for you, not for me, not for anybody.

THE GANGSTER

"When you were a gangster, did you do drugs?"

The question rolls easily from my tongue. Just a stray thought floating by our bodies lying peacefully on the bed, the dreamy way thoughts do after people make love.

"Well, I'm gonna say something. Gay men do meth in order to have sex. Gangsters do meth in order to kill. Because when you're doing meth, you *don't give a fuck*. And that's all I'm going to say."

These words don't float. They sit right down before us like giant boulders blocking a trail. Not threatening us, but not going anywhere either.

As always, he has said a lot by saying very little.

He is a man of few words. He speaks in crisp sentences assembled from the limited vocabulary one acquires in prison instead of school. He reads only with difficulty. And yet I learn so much from him.

I learn how to light a joint in a prison cell without matches or a lighter.

(An elaborate process involving pencil lead, toilet paper,
a Q-Tip, and an electrical outlet.)

I learn how to deliver drugs to gang leaders in solitary confinement.

(An even more elaborate process involving swallowing
drugs in a way that allows you to pull them back out
of your esophagus, then assaulting a prisoner the gang
leaders have sentenced to punishment, which gets you
sent to solitary yourself, and then a lot more stuff once
you are there.)

I learn how gangs enforce discipline in prison.

(He and his cell mate were once tasked with meting out
discipline decreed by gang leaders. The man arrived in
their cell at the appointed time and just stood still, waiting. It took hours to clean up all the blood and hair and
flesh in the cell once the discipline was administered.)

I also learn a good deal about freedom. You see, he never has a bad
day.

I spent five years of my life *living in a cage*. Now I am in
San Francisco. I get to hang out drinking beer in bars
with gay men. So my day is *great*.

These are not empty words. He knows what a bad day is. There was
the day he was arrested for slicing up a man with a box cutter. The
day he was convicted for assault with a deadly weapon. The day they
slammed the prison door. The day of the prison riot that got his
sentence extended. So if he is in San Francisco, can go where he likes,
and can share a beer with friends at a gay bar after work, it cannot be
a bad day. And it is true: every time I see him he is having a good day.
Every single day.

I also learn how profoundly a man can change his life. I knew a man can change from straight to gay, can quit meth cold turkey, can heal from a broken heart and another and another, can lose everything and carry on, can find God, can lose God, can get grumpy with age. But this man changed *everything* in his life. Walked out of prison and never looked back.

He maintains an outward calm that is striking, and is remarked upon by everyone he knows, all of whom will tell you that you could never meet a nicer person or have a kinder friend. More than one man has described him to me as a sort of angel. But inside he remains tightly wound from a life shot through with violence. His entire history is present in his body. I suppose that is true for everyone, but not everyone has his history. Tension and ease, violence and peace, rage and calm, all coiled up inside. If that coil was sprung, he would *go off.* Do real damage. He knows how to fight to kill, is skilled at it. That's not going to happen though. I know that, because he knows that. Knows it deep in his bones.

He relieves some of the pressure by smoking copious amounts of marijuana, and by making art, for which he has serious talent. Mostly he draws faces of birds. Again and again. Fills entire notebooks with them. Then draws more. Once he told me how much he was looking forward to an airplane flight of several hours as he was planning to spend the entire time drawing faces of birds.

He gets to have sex now. He celebrates this amazing development by having a lot. He has his main lover in California, another in Michigan, another in Vancouver, and then a whole bunch of guys in between, like me.

I wonder, have I been searching for him for a very long time? A man who has been steeped in violence. Not the negotiated and staged violence of BDSM. Violence without consent. Deadly violence. Assault.

And I can be naked with him. I can kiss him while he kisses me, can be in him and he in me. And we can be wild and crazy and dominant and submissive and full-throttle and no-holds-barred and then hold each other tenderly in silence and let the world float by and ask dreamy questions and even if the answers are shocking it's all good and perfect and love wins the day.

He has a real thing for old men. I know many guys who have a thing for *older* men, but he likes *old* men. Those are his words. "I just really like old men." He has no interest in anyone else. He likes to touch old men, kiss them, hang out with them, talk to them. He likes to fuck them, which definitely marks him as angelic in the minds of many. I once invited him to a party that was the hot ticket in San Francisco. Lots of beautiful men in every stage of undress engaging in unspeakable revelry and debauchery. As an ex-con working for less than minimum wage he has very little money, and I thought he would appreciate the free ticket. He thought for a moment, then asked, "Will there be any *old men* there? No? Well, that party wouldn't be for me."

He does, however, have a real thing for me.

And that is how I know that after this long, crazy journey of so many years, I am finally old.

PART 4

*Master and servant – or master and man relationship is, essentially,
a polarized flow, like love. It is a circuit of vitalism which flows
between master and man and forms a very precious nourishment to
each, and keeps both in a state of subtle, quivering, vital equilibrium.
Deny it as you like, it is so...*

*It is good for Sam to be flogged. It is good, on this occasion, for the
Captain to have flogged Sam. I say so.*

– D.H. Lawrence, Dana's Two Years Before the Mast

SUMMER CAMP

The bus pulls away from the airport and heads for the children's summer camp in the woods, but there are no kids on this bus. Just grown men, mostly in their forties and fifties. They have come from all around the country and beyond for four days of bondage and sadomasochism. BDSM in the vernacular. I am one of them. But, am I one of them? How did I get here?

A while back a dear old friend called me on the phone.

"You like to do crazy things, right?"

"Ummm, sure. Do you have a particular crazy thing in mind?"

Indeed, he did. A friend of his was an internationally-known dominatrix. A client from London was arriving the next day to spend an entire week in her control. This was a man of considerable means, and he had ordered custom bondage gear from around the world for the dominatrix to use during the festivities. She was, at this very moment, sitting on the floor of her dungeon surrounded by boxes of gear she had never used. Given the amount of money the client was paying, it would never do for her to be fiddling around trying to figure out how some of this stuff worked. She needed someone to be her crash test dummy so she could try everything out, and she needed that person right now.

Well. I *do* like to do crazy things. I was intrigued. I understood that even the most vanilla sex has some element of domination and submission. And I knew that when I am fully engaged in sex, sensations that would otherwise be painful can become pleasurable. I knew there was a whole world of bondage and s/m out there that beckoned, but I had never found a way in. I put the phone down and jumped on my bicycle. By the end of the afternoon I had been bound in a leather straight jacket, zipped into a leather mummy bag, hung from the ceiling in a leather postal sack, and I can't remember what else. Lo and behold, every time I got locked into something, my dick got hard.

"I think you like this," she said.

"I think you are right," I answered.

I got home and called another close friend who I knew was way into the bondage scene and told him of my discovery. He in turn told me of this upcoming gathering at the summer camp. It was not set up as a wading pool for those learning to swim, more like a high dive into the deep end. But my friend had authority to sponsor in one newbie, and I like diving right into the deep end of things. So here I am, just a few weeks later, on the bus to summer camp.

I am the only rookie on the bus. Everyone else is a veteran of this very private club. Will their sexual practices become mine? Will they be my people? On the latter score, things are not getting off to a great start. The men on this particular bus seem to be a singularly humorless bunch.

Most of the small talk revolves around military matters. Some men had just come from a similar event in another part of the country (though not held in a children's camp) which had been attended by a naval "flag officer," an admiral of sufficiently high rank that a naval ship graced with his presence had to indicate that he was aboard by flying his own particular flag. The admiral had brought his flag to the weekend of sadomasochism and had "flown" it there, alongside the gay flag and the leather flag and the club flag. The men on the bus are very impressed by an admiral flying his flag at a bdsm event. One of the men is in the Navy now, a career Navy doctor whose present job is treating the many severe head injuries of wounded American soldiers returning from Iraq. He says he is looking forward to doing some "cutting scenes" at our summer camp. Here is a man who patches up wounds for his job, and inflicts them for sexual pleasure on his vacation. I'm trying to accept this information as just another unremarkable piece of chit chat to pass the time, but my mind is stubbornly refusing to go along. I am trying to swallow the conversation, but this fact has stuck in my throat like a chicken bone, and is blocking my digestion of the stream of words that follow.

I have the feeling one gets on a roller coaster as the cars get slowly cranked up the first big hill, and you are strapped in, and you realize as the ground moves farther and farther away that you actually cannot do this, your fear of heights is too great, but there is no turning back, the train has left the station and even though you cannot do this, you will do this. So you hold on, try not to look down, and try to occupy your mind until you reach the crest of the hill and all is lost in the rush of noise and motion.

*

I get off the bus and pick up my bedding and walk to the cabin where I will be staying, Cabin Q. I learn that Cabin Q is also known as "Harold's cabin." Harold is the founder and spiritual leader of this entire event. Harold is just the second man I have met here, and he is another military man whose unusual work and sexual fetishes bleed into one another in disconcerting ways. Harold is a former Army sergeant, and will tell anyone who will listen that his specialty was training American soldiers how to survive prisoner of war experiences. For many years, he says, the US government paid him to put men into bondage and terrorize them, while he coached them through how to survive the experience. Upon retiring from the Army he set up a private training program for anyone who wants to find their inner prisoner-of-war. He uses the trainings as a recruitment tool for summer camp. He runs this program from his house, which features five fully-functional jail cells, which Harold rescued from demolition. Harold is sufficiently well-known in jail cell circles that from time to time, when a jail cell is no longer needed, someone calls Harold and asks if he might want to bring his truck, dismantle the whole thing, and take it home.

I have never met anyone like Harold. To say that he is a character doesn't begin to get it. He basically holds court here, and seems to be a very benign ruler. He's got "Army sergeant" coming out of every pore. He speaks in a strong southern accent, and what he says is often funny, very funny in a very dry way. Parched dry. Desert dry. Torture through dying of thirst dry. But funny nonetheless. His humor becomes more notable as the weekend wears on and it is revealed that he is one of perhaps three or four out of a couple of hundred men here who have any humor whatsoever.

I have not even set my bags down before Harold corners me and slaps a pair of handcuffs on my wrists. Not just any handcuffs, 1910 cuffs. Harold has brought a collection of handcuffs that includes entries once every few decades from the mid nineteenth century down to the present day. I am cuffed in the 1910s and Harold is

playing with my nipples. Soon he has clothespins on them, then
starts playing with the clothespins with a vibrator. He is very
impressed with me. He keeps saying I am "tough," which is apparently his highest compliment. In his dry southern drawl, he declares
that I will be a nice "slab of raw meat" for the club, and that sadists
will flock to me "like bees to honey." Soon he decides that I am going
to be the sub for his "interrogation demo" tomorrow afternoon. I am
not consulted regarding this decision. Harold assumes my unques-
tioning acceptance of this decision as a first act of submission.

*

Dinner provides no relief from the sense of utter strangeness that
envelopes me. Here are some two hundred men, most in their fifties
and perhaps sixties, some in their forties, a very few in their thirties.
Harold is seventy, and there is one baby in his early twenties – an
orchid of youth in a desert of age. Men wearing every conceivable
kind of fetish wear: leather, army uniforms, Nazi uniforms, handcuffs, chains, boots of all descriptions, and jockstraps. The baby
of the group wears combat boots, a chain collar, and torn Fruit of
the Loom undies. Into the middle of it all come the regular camp
staffers, who have stayed over after the last of the summer's camp
of children to earn extra cash working for us perverts. They seem to
be mostly eastern Europeans in their early twenties. Here they are at
dinner working the food service, keeping us supplied with forks and
knives, and ketchup and relish for our sloppy joes, and thousand
island dressing for our iceberg lettuce. Then the owner of the whole
place comes out and takes the mic to tell us, "Thank you for coming,
and thank you for being who you are."

I have slipped into a parallel universe. If I can replicate this experiment in the laboratory I will win a Nobel prize in physics.

*

After dinner I wander over to the main "dungeon," which the rest of
the year is a gymnasium. Harold is whipping a man with a four-foot
single-tail whip. The target of the whip, it turns out, is yet another
man who has a military career back in that other universe I used to
inhabit. In fact he is, or at least he says he is, a professional interrogator, exactly where and for who is, I am told, "classified." This makes
the first *three* men I have met here soldiers whose professional work
and sexual fetishes seem to merge – perhaps separated only by a
change of polarity, positive to negative, or the flipping of just one bit,
zero to one. Or maybe their war lives and sex lives are not separated
by anything at all. Maybe this is not a parallel universe. Maybe I am
just getting a more complete view of the one universe I have always
inhabited. Maybe *all* military men find sexual pleasure in interrogation and incarceration and torture, in war. Am I learning a profound
truth about the human male? Or have I simply voluntarily isolated
myself in the woods with a bunch of really fucked up dudes?

Harold's whip is raising large purple welts across the mysterious
interrogator's back, but he doesn't scream. He doesn't whimper. He
doesn't make a sound. He doesn't even flinch. He just stands there
like a fire hydrant, and when Harold is done, the man impassively
puts his shirt back on, as cool and collected as if he were just finishing his morning shave. Harold explains to me that normally topping
in an s/m scene is all about reading the sub's mental and physical
state, knowing how to take him to the edge, knowing how to take
him past where he ever thought he could go, and then knowing the
point at which to stop, the point beyond which he really *can't* go.
But none of this applies to whipping the interrogator. Reading *him*,
Harold says, "is like trying to read a fencepost. Come to think of it,
he is probably about as intelligent as a fencepost. Except a fencepost
would never allow itself to be put in such a position."

Harold is known as a master practitioner of the single tail whip, and like the soldier he was, he has a very particular and ordered way of going about it. Harold's lashings come in three groups of one hundred. The first hundred are "feather touch" lashings to "get the chemicals going." (The chemicals your body produces, that is. There is a very strict ban on recreational drugs here.) Then there is a break. The second hundred lashes build very gradually, almost imperceptibly, to a level that inflicts serious pain but leaves no marks on the sub's skin. Then another break. At this point the sub can decide whether he has had enough or is ready to continue to level three. Level three is for big kids. There will be marks: hot red streaks, or dark purple welts, or bright red gashes oozing blood, depending on how Harold is reading his victim. But the victim is expected to take it. Agreeing to continue after the first two hundred lashes means handing yourself over to Harold, trusting that his read of you will deliver something you can take, and even want, and also trusting that he has the skill with the whip to administer exactly the blow he aims to inflict and no more, in exactly the place he intends and not an inch up or down. This takes considerable skill. The slightest miscalculation can turn what was intended to be a purple welt into a bleeding gash, or a blow intended to land between the shoulder blades into a whip wrapping around the victim's neck in a most horrific way. The interrogator wanted welts but no gashes. It is just the first of four nights at camp, and he has big plans for the next few days. If he is whipped to the point of bleeding tonight, he will have to curtail the coming festivities. Harold's technique indeed seems impressive: the man's back is covered with welts but no skin is broken.

Harold does not take the time to explain all this to just anyone. Harold is king here, and he is holding court. Somehow, I am being treated like a royal guest. According to most everyone here, Harold is a benign and fair ruler.

I struggle to absorb it all. Here I am. In a children's camp. In the gym. Strewn around the gym are strange apparatuses: tables, crosses, stocks, benches, scaffolding, mattresses, and things I have no name for. Men are being whipped, flogged, shocked with electricity, bound and gagged, and mummified. The scoreboard on the wall shows the final tally of the last basketball game played by the last group of eager young campers, but the screams that are now reverberating off the hard gym walls are not cheers. No, a career army sergeant is happily explaining the technique he has just used to administer a bull whipping to an active-duty military interrogator. I start to slip into sensory overload. I can no longer follow the conversation. I am losing the thread. I *think* that Harold is explaining all of this to me because he wants to whip *me*, but right now I am feeling dizzy, and my focus is simply on remaining vertical and eventually walking out of the room under my own steam.

After a while I find a guy who is way less intimidating than Harold. Younger than most of the men here. A very nice and nice-looking guy, shortish, with shaved head. He proposes putting me into leather bondage tied to a tall wooden rack extending straight up about ten feet with horizontal slats every few inches up. Can I do this? Am I ready for this? I can find no answer to these questions. Down below, in the place where I normally make decisions, there is no one at the controls. No one is present to read the dials and meters, or to hear the humming and ticking of the engine. The questions I send down read out to an empty room and no answer is returned. But back up on the surface, somehow my head is nodding consent. He tells me to strip and opens his bag. All the tops carry around their implements of torture in large gym bags, or suitcases on rollers if their tools of choice are too heavy or if age or lack of exercise has left them with a bad back. They look like country doctors making house calls. Or factory mechanics from the 1930s. Out of this particular gear bag come leather straps, buckles, cords, and a hood. Soon they are all on me. The most intense thing is the hood. A very intense hood. Lots of pressure up under the jaw so you can't open your mouth.

The hood plays on my fear of not being able to speak, of the sound in my throat losing its way to my mouth. This fear permeated the nightmares that used to plague my sleep, nightmares full of psy-chotic men trying to kill me. I would try to scream for help but no sound would emerge. Sometimes in my waking life I have been unable to speak in the face of sexual advances I did not want but could not find the voice to reject. Some of those situations had last-ing consequences. Like the man who tore my shoulder and it took me nearly a year to heal. Or the man who gave me HIV. Now there's a consequence for you. And then there are the far more numerous times when I have wanted to voice disagreement in non-sexual sit-uations with something someone is doing or saying, and my fear of displeasing them freezes my larynx and no sound emerges. I could fill pages with these moments.

Hoods play on these feelings, and the more intense the hood, the more intense the fear. I remember very clearly the first time P____ put a hood on me. Fear that I would not be able to speak began to crawl over me and into me and through me. This same fear was even more powerful the first time I really blasted off into my lizard brain the second time I saw him. In that hood, in that bondage, I began to fear not simply that I would lose my voice but that I would actually lose my mouth. I would want to speak, to say "I can't do this any-more, please stop," but when I would go to speak I would not be able to find my mouth. I would be lost in the dark. Not even one photon of light. I would seek my mouth, the muscles in my face that sur-round it, that pull at the jaws and lips and tongue to produce speech. I would feel for them, the way you gently wave your arms in front of you as you slowly walk, one step at a time, through a dark room feeling for the wall, or the bedpost, or the chair. I would look for my mouth like that. Except I would not be able to search one step at a time because my feet were bound, and anyway I would not be able to find my feet any more than I could find my voice. And I could not hold out my arms to feel ahead in the darkness because my hands were bound, and anyway I probably couldn't find my hands either. I would lose my mouth. Not my throat. I felt fairly confident of my throat, because I can always find my breath. You can always hear your breath. If the hood covers your ears it only makes the sound of the breath louder, because you then hear it from the inside and the sound has less competition from the noisy world outside. I was sure I could find my throat, but I would not be able follow my throat all the way to my mouth. Like paddling a kayak on a river on a cloudy night with no moon or stars, looking for the way downstream to the mouth and not finding it. It is so dark you cannot tell the current from the eddy, and anyway there are whirlpools everywhere and no detectable direction of flow. No mouth.

What would happen? What would happen if I lost my mouth and he started hurting me more than I could stand but I was lost in the dark and could not communicate? What happens when you are hurt more than you can stand but you cannot stop it? This question is an abyss. Of course, you would have to stand it. There would be no choice. But you cannot. There is no choice about that either. What happens when two iron-clad no-choices collide? There is a truth hidden in that question.

Hoods are a direct route to this whole terrain. Hoods have a subtlety and nuance I scarcely imagined. Each is its own story, its own world. Each imposes its own reality. Some fit lightly on your head with no pressure. You can breathe easily, and even though your eyes may be covered you can see through the hood sufficiently to make out at least the outlines of the world outside. On my journey to summer

camp I had visited a man who put me in a very intense leather
hood. I could see nothing. My eyes had not been turned down but
turned off.

it is very tight in here. the hood presses up against my jaw making it
impossible to open my mouth. now I am uncertain whether I will be
able to speak even if I can find my mouth. I try a test run. yes, I can
speak, just a tiny sound between clenched teeth. yes, he can hear me.
but not being able to open my mouth heightens my fear that I will
lose it in the dark. then he ties down my head. this ratchets things
up many notches. the power of this simple act imposes itself. the
attention is immediately drawn to the frailty of the neck. having
one's hands bound together is one thing. maybe the simplest thing.
having the hands bound *to* something is another step. having the
feet bound comes next, having the feet bound *to* something follows.
what comes next is a ladder with many rungs: bondage of all kinds
that close in on different parts of your body in different ways. at the
top of the ladder, at the top of the body, is the head. having the head
immobilized is the last stop. it is not possible to remain in normal
reality with the head bound. ties to the normal world become tenu-
ous. tethers start snapping.

When pain administered to my body starts to become intolerable, I
retreat into my breath. It is a meditational practice similar to yoga. I
try to control my consciousness – actually no, "control" is not at all
the right idea. Consciousness cannot be controlled. Understanding
this is step one. But consciousness can be directed, or better, herded.
Consciousness can be herded from one part of the body to another.
As pain becomes unbearable, or as I lose track of my limbs in hoods
and bondage, I herd my consciousness into my throat. I herd it into a
tighter and tighter flock, trying to concentrate it at the precise point
at the top of my throat where the throat opens out into the mouth,
the river runs to the ocean. Yoga asanas are one way of herding the

consciousness into this point of breath where the self opens into the ocean. Erotic pain is another.

The breath reminds you that consciousness cannot, in truth, be herded at all. It is not a flock of sheep. It is a cloud of breath. A cloud moves with the wind, but you cannot blow wind inside your body. What you can do is create vacuums, empty spaces you want your consciousness to fill, or to hide.

But what if consciousness is not a cloud either? What if it is an army of ants?

Above the spot at the top of my throat where the sound of the breath resides and where I hide myself is the head. The mouth, the nose, the brain, the top of the head where the body regulates its temperature, the two eyes which are turned off in the darkness of the hood, and the third eye, which the yoga tradition asserts is the most important. The top of the throat opens out to all of this. Herding the consciousness up to the top of the throat is like watching a blackout move through a city at night, starting from the soles of the feet and moving up through the body atom by atom. But when the head is bound in a tight leather hood, and then the hood is tied to a rack, tied there by a man who has been exploring this terrain for decades, whose desires in this direction are so overwhelming that he has created his own dungeon populated by devices of his own design and construction, a man who likes to lick blood from the wounds his whip carves in other men's backs, when this happens there is a counter movement that starts at the top of the head and moves *down*. All that is the head is lost. The crown of the head that is the connection to temperature and sky. The ears, the connection to the barometric variations we hear as sound. The eyes, even the third eye. The mouth. Suddenly that point at the top of the throat where consciousness takes refuge in breath opens out to *nothing*. Nothing but the ocean at night. There is no self in the ocean. The ocean doesn't care. The pattern of energy that constitutes the self cannot maintain its essential integrity. As it flows into the ocean the pattern simply comes apart in the dark waters. How to face this moment without panic?

So here I am, my first night at camp and I am in an intense hood and I am starting to panic. Can I find my mouth? Can I speak? Can he hear me? I make a test. Yes. He responds. He is very reassuring. But what if it gets noisy in the room? There is whipping and flogging going on around me. Screaming. It is loud. It is a dungeon. There is music. What if he cannot hear? What if I lose my mouth? The panic quickens. But then it becomes clear that this man is not really a sadist, he is just into bondage. Once he has me in his control, his "play" is simply to continually rearrange the bondage. Tighten a buckle here. Add a strap over there. Move my arm to a new position that has just occurred to him. I begin to relax. I can do this. It's easy, actually. A piece of cake. I can relax right into it.

*

Back at the cabin it is time for bed. So hard, this cabin is so very hard for me. It is essentially a military barracks. Harold is the commanding officer, complete with his army footlocker at the foot of his bed full of implements of torture. There is an Army banner hanging over one window and a Marine banner over the other. Inside are men in full military dress. These are not Castro queens putting on military drag but men who have spent years in actual armies. Several of them are in those armies even now. These guys have to wear this shit every day, year in year out, and violence and control is their job. And what do they do for their vacation? They come here, and wear the same shit, and play with the same violence and control.

No, they are not Castro queens in military drag; they are military queens in military drag. Queens all the same, but these queens have permission from the state to actually hurt people. One of them was for years the commander of a military brig at an "undisclosed location" where, he tells me, "real bad guys" were held. The whole notion of "real" bad guys as a separate and identifiable breed seems as obvious to him as the nose on my face. I wonder how the treatment of the real bad guys differs from the treatment I would receive. And what am I? A good bad guy. A bad good guy? A good guy in bad guy drag? What the fuck am I doing here?

Many of the men here have a uniform fetish. They strut around in uniforms of every kind: army, marine, cop, sailor, Nazi storm trooper. There is a German guy who comes all the way for Germany for this camp ("I wouldn't miss it!") who has brought two uniforms for each day of camp. He's got them all neatly hanging in the closet in Cabin Q. You know he has done his daily change when you see him strutting around smoking a cigar in his new threads and looking like an imbecile. But a very happy imbecile. I am almost envious of what it would be like to be so stupid that putting on the clothes of authority would bring such happiness and content. But only almost. Instead, he makes me angry. What right does he have to be such an idiot? Are we all idiots here?

A thought occurs to me that will return over and over throughout the weekend: I could never explain to my old *compañeros* in Central America what I am doing here with these men. No way. And the barrier I would confront if I tried is not the one kinksters typically encounter. When revealing a bdsm practice to someone outside of the subculture, you might expect to encounter fear, disgust, incomprehension, moral disapproval, or concern for your physical and mental safety. But I think my old *compañeros* would see my presence here as *betrayal*. An impossibly weird, confusing betrayal.

Fraternizing with the enemy and throwing myself at their feet. I would henceforth be utterly shunned. Not worthy of even the most trivial confidence. And I would understand them, because I myself am experiencing this betrayal. I feel it in my presence here, in this cabin, with these men, with these Marine banners over the windows and the military footlockers and the implements of torture.

first night dream:

> i go off to the mountains with a bunch of others to die of aids. it is our time, we're going to die that night. friends from el salvador days are there. juana. i think joel. not clear who else. pretty sure no gay people i know. during the night all of us with aids feel sicker and sicker. a forest fire starts. one by one everyone dies. soon i am the only one left. i feel extremely sick. i start to die but can't quite finish the job. someone else is there in the same predicament though i can't remember who. in the morning we go back to town, certain we are going to die at any moment. i wonder what to do with my last breaths. at some point it dawns on me that i am still alive, and begin to wonder if i am really going to shuffle off this mortal coil or not. wonder if i should even hope i will not, because at the moment i am ready to accept death, and if i start to hope for more life i will no longer be ready. thinking of people to call or say goodbye to. juana is the big one. try calling her but my cell phone doesn't work. by now i have inhaled a few drops of some drug that appeared from nowhere, that might give me just the boost i need. i decide i can allow for a little hope, though i am still not going to go for life with everything i have. what to do? i decide to run. i know it is crazy but i think somehow i might outrun this. i connect with juana. at

first she is upset that i am dying, then confused, but she starts to run with me. i wonder where i'm going to go. after all, it is very unlikely that i will outrun this, and probably the running will be the last straw. deathly ill people are not supposed to run. should i run home to family? i decide yes. run all the way to my home town, with juana next to me. i get there. i only see two of my sisters, but everyone is there whether i see them or not. they are crying hard, but when i see them i realize that i am going to make it. i will live.

*

Saturday morning. Harold tells me over breakfast that we should spend a little time during the morning investigating whether I will be an appropriate "slab of raw meat" for his demonstration this afternoon. Back at the cabin, Harold explains that this will be an "interrogation demo" involving "endurance torture." The basic idea is that he will tell me to perform various exercises which I will have to continue until I cannot do them anymore. As I start to falter, he will demand that I keep correct form and if I don't he will hit me with something that will hurt. A lot. A strap, maybe. Or perhaps a cattle prod. Harold asks how much I have played with electricity. Never, I reply. Harold takes a moment to absorb this information, then suggests he should hit me with the cattle prod right now for practice.

Harold puts me through some exercises and declares that I do a beautiful push-up. As we proceed he holds forth on his theories of bdsm, something Harold does quite a lot. With most people I would eventually find this excruciating, but Harold is generally interesting and funny. The idea that interests him the most is that bdsm is really all in the mind. He is fascinated by finding ways to administer what his victim would experience as earth-shattering pain but would involve little or even no "real" physical pain. Another big interest is men who can tolerate a lot of real physical pain. He is fascinated, enthralled by this. He tells me that after decades of careful consideration, he has concluded that there is a genetic basis for some men's ability to withstand extreme physical pain. He says that the training that Navy seals go through is not actually about training them to do anything, but rather to weed out those who cannot take a lot of pain. The Navy wants seals who are genetically programmed for pain. Another big interest is men whose wounds heal exceptionally fast. When I asked him last night how long the welts his whip leaves generally last, he answered that it depended on the person, and that he is always on the look-out for "quick healers."

Harold has gathered around him in Cabin Q an entourage of men he has assembled over many years who can tolerate exceptional amounts of pain and heal quickly. These are his people. He loves them, and they love him back. And he thinks that I may be one of these kindred souls, that I may have the special genetic make-up. He keeps telling me I am a "most intriguing individual," which makes me a bit squeamish every time he says it.

Harold knows something of what he is talking about. For forty years in the army, he says, his job was to prepare people for being prisoners of war. An important part of his duties was to tell the Army with some degree of accuracy which of its soldiers would hold up under torture and which would not.

Eventually my practice session with Harold unravels into Harold's storytelling. I discover that, as interesting as he is, there is still a point beyond which he becomes another old man lost in his stories, some of which seem to be slipping into senility. He explains how Saddam Hussein might indeed have been hiding weapons of mass destruction at the time of the US invasion of Iraq, but we will never know because the State Department "subverted the mission to find them by sending a gay guy to do it and then exposing him, pulling the rug out. *And he's here.*"

Harold finally announces we are all ready for the afternoon demonstration. He has completely forgotten about testing the cattle prod on me, and I don't remind him. I politely excuse myself.

This is strange and difficult for me. This has no connection to what attracts me to this world. I am here trying to develop an ecstatic sexual practice using the boundary of pain and pleasure to explore psychic places I have never been. Like yoga but different. Nothing to do with marines or interrogation. Yet here I am. Did I get lost? Take a wrong turn? Or did I simply not understand the direction I was heading? One way or the other, here I am alone with the US Army's prisoner-of-war-experience expert, and a cabin full of army footlockers, fatigues, and combat boots. Just a few weeks ago this would have been suffocating. I would have had to run, or vomit, or pass out, or all three. I am starting to escape from the grip of that nameless fear.

At lunch, I mention in passing that I will be the sub in Harold's afternoon demonstration. The man with whom I am speaking looks very startled and quickly looks away. "Well, good luck with that," he stammers. "I won't be there. I'm just not into that." He excuses himself and wanders off. This exchange leaves me feeling a little unsettled. By way of experiment I casually mention it again in my next conversation. "What's he going to do to you?" the man responds. When I indicate I don't really know, the man is perturbed. "Does that *concern* you at all, that you are going to be in Harold's demo and you don't know what he is going to *do* to you?" I plead ignorance. "Well, you should know that the last time Harold did a demo, the guy had to go home afterwards. He just couldn't take anymore; it was the end of his camp." This is even more unsettling.

I find my friend who sponsored me in here and report these conversations, but he assures me that nothing will happen in the demo that I can't handle.

Demo time arrives and a crowd of men gather on the tennis court. Harold holds forth from behind a table of his favorite toys, with his interrogator buddy and me (?!?) at his side. It turns out that my friend is correct. Nothing happens I can't handle. In fact, nothing happens at all. At seventy-five, age is catching up with Harold. It is not clear whether he changed his mind, or got confused, or simply forgot, but no pain or terror is administered. Instead, he just talks and shows off his toys. The one he is most proud of is what he claims is a genuine hood from the US prison camp in Guantanamo, the same hood you see in news photos of Muslim prisoners in orange jumpsuits. Harold is especially proud of this hood, because it is not an easy thing to come by. Evidently, he still has good contacts in the military, men who understand and are sympathetic to his extracurricular interest in bondage and torture.

As it becomes clear that this "demo" will involve nothing but Harold's war stories, I relax and my mind wanders as my eyes scan the assembled multitude. The men gathered around are clearly titillated by Harold, his Guantanamo hood, his interrogator sidekick, and his years in the army. It dawns on me that the wall that I am trying to will into existence, between the outer world of prison camps and torture and my inner landscape of sexual desire, is something that Harold and his posse have spent years working equally hard to demolish. One man asks Harold if the interrogation methods he is suggesting as fun tools for erotic play are actually used for prying evidence out of real torture victims (the implication being that his sexual interest will ratchet up if the answer is yes). Harold responds by telling stories of American soldiers throwing Vietnamese out of helicopters as a way of making their comrades remaining on board talk. I resolve at that instant that I will *never* engage in any sort of "play" with Harold or *any* of the military men here.

*

Saturday night is busy. It begins with a scene with me and a very heavyset man. He has no bondage gear, so he puts me on a sort of bench, plays with my nipples, and spanks my ass with a crop. He was going to put toys up my butt but ran out of time, and anyway there was no lube or condoms around. Butt play of any kind, including fucking, does not really happen in public here. This is way the Harold wants it. I asked Harold if he liked fucking. "I have no interest in sex," he replied. "I had sex three times: once with a man; once with a woman; then one more time with a man just to see if there was anything I missed the first time. There wasn't."

The scene gets quite intense. Having no bondage gear puts things in a different light. In a way it makes the experience more submissive – not being tied down, but having to discipline yourself, force yourself to stay put and take it nonetheless. I blast off into my lizard brain and, as is often the case, it takes me a long time to come back. Or at least, longer than seems to be the norm around here. The man gets worried. The dungeon safety monitor gets worried enough to come over and ask if I am OK.

I learn that I must warn people ahead of time that if a scene gets intense it might take longer than they are accustomed to for me to return to the land of the normal, and that though it might seem to them like I am not OK, I probably am. That's a difficult one. If you play this far out on the edge, you want your partner to be constantly checking in to see if you are OK. The last thing you want him to do is assume you are OK if you seem like you're not. And yet, if I just do what comes naturally, and go where I naturally go, men seem to read this as "problem." Not sure what to do about this. More typically, men here engage with levels of pain which would send most people into shock, then nonchalantly dust themselves off and saunter away. Is that what happens if you do this kind of thing long enough? Does it mean anything for them anymore, or are they just here out of habit?

Next up for me is a scene in the main dungeon. Maybe I am finally getting into the groove here. A man ties me down to a board, a very elaborate process which takes a long time. I am blindfolded so I cannot see, but at the station next to ours a man is being tickled, and he is laughing, shouting, screaming at the top of his lungs: "OOO! OW! OH! HA HA HA! THAT'S MY BELLY BUTTON! OUCH! NO! HEE HEE HEE!" and so forth. The utter incongruity between the sound and the other sensations that are arriving at my nervous system is partly hilarious and partly disconcerting. This man is reliving being a five-year-old on his daddy's lap. Very loudly and with no inhibition. In the midst of a dungeon where men are being flogged and tortured. One of these men is me.

When the tying of ropes is done, I can't move anything except my head, which I can raise perhaps an inch. Then come the clothes-pins, lots of them. Super intense. Clothespins hurt. A lot. They also fuck with your head, because you know that for the few seconds after they are removed the pain will be even more intense. So you have to calibrate your awareness to the pain that is present even as you prepare yourself for the greater pain that is coming. A real head trip. The limiting clothespin is on my right nipple. I indicate that I cannot take it anymore. He starts removing them, and I blast off into the void. Now he puts a cock ring on me with a vibrator wedged between the cock ring and my dick. Then he starts in on my nipples with a pin wheel, a devious device that features *very* sharp metal pins on a little metal wheel held by a handle. The pins are so sharp that the lightest touch to a sensitive body part can be like an electric shock. In fact, I believe I *am* being shocked with some sort of electric device. I only learn of the pinwheel when the blindfold finally comes off. Lost in inner space, I become vaguely aware that up on earth another man has joined the first one, and is squeezing my nipples with his fingers. Hard. There must be just enough play in the ropes to allow me to thrust my hips ever so slightly, or maybe I am not moving at all but simply contracting my muscles, but one way or the other I feel like I am fucking this vibrator. It is intensely pleasurable. When I cum it is a volcanic eruption. Aftershocks course through me for a long time. I hear exclamations of approval from what must be a group of men who gathered to watch the show. Apparently we drew quite a crowd. I had no idea and I don't care, because I am far away, falling through a black hole in a remote corner of the universe.

Too soon, I become aware that ropes are being untied. The blindfold is coming off. Next thing I know he is rather impatiently asking me if I think I can get up now. I say I am not sure. He says it has been forty minutes since I came. I was thinking it had been maybe five. Again, he is concerned if I am OK. Yes, yes, I am OK. More than OK. I just need time. But time is something he doesn't want to give me. He is done, outta here. I ask him if he will walk me back to my cabin, as I am not at all sure of my coordination. He consents grudgingly, not hiding his annoyance.

All in all this has been a very weird experience. I felt wild sensations, both emotional and physical. I went to someplace deep. But I had absolutely no connection with this guy, and he didn't seem the slightest bit interested in me. He was not attractive, not nice, not the least empathetic. In the end, it feels like I have been through a medical procedure. In fact, I think I have had more connections with doctors and nurses than with this man, who lugged all this gear, and all of his big beer belly, up to this children's camp in the woods to repeat this fixed set of procedures on a stream of male bodies he doesn't care about. Really it seems quite inefficient. If he had a little entrepreneurial spirit he would assemble a crew and set up an assembly line. Male bodies could move down the line as incommunicado as car chassis, with the prescribed set of procedures completed at each station, finishing with a mechanical device to suck out the semen just before the finished bodies are ready for delivery.

As spent as I am, if there were a way out of here – a bus I could jump on, a car with a key in the ignition, a rocket – I would leave right this minute.

*

I wake up the next morning feeling somewhat refreshed. I see sunlight through the window. Yes, I actually am in a sort of pleasant place in the woods.

At breakfast I notice again the youngster in the torn underwear, chain, and boots. He is one of the few here I would describe as attractive, mostly because he has the sheen of youth, which stands out all the more among these men who seem even more tired and sullen and sunk in their ways than their years alone would suggest. My attention keeps returning to the kid, and I am getting ideas. He is short and slight, of Filipino descent. I ask how his time here is going. Wonderful, he says. He has been suspended in rope, mummified, flogged, and tortured in all kinds of ways. I ask if he might like to get with me. Sure, he replies. "What do you have in mind?" "Have you been fucked here?" "No." "Would you like to be?" "Hell yeah." "How about we leave this dungeon scene, go down in the grass by the creek, get naked, and fuck?" He is enthusiastic, but first he must get permission from his master. He is a slave and is here with his master, a much older man with yet another huge belly. He scampers off and gets permission, and off we go, me in my usual jeans and t-shirt, and the slave boy in his torn underwear, chain collar, and army boots.

We cross the road under an overhanging sign that reads *Watch Children*. Through a fence, around the swimming pool, across the baseball diamond, and into a large grassy field by the brook. It is a beautiful day. The sun is shining. You can hear the gurgling of the brook and even an occasional bird. I am going to get naked and intimate with a cute young man, by the brook, in the grass, under a tree. Whew.

We look for the perfect spot. We find one under a beautiful old tree, but it is already occupied. A naked man is standing under the tree, facing the trunk. His wrists are tied together, and the rope that binds them is also tied around the tree. He is being whipped, hard, by another man. A camp counselor, a wholesome looking young fellow who is obviously not part of the kink crowd, is meanwhile circling the tree, mowing the grass on a ride-on-top lawnmower. Around and around he goes, paying them no more attention than he would two cows grazing in the field. *Snap* go the lashes on the man's back.

One can find humor in almost everything that happens here, but this scene is another level. Slave boy and I decide to go a little further on, and do indeed find a most beautiful spot.

Immediately I grab him and plant my mouth firmly on his, while pinning his hands behind his back. I am a big strong guy and he is not. I can completely dominate him. No rope. No hood. No gear. No bag full of implements. Lots of skin, tongue, lips, spit, and germs. I blindfold him with my t-shirt, whip off my belt and tie his hands, and force his mouth down on my dick. And then I am fucking him, and it is indescribably sweet. Fucking naked under a blue sky in the green grass by the brook. I am amazed at how dominant I am. I *never* talk during sex, but words are jumping out without my meaning them to. I am dominating him verbally, but it is not really "role play" because I am playing myself and I mean it. I stuff my t-shirt into his mouth and then demand that he speak. He cannot. *Slap.* C'mon man, talk to me. Tell me something. He is furiously shouting back but all that comes through is a muffled whisper. *Slap.* I fuck him even harder and yank the t-shirt out and kiss him even harder still and then more fucking and slapping and fucking and biting and fucking and gagging and gagging and talking. I put my face right up to his and look him right in the eye as I push the pain right to the edge of his tolerance and hold it. "C'mon now. You wanted this. You can tell me to stop anytime you like and I will, but then you won't get fucked anymore, and this is what you came here for, because you wanted it. So take it. You can do it." And it is so sweet. So aggressive but tender, intimate yet on edge. Kind but severe. I am all over him all at once, he has no chance to protect himself. And then he shoots warm beautiful boy juice all over himself and we collapse, skin on skin, sweat on spit.

Bruises. We both notice at the same time. He is covered with bruises. Deep purple bruises streaking across his pecs and his butt. Wow, I have made a real mess of his pecs. And a great big hickey on his neck. When did that happen? We lie with each other. It is the first skin to skin contact either one of us has had here. It's beautiful.

So what does it mean to be a slave? I ask him. He explains that his master has him as a slave and another man as a "sub", but it is not a triangular relationship. The master has one relation with his sub and another with his slave. The master and his sub are considered a couple. The slave is not at that level, he is a slave. One big happy family. Family values.

His master never fucks him. There is not even much oral sex. This is in keeping with what is going on here at camp. There is almost no genital sex. I had even asked Harold if fucking would be allowed. Sure, he replied, if you went off and did it in private.

Well, I fucked him. More or less in private. And it made both of us very happy.

He tells me more about his life, how he got messed up on drugs and dropped out of high school and then things had just fallen apart, but that becoming a slave had been a turning point and now he is much more stable. Listening to him, I am less sure than he that this slave thing is really all that good for him, but it is not my problem. We have a leisurely walk back to the main camp. He doesn't give a second thought to the bruises covering his body, but is nervous about the hickey. Bruises? Those are a matter of course here. But a hickey? He expects to get teased about that. Are we in high school?

I see him walk over to his master and report on the morning's events. The master looks him over and casts a less than friendly look in my direction. I decide I am needed elsewhere.

*

By now my dance card is filling up. Literally. When you check in to this summer camp, you get issued a dance card with which you can schedule sexual appointments hour by hour throughout the four days. I have just fucked my brains out and I have two more scenes scheduled before bed. The first is set for after lunch with a guy named Jim who seems reasonable and nice, actually smiles, does not strut around in uniforms, and can see his belt buckle when he looks down. It is a perfect early fall day and we decide to find a place outdoors to do whatever it is we are going to do. He has some very particular rope bondage he wants to put me in, which will require two sturdy trees a certain distance apart. So we go wandering around the camp, through soccer fields and fire rings and little amphitheaters and stands of trees in fall foliage, examining all sorts of trees, posts, and fences – none of which are just right. Finally we arrive at the swing set, with swings suspended from a large rectangular wooden frame that disappears into the sand box the whole thing is situated in. I point out that we could take down the swings and have a sturdy wooden frame, and he points out that the iron rings on the top of the frame from which the swings were hanging would be perfect for what his has in mind. The swing set it is.

Jim ties me into a very elaborate rope harness which runs the length of my torso, around my hips and down both legs. A full-body harness of rope. Then he begins tying the body harness to the swing set frame. This is intricate, detailed work and takes a long time. Thankfully, he has blindfolded me. Being wrapped in darkness, my sense of hearing rises to an acute pitch as my vision shuts down. Were it not for the darkness, the waiting would be tedious. But from the moment my eyes are turned off, I experience everything as... what? Sex? I don't think sex is the right word. Not sure I have the right word.

I am not sure other men here have the right word either. In the standard shop talk of the camp, the correct words are "in the scene," as in: "from the moment my eyes were turned off I was in the scene." Like when people used to say they were "in the life." Not something you *are* (like gay, homosexual, queer, pervert, or invert), nor something you *do* (like sex, love, or torture), but some place you *go*: into the life. Actually, torture is not a word used much here, and I am glad of it. I have friends in El Salvador who were horribly tortured, and not for fun. Real, barbaric, unspeakable torture. I live in a country where the state now routinely engages in torture as a matter of policy, even runs a global network of torture in which it kidnaps people from the streets of other countries and hustles them into planes destined for clandestine torture chambers who knows where. Some of the men at this very camp might participate in that system, or train others to participate in that. This is not me. This has nothing to do with me. I am not here to be tortured. I want to delve into the ecstatic potential of my mind and body. How did I end up in the woods with these uniform creeps? What am I doing in Cabin Q with interrogators and jailers? What is happening to me?

This sort juiced up nervous thought excursion can really fill up your head while waiting for a dom to complete some complex rope bondage. You can learn a lot about yourself.

And then I am trapped in a spider's web. The spider in this case is Jim, and his web is spun on a swing set located in a sandbox. I am his fly. Despite not being able to completely leave behind the humor in the situation, I have to acknowledge: this is interesting. I can move but very little. The web fills the entire swing set frame. Jim clearly knows his way around rope. Though the rope pulls at me tightly, the pressure is evenly distributed around my body, making it quite bearable, even comfortable. I have no lateral movement at all. As I am tied from above and from both sides but not below, I can bend my knees a little, lifting them up toward my chest. But there is another kind of movement that far more interesting. He can stand in front of me and with the gentlest push send me floating backwards as the web tensions back like a sling shot, and then I'm shot forward, then back again, oscillating back and forth until I come to rest centered between the posts. There is a distinct feeling of weightlessness. This is fun. If this were a ride at a county fair there would be a long line to get on.

He starts to [＿＿] with me. (There's that missing word again: play?

torture? "do bdsm"?) He sends me flying backward, and I never know what will be waiting for me on the rebound, pain or pleasure. He has tools for both, including the same ultra-sharp pinwheel the guy last night had. *Ow.* That is almost too much. Maybe it *is* too much. How do I know what is too much? I have only an instant to think that question, and no time to answer it. Dealing with this much pain and pleasure requires shutting down that sort of thinking and taking my mind fully into my body. He puts nipple clamps on, very tight ones, *oww*, connected to each other by a chain. *Owwwwww.* This is way, way intense. He ties a rope around my balls, then ties each end of the rope around one of my feet. The rope is just short enough to prevent me from straightening my legs and I must focus on keeping my knees bent or the pressure on my balls will be intolerable. Then, with this excruciating pressure on both my balls and nipples, he gently strokes my dick. This is wildly sensual and erotic, and the floating back and forth in space part makes it other worldly. I orgasm. A huge, shattering of cumming that convulses my body in ways I cannot possibly control. An epic could be written about the journey of every muscle, nerve, and organ in this orgasm and the tornado of chemicals in my brain, but would abruptly end after the first sentence, for a region of my brain over which I have no control has ordered my body to stiffen like a board. My feet shoot down into the earth as my legs go perfectly straight. This is not possible: the rope tied around my balls and my feet is not long enough to permit my legs to straighten. But it is likewise impossible not to drill my legs straight into the earth like I was drilling for oil. The two impossibilities collide, and the pain is searing. Too much pain. Not the "too much" that makes you ask yourself if it is too much, because you know in an instant. At that very moment he seizes the nipple clamp chain and *yanks* off the clamps. The pain hits like a sledge hammer to my head, no, *inside* my head. The pain is not erotic. It is not pain/pleasure or pleasure/pain. It is not subtle or nuanced.

There are no dark corners to investigate, no place to relocate my awareness, no door that opens to another place I can safely move my awareness. The pain is a blaring fluorescent light in a white room with no windows or doors, a hospital room with stainless steel furniture and surgical tools laid on a tray. I vaguely remember pain like this when I woke up in the recovery room after life-threatening surgery. Something starts at the base of my nipples and shoots up through my chest and throat and out my mouth, a ball of pain and blood and claws and bones and rocks and battery acid and rusty nails and fur and teeth, and it flies out of my mouth, and about three feet into the light of day it explodes into pure energy which for all I know is the big bang of a new universe to which I have just given birth, but back here on earth it is perceived as sound which I cannot describe or even imagine but I am certain is very loud.

There is nothing left. I am empty. I am being untied from the web like an accident victim is cut from the mangled remains of a car by highway cops. I am being helped to the grass where I collapse. Time does something, I don't know what. Stop? Extend? Give up? Up above, through fifty feet of dark red Jell-O where it is a sunny afternoon in a children's summer camp, I can just make out two men talking with Jim. They are old, even old by the standards of the men here at camp, which means they are actually elderly. They have been watching the scene intently from a nearby playground bench, and they are here to testify that what just happened was really something. Old school, they call it. They have to dig back to a night in Chicago at a national leather gathering decades ago to think of something equivalent. They are congratulating us. Well, they are congratulating Jim. I am wrapped in two hundred pounds of Jell-O. They want to tell us we have won their respect. We have transported them back to a time when they were not very old men. My pain has taken them back to a younger man's place and time. They are happy.

Do I get a merit badge?

The old-timers have gone. The implements of torture have been put away. The rope has been neatly coiled and stacked in the bag. Jim is bending over me in a kind, friendly way and telling me that I can stay under the Jell-O for longer if I wish, but dinner is already under-way in the cafeteria if I want to eat.

*

And then I am at dinner, watching sulking eastern Europeans who, after a summer tending to the demands of preteen angels and monsters for bargain basement wages, now must tend to a couple of hundred perverts in rubber and leather and latex and bruises and blood and chains and spit and welts and scabs. I meet a very beau-tiful man with a shaved head and a Buddha smile. Something very intriguing about him, an inner calm I can just glimpse behind the smile. Always smiling, never talking above a whisper. A gorgeously muscled and toned body. His partner is here, also with a beautiful smile but similar in appearance to many of the other men with tummies that are larger than they would like and more years on their faces than they would like and just generally ragged around the edges. The two men are a dom/sub couple, the ragged dom and the glistening sub who, I am not surprised to discover, spends many of his waking hours at the gym. He has also recently had surgery to replace both his hips. Yet here he is, on crutches, slowly hobbling with his partner's assistance from the cafeteria to the gym where he gingerly limps up to a Saint James cross, leans his crutches on one side and his Adonis frame on the other. His ragged partner care-fully ties him to the cross so as not to aggravate his wounded hips, then beats the daylights out of him with a leather flogger. His smile never disappears.

A lot of the men at dinner have that special uncomfortable air of people who know that they are supposed to be having a good time but are at a loss as to exactly how to do it. They arrange themselves in the proper poses and groupings, and make themselves willing vessels for an inspiration that might transform the mimicry of fun into the real thing. Like Pentecostal Christians who stand and sing in church, arms outstretched to heaven inviting in the Holy Sprit, but here the sprit of good times never seems to actually arrive. The campers have traveled long and arduous paths to arrive at this place, have come to terms with desires that are way out of bounds, that make them pariahs and monsters in the eyes of almost everyone else in the world. They have explored these desires first tentatively, then determinedly, and finally obsessively. They have broken whatever bonds and constraints and taboos kept them from this. Many (like me) have traveled a long way, some (unlike me) with large collections of arcane fetish gear they have painstakingly assembled, not stuff that you just go buy at the leather store and announce you're a leatherman, like you can take a credit card to Ikea and walk out a yuppie. No, some of these guys are genuine originals.

One man constructed a scaffolding maybe twenty feet high. From the top he suspended a series of bungee cords which ended in a harness of the sort a skydiver would wear attached to the parachute. A collection of wet suits hung from hangers placed on one of the scaffold's crossbars, neatly arranged like business suits at a men's clothing store. Originally intended for surfers, there are wet suits of every shape and size to accommodate anyone who wanted to partake of the experience this man has gone to such lengths to prepare. Men who wanted to go on the ride would put on a wet suit and then be strapped into the harness attached to the bungee cables. A butt plug would be inserted in their rectum, and some sort of electric vibrating device would go on their dick (holes had been cut in the wet suits in the appropriate places). The contraption was constructed such that if the rider flapped his arms like a chicken he would bounce up and down in the bungee cords, which in turn would cause the butt plug to fuck his ass and the vibrator to masturbate his dick. The riders would fly through the air flapping their chicken wing arms until orgasm. It is impressive to contemplate how many iterations the contraption must have been through – the parts collected, the thing constructed, adjusted, revised, tinkered with, and discarded – before the inventor had finally hit on this, the holy grail. And then he had taken the entire thing apart and transported it to this summer camp in what must have been a good-sized truck, where he reassembled it for the enjoyment of all. Dungeon meets amusement park. If you are taller than the wooden clown you can ride this ride alone. No charge, just say thank you.

So here is a cafeteria full of driven men who had come so far to finally arrive at this place at this time with others like them, their *people*. And here it is, the happiest of all days, Thanksgiving and Christmas and the Fourth of July and gay pride day all rolled into one. And as so often happens at holiday gatherings, once everyone is seated at the table no one really knows what to say or do to make it actually fun.

OK, I'm exaggerating. Really it's not that bad. Men *do* have fun. They meet and fill in their dance cards: flogging at three, mummification at eight, lie down and have others piss all over you in the water sports cabin at eleven. Fun.

*

After dinner my dance card shows a date with Domasan. Domasan is an Asian guy who is something of a bondage genius. He ties men up in rope so beautifully he has exhibitions of his bondage in art galleries in Los Angeles. He is pretty much the hottest ticket at camp. Everyone wants Domasan to tie them up. I asked to add my name to the queue, and he fit me in at ten-thirty tonight, which gives me three hours of empty space after dinner. Perfect. The bomb that went off in my head while tied to the swing set is still reverberating. There is something definitely wrong about this. It is not supposed to be this bright in one's head. There are supposed to be shadows. The inside of your head is supposed to be lit like a cozy reading room with a nice antique lamp on the desk, and perhaps the flickering light of flame from the fireplace. Not the hot white glare of an operating room. I need sunglasses inside my head.

I walk gingerly through the campgrounds in the twilight. I take a few hits off a joint, which definitely helps. (Yeah, I know, recreational drugs are taboo here. There is something comforting about being able to break a rule in this place.) I just wander around and try to be as empty as possible. It is a perfect summer evening. A cricket chorus is singing a stochastic oratorio to the strange goings-ons. The country darkness cools the overheating in my brain. I walk though ghostly tennis courts and empty baseball diamonds. I walk past the water sports cabin and the fisting cabin, strangely silent and calm. I walk past the lower gym which only allows scenes which are quiet, no yelling, screaming, or laughing. No talking among bystanders or onlookers. Classical music softly floats from a pair of speakers up through the gym rafters. Groups of men are huddled here and there doing mysterious things I have no desire to investigate up close.

I watch the sun go down. Darkness falls. I sit and wonder and listen to the sounds of dusk slowly transition to the sounds of night. I maintain this still solitude until the last minute. At the appointed hour I appear at the upper gym for my date with Domasan. He is tired. He has spent two days tying up one man after another. He is developing tendonitis from repetitive motion stress of tying and untying all that rope. For my part, the reverberations of the searing pain in the swing set have become faint though still not fully subsided. The sensible thing for both of us would be to forego this encounter and go have a cup of tea. But then, who is doing anything sensible here? We seem to actually like each other. He smiles incessantly, a soft smile, which is not standard fare here. His dance card is completely filled in for the remainder of the camp. This is our only chance, and we go for it. He is going to fully suspend me in rope.

Domasan works fast. Suspending a living human body in rope is an exacting task that requires considerable skill to do safely, and even more skill to do in a way that makes the person comfortable enough to tolerate the suspension for more than a few minutes. Domasan is a master craftsman, working with a speed and assuredness that are something to behold, creating bondage which distributes the pressure from suspension across the body so that, while certainly uncomfortable, the sub can last long enough to investigate the uniqueness of the experience. This is also facilitated by the rope he uses, soft red and black rope intended for use with livestock. ("*Perfect*," Domasan says with a grin.) Many doms who are into rope specialize in one or two basic schemes, and then all the bondage they do is some variation of those. (Jim's spider web, for example.) Domasan creates something new every time. He has been going for two days and has yet to repeat himself. As an improvising musician, this immediately draws my attention and respect. In no time he has me harnessed in a fresh creation, which he then ties to another rope looped over a wooden cross bar overhead. He ties one of my legs up so that my knee is bent and my heel is gently pushing into my butt. Finally, he ties yet another rope around my balls, pulling the remainder of the rope straight out in front of me and fixing it to something I cannot see as I am blindfolded. I am left in an awkward and interesting predicament: the roped tied off in front of me pulls constantly on my balls just enough to be painfully erotic. I am precariously balanced on my left foot. It is all I can manage not lose my balance. If I fall the ropes will catch me, but falling would shoot the pressure on my balls into a different realm entirely. So despite the blindfold, the constant pressure on my balls, and the pain from the bondage of both my arms and my right leg, I put all my concentration on maintaining my awkward balance. This is yoga: painful, perverse, erotic, pleasurable yoga. I have long had a yoga practice, and Domasan is fascinated by my ability to hold this position. He whispers in my ear that, in the lit world outside the blindfold, we have attracted a crowd.

When Domasan judges that I have held this position long enough, he ties another rope around my ankle and yanks, and suddenly I am sailing through the air. He ties this rope off to a point somewhere off to the side. I signal for his attention and his ear is by my mouth. The pressure on my leg is too much, I whisper, I feel like I may be injured. In one moment he has made the perfect adjustment, and there I am, fully suspended in a rope spacewalk. I have left the rocket to perform a scientific experiment in space walking. I cannot remember just what the experiment is, but no matter. I am walking, actually floating in space with pain and confinement and weightlessness and freedom crawling over my skin and through my muscles in constantly shifting combinations.

Soon I am not floating but swinging. Domasan has grabbed hold of the end of the rope tied around my balls and is swinging my whole body with it, back and forth. As the arc of the swinging grows wider and wider, I fly higher and higher. This is what I imagined, or hoped, bdsm could be. Domasan has finely tuned this whole scene to my edge of pain and pleasure, and gradually moved that edge farther and farther out. I am flying through that expanded space, and it feels great.

Eventually a safety monitor comes over and points out that if Doma-san swings me any higher the entire ten-by-twenty-foot wooden frame I am suspended from could tip over, and thus the scene is brought to a close. It has been the perfect counterpoint to my experience earlier in the day. It ends with me wanting more, totally buzzed and incredulous.

*

Now it is my turn to do a work shift staffing the information desk, or "command central," from midnight until four in the morning. I share this duty with a truly strange man. Even in this crowd, he stands out. There is something creepy about him in the same way there was something creepy about the piano teacher the Betty Davis character hires for her planned comeback in *Whatever Happened to Baby Jane.* And it turns out that he is, in fact, a public school music teacher and church organist. I ask what his particular sexual quirk might be. Anal play, he tells me, as if revealing a state secret only he has clearance to know. A *particular kind* of anal play, of his own invention, using highly specialized techniques only he knows.

"My goodness," I reply. "Tell me, tell me."

He pauses to give the impression that he is weighing whether or not I am worthy of such knowledge, though it is clear he cannot *wait* to tell me. Telling people is the reason he is here.

His secret technique is really a secret ingredient, he explains, something very special to put up men's butts that only he has thought of.

He leans forward and in a stage whisper explains:

"*Eggs.* Hard boiled eggs. Lots of them. The key is that they distribute the pressure evenly. It's not like a sex toy that is just one size, you can always add another. It's organic matter, so if one gets stuck up there it's no problem, it will just come out the next day."

I can't resist. I ask if it matters if the eggs are from free range chickens. He assures me it doesn't. "How about white or brown eggs?" No, he says, none of that matters. That's the beauty of it.

*

In the morning I wake up feeling like a spent piece of used jet trash, and drag myself to breakfast. Over pancakes, a nice man named Tom suggests that he mummify me. He promises it will be easy and dreamy, no pain, all gentleness. I ask him how long he has been into mummification, and he replies that he had his first orgasm when he accidentally wrapped himself up tight in a blanket while rolling around in bed as a child. By the time of his second orgasm he had cellophane wrapped around his chest. Precocious.

We head to the lower gym. Rays of soft morning light filter in from the surrounding woods. Graceful notes from a piano sonata are quietly moving through the room like a light mist. Tom has brought an industrial-size roll of cellophane. He tells me to relax, this will be easy, and begins to wrap me up. Yards and yards of the stuff, more and more, tighter and tighter. But I'm not quite getting the point. Once I am fully wrapped it takes three guys to lift me off the ground and place me lying on a table. And then there is yet more wrapping.

Then he puts a gas mask on me. Now this is weird. I had seen pictures of men in bondage wearing gas masks, and was mystified. What was the fetish? WWI? Poison gas? Something I was missing entirely? Or was it just a random burst of inspiration by a bondage top who had wrapped someone up in duct tape, cellophane, rope, and chains, then stepped back to admire his handiwork when suddenly it hit him: a *gas mask* would be the finishing touch, the *pièce de résistance*? But when the gas mask goes on I discover that it is all about the experience. Maybe for the top its appeal is in its appearance. It must have *some* visual appeal, because it is such a strikingly odd thing to put on someone. But from inside, a gas mask with the eyeholes blacked out is a world in itself, a black hole. Even the most intense hood leaves a hole for the mouth, even if it is just a straw. Or if there is no hole for the mouth the hood must be loose enough for air to get in somewhere. But a gas mask has none of that. Everything is tight. No holes. That's the whole point of a gas mask: if it wasn't tight gas would leak in. Air enters only through filter at the end of the hose, which in no way feels like an "opening" to the outside world.

As for the mummification, it just isn't doing much for me. But then again, this is what I wanted after the excruciating pain of yesterday. Something nice. Nice and easy. I had told Tom that, and he is going to great trouble to give me exactly that. Thank you, I think, and I sink into the flow.

And then it is time to unwrap, which is a production in itself, though not as involved as the wrapping, since now the whole thing can be cut off. As the layers of plastic are cut, I notice another scene going on in the gym to my left. I cannot make out the details, but I can see enough to know that I do not want to see more. A group of men is standing around a table on which another man is lying. One of the standing men is wearing a headlamp of the sort a surgeon might wear, and he is holding the lying man's penis up with some kind of stainless steel medical instrument. Quick as I can, I turn away. These medical sorts of scenes are *not* for me. No way, no how, not even for a second, not even just for a look. There was a "cutting" scene in here yesterday involving the naval surgeon I had met on the bus the first day, and I fled from that one as well. My revulsion is so strong that I carefully position my head so that whatever is going on over there is outside my field of vision.

The rest of the mummification is removed. The clear plastic wrap is more suggestive of a larvae than a mummy. Will I emerge as a butterfly? No, I emerge with the same tired aching body as before. I stand up a little unsteadily, then carry my not-butterfly-like body out of the gym, my hands cupping my eyes like binoculars allowing me just enough tunnel vision to direct myself through the door, carefully avoiding any glimpse of the scene going on to my left.

Outside I run into a club board member who says there has been an "accident." A scene went bad and an ambulance has been called. All play in the camp is suspended, and everyone is supposed to get inside whatever cabin they can find, put on normal clothes, and wait until the ambulance has come and gone. Where did the accident happen, I ask? In the small gym, he replies. It was the scene I couldn't watch. The headlamp and stainless steel flash through my mind, the memory becoming covered with blood.

This is most unpleasant news. Sure, this camp is full of slightly crazy men doing strange and painful things to each other, but nothing is supposed to result in actual injury. The possibility that I could end up cut out of the spider's web or the plastic larvae by paramedics, that I might leave here in an ambulance instead of a bus — this had never crossed my mind. In my anxiety about coming here, among all the scenarios that played through my head about what might possibly happen, this is one I never considered. The realization that this was a real possibility envelops me like a toxic cloud.

Eventually the ambulance is gone and the campers emerge from the cabins and head to lunch. No one seems particularly bothered about the "accident." Shit happens, life goes on. What's next on the dance card? It turns out that the scene involved inserting stainless steel rods into the man's urethra and then all the way down his penis. Among aficionados this is called "sounding." In fact, the scene was actually a workshop in which the camp sounding expert was demonstrating how to do this safely. One of the rods apparently went in too far, and the result was a flood of blood. Oops.

I am done. Completely finished. Can I go home now? Can I get as far away from this as possible? Can I teleport to a tropical beach where I can lie naked with a beautiful man and we will touch each other gently, and be kind to each other, and let the waves wash over us?

Walking to the salad bar, I see a man in a t-shirt that features a photo-realistic image of Jesus' arms outstretched on the cross. The nails are rendered in fine detail, and blood is oozing from the wounds. Text running across the shirt under the image reads *I Love You This Much.*

I crack up. I have to ask, "Is that a Christian shirt or a bdsm shirt?"

Without any sense of irony or humor, the man wearing the shirt answers, "As a practicing Christian who is into bdsm, I don't see any difference between the two."

Good grief.

"Well, did you buy it in a church or at an bdsm party?"

"At church."

This is not the answer I was expecting. I remember that the day before he wore a shirt with a similarly realistic and gory image of the gashes on Jesus' back after he had been whipped, with the words *Read Between the Lines.* I ask him about that one and yes, he bought that one at church as well. I think of all the men I have met here who say they are, or were, Christians. That would include nearly everyone except the military men. Almost all Catholics, plus a few Anglicans. I myself was raised Anglican. It hits me: we're at a church camp. A church camp for middle aged men whose erotic landscape was formed by the combination of Christian guilt and the sadomasochism of the whole sordid Christian tradition of crucifixion and martyrdom. And no one seems to find any humor in this. To the contrary, most of these guys still go to church. The egg man last night is a church organist!

I need to get away right now. I walk to the creek and practice yoga on a rock in the middle of the stream. This is all I want. The sound of the creek, the light on the water, the calm of the yoga.

The rest of the day is a blur. I had talked to a guy about doing a "fire scene." Even at this camp, fire scenes are considered risky and esoteric, but this man came recommended as the best. He teaches workshops in how to engage in fire play safely. Just like the workshop in sticking steel rods up your dick safely that ended up in an ambulance. I cancel my meeting with fire man.

*

It's the last day. Men are covered with bruises, scabs, and blood. Some real horror shows. There is an "iron butt" spanking contest in which really fat men bend over and take it, without showing any outward sign of pain, pleasure, passion, or anything at all, until their asses are the consistency of raw ground beef. It is yet another shockingly ugly sight I try to avoid.

At dinner a nice faery-looking guy propositions me. I tell him I have no stomach for more bdsm, but if he wants to take a blanket into a field and lie and watch the stars I would be happy to have his company. In the field we lie down and talk and kiss. I tell him how alienated I feel from the men here. They all seem stuck going around in circles, ruts leading back to the same fetish over and over. Like addicts. He disagrees. He thinks most of the men here are on paths of spiritual growth. For an example, he mentions a friend he is camping with, who declared himself a "sex addict," and joined Sexaholics Anonymous. He is proud of this friend and is here to support him. "He has made his boundaries and is living by them." For instance, last night his friend did an "abrasion scene" and really stuck to his limits. "He didn't take his clothes off, didn't suck the guy or fuck him."

This strikes me as hilarious. A "recovering sex addict" comes here, of all places, and fills up his dance card with scenes, and as long as he doesn't take his clothes off, suck dick, or get fucked, he is on the wagon? But my new friend sees no irony at all. He tells me that he himself is here on a quest. He is deeply involved in "earth-based religions." He is Wiccan. He talks about Wicca and witchcraft and how earth-based spirituality has led him to this place and this sexual practice.

"So were you raised religious?" I ask.

"Oh yes, Catholic."

I walk to the midnight snack area but the Iron Butt contest is there, heading for its bloody *dénouement*. I join the men in the next room who are trying to socialize without subjecting themselves to the sights next door, and *finally* find someone with a sense of humor. He is standing among the usual crowd of uniform fetishists with cigars, but wearing a camo baseball hat and camo onesie pajamas, the legs of which are tucked into camo rubber galoshes. He is holding a teddy bear wearing a leather harness, and pinned to his chest is a camo shoestring tied to a pacifier. I burst out laughing and walk right over.

"Thank you. Thank you for this. You just made my night."

"Oh, but you haven't seen everything yet."

He unzips the pajamas to reveal a diaper, complete with camo over-pants. He has spent his evening in the "water sports" cabin.

*

Getting on the bus to leave summer camp feels like a jail break. The sky is blue. The day is warm. The trees are green. The bus pulls out of the woods into suburbia and for the first time in my life I am glad to see strip malls. The normal world is still here. And all I can think is: I will never go back to that place.

*

I never did go back to that place. But I did find meaningful and even loving ways to play sexually with pain and pleasure, freedom and control, and domination and submission. Never once, however, have I been at a gathering of people brought together by these interests where I felt among my people. It is not my community, not my world. As is so often the case, I find myself the outlier.

I have thought a lot about Harold over the years. Such a strange man, which is just another way of saying unusual. He certainly had an unusual set of desires. His statement that he "had sex three times: once with a man; once with a woman; then one more time with a man just to see if there was anything I missed the first time" is not a sentiment I expect to hear from any lips but his. As far as I could discern, he had no desire to experience pleasure, but he was endlessly fascinated by pain. Administering pain. Dissecting pain. Watching pain. Watching people recover from pain. Learning how pain played out on this body as compared to that one. He was deeply drawn to men who desired, and could tolerate, all the pain he wished to administer, and went to extraordinary lengths to gather them around him. He built a career around it, got the US Army to provide the money and resources to do precisely those forbidden things he was driven to do. He built a world of kink around it, starting at a time when there were definitely not images of women in leather with whips being used to sell cars. His life partner of many years is a man who can take an amount of pain that would make even the heavyweights of summer camp blush.

He enforced a strict compliance of consent at summer camp, and in his other activities during the rest of the year. He taught others how to think about consent intelligently. He was looked up to by all as a fountain of wisdom on the ethics of extreme bdsm.

I never heard him say anything about respect for the Army, love of America, hatred of commies, or anything of the sort. His life partner was an outspoken anarchist who often talked about his hatred of the US government, which did not seem to bother Harold in the least. Harold talked about pain, and control, and fucking with people's heads. I doubt he ever tortured anyone (caused pain without consent), and I suspect his vague references in that direction were just bluster. Of course, I do not know this for fact. There is so much I don't know about the man.

I have a very different sense of some of the others at Cabin Q. One in particular, the "interrogator," who stood as still and expressionless as a fence post while Harold whipped him. That was a scary guy. Never showed emotion of any kind, but he wasn't just blank. It was like he had invisible armor on that would burn your flesh if you didn't get out of his way in time. I have no idea if he really was an interrogator or in any military or intelligence or whatever, but I am certain that if he was an interrogator, I would not want to be questioned by him.

And then there's the surgeon who came to summer camp to do cutting scenes. Fine by me. The man knows what he likes. Many people find anal and oral sex between men to be utterly abhorrent, but I like it and I do it. So there. Find your bliss.

But my encounters with these men are pieces of a puzzle I have been trying to solve for a long time without necessarily knowing it: the interrogator who does interrogations scenes; the surgeon who does cutting scenes; Harold and his prisoner of war program; even the man I met long ago whose obsessive sexual fetish was the leather pants he wore to work every day as a motorcycle cop. Putting these pieces together leads me back to my encounter with the real killer and torturer, Roberto D'Aubuisson, and the swarm of questions following him around which constituted the weird sexual energy he exuded. Did he bring that sexual energy into the torture chamber? Did he get off on it? Did his victims sense it? Did he get off on killing?

I think I have solved the puzzle, and the answers are yes, yes, yes, and yes.

Men become cops because they get off on control, and the clothes that symbolize control.

Men become surgeons because they get off on cutting people open.

Men become torturers because they get off on torture.

It might be rare that a surgeon gets off on cutting to the point that it becomes a sexual fetish. And not every cop gets off on control and uniforms so much that it becomes a sexual fetish. These are continuums, just like even the most vanilla sex has at least some small element of domination and submission, but not all sex involves whips and hoods and handcuffs. As you move far down these trails you arrive at terrain where you have to think carefully about ethics and boundaries. This is not all that difficult to do. But continue on even farther out and you arrive at monster land, inhabited by those who have thrown ethics into the trash. My point being that you cannot account for the extremes of human violence without taking into account the sexual energy at its core. Not everyone who is capable of extreme violence commits it. Circumstances must be right. But if, for example, you are the morally bankrupt owner of a vast hacienda and find yourself urgently needing a thug willing to dirty his hands protecting you from the wrath of those who are working themselves to death on that land, you can be sure that the man who answers your call is going to be a man who gets off on killing and torturing. If you want to understand why the world is the way it is, you are going to have to understand that.

CODA

On June 3, 2007, an article appeared in the *New York Times* titled "Soviet-Style 'Torture' Becomes 'Interrogation.'" According to the *Times*, the torture techniques Americans used on prisoners at Guantánamo Bay, in Afghanistan and Iraq, and at the CIA's secret overseas jails were developed from a Cold War era Army program called Survival, Evasion, Resistance and Escape (SERE). SERE was designed to prepare American military personnel to survive Soviet torture. When the CIA got the green light to torture prisoners after 9/11, like any bureaucratic organization, they looked around for a manual for how to do it. They found the old SERE program and reverse engineered it, essentially reinventing Soviet torture techniques from the cold war. Or rather, Harold's fantasy of what Soviet torture techniques might have been. If Harold's stories are true, then SERE was Harold's program, and he recruited the initial corps of his summer camp from its veterans. The *Times* missed this link. A more complete headline would read *Soviet Style 'Torture' Becomes 'Summer Camp' for Men Becomes Guantanamo 'Interrogation.* Harold is the missing link between Josef Stalin and George W. Bush – and me.

PART 5

He was a man, take him for all in all, I shall not look on his like again.

– William Shakespeare (Hamlet)

HANK

The phone rang.

"Hello?"

"Hi, how are you?"

"Not great actually." I launched into a series of complaints about things so trivial I cannot remember what they were. After I had carried on a sufficient amount of time, I said, "So, Hank, how are you?"

"Oh, I'm fine, I'm fine. I mean, I have lung cancer, but you know, I spent the last few days at the library reading about it and what I learned is that people who have lung cancer don't think they have any rights because they are all smokers, so this will be fun."

(Hank never smoked in his life: tobacco, marijuana, or anything else. In his drug use as in everything else, Hank was extremely modest. Modest in everything except sex. In sex he was a hedonist.)

If it had been anyone else I knew, or maybe anyone else in the world, I would have heard that last statement as a facetious way to soft pedal the terrible news. But Hank wasn't joking. His very real intention was to make lung cancer fun. And he would make it fun by making it an opportunity to work with yet another population who didn't think they had any rights. Maybe they could get together and go get some.

I knew he meant it because he had done it before many times over. For twenty years he had managed a 150-room flophouse hotel as an unfunded DIY hospice for indigent people dying of AIDS, and made the work fun. He had founded organization after organization through the bright lights of the gay liberation years and the darkest times of the AIDS epidemic, went through AIDS himself, and made all that fun. Now he would make lung cancer fun.

I had my doubts.

When someone tells you they are terminally ill, the nature of your relationship with them flashes through your mind. But who were we to each other, Hank and I?

The day we met he said something equally absurd yet compelling, which has stuck with me through all the intervening twists and turns. A gay stand up-comedian had run a long-shot last-minute write-in campaign for Mayor of San Francisco against the most powerful politician in California, and surprised everyone including himself by forcing the first round of voting into a run-off between the two. The next day I went to the campaign headquarters to volunteer.

"Hi, I am here to volunteer. What can I do?"

I was directed to a strapping man with square shoulders, a swimmer's chest, and a wry smile. A big man with a small ego, who seemed to be taking up less space in the room than a body like his would typically require.

"Here, answer this phone."

"OK."

Ring.

"Hello, Tom Ammiano for Mayor headquarters."

"..."

I put my hand over the receiver. "Hank, excuse me, it's the newspaper. A death threat has just been made against Tom. They want a statement."

"You can make it."

"What?! Ummmm. Hank, I just walked in here. You don't know me. I don't know Tom. I don't even know you. I *cannot* make a statement to the press about a death threat!"

Finally I got Hank to take the phone and make a statement.

Who was this guy? He seemed to be in charge without taking charge. He was making decisions that would normally get you bounced out of an electoral campaign right quick, yet everyone was deferring to him. I was intrigued.

It took a while to learn his extraordinary history at the center of gay activism in San Francisco, and of his particular focus on working with those at the very bottom of the food chain: the homeless, the drug addicted, the very young, the trans___. Hank had been doing the work for so long that the terminology had gone from transvestite and transexual to tranny to transgender. Hank was not interested in words. He was interested in people. In the end he became a sort of quiet hero to those who stuck around long enough to notice who was actually walking the walk. After he died, I taught myself to make movies so I could make a documentary about his life.

So, who were Hank and I to each other?

Not long after we met, the subject of sex was broached. True to his colors as an older gay man who had come of age in the pre-AIDS pre-internet era of cruising, his response was immediate and direct: "I'm on my way." Soon he was at my door, a bottle of massage oil in hand. The massage turned into sex. It was nice. Nothing earthshaking. The post-coitus cuddle was perhaps the most comfortable part.

The next day the phone rang and it was Hank. Oddly, I feel private about what he said. Even all these years later, even in a book where I tell so much, I will keep that conversation between Hank and myself. But the point was that he didn't think a sexual connection between us would work. So instead, we settled into the relationship that would continue between us until his death.

But what were we to each other?

We saw each other often, and talked on the phone even more often. By this time the hotel was in the past, and he was running a free breakfast program for homeless people with AIDS. Something like three hundred people a day ate breakfast there. And then there were all his political projects. He never tried to recruit me for a single one, though he was an extraordinary organizer and I was an experienced activist. He never asked me to volunteer at the breakfast program, though he was the sole paid employee and needed volunteers. He never introduced me to his close friends, whom I finally met when we were all gathered around the hospital bed on which his lifeless body lay.

He never invited me to his dingy, roach-infested, one-room apartment where he slept on the floor. Didn't even own a bed. Hank found joy in living on less than most people thought possible, and having fun doing so. Who needs a bed? Once you get used to it, the floor feels fine. The activist group ACT UP would send him to AIDS conferences with a per diem for food which he would hand back upon return, having snacked at convenience stores instead of eating meals, to save money. Which was fun. It was fun because if you didn't need money you could provide services for the indigent at your hotel which exceeded the services offered by agencies funded with public money.

Somehow, he chose to keep his relationship with me apart. His life was such a whirlwind, maybe he wanted to keep hold of one connection outside the storm. We talked about everything: life, love, joy, sex, trouble, loss, pain, power, oppression, resistance. Most of all we engaged in a sense of humor we shared. We went to lots of movies. Movies were the one respite he would pay for. He loved to dissect movies with me late into the night afterwards.

Whatever our relationship was, I came to accept it and feel comfortable in it and treasure it. I had hoped we might become more of a "couple," but he appeared to want something else. He was a very unusual man. His entire life spent in service to others. Whatever emotional needs he had, they did not seem to include the things that most of us seek to fulfill in a couple relationship. Shoulder to cry on? No need. Talk late into the night? We did that. Vacation and travel buddy? Hank didn't take vacations. The one exception being that every so often he would take a day to go swim at a river resort frequented by gay men a couple of hours out of the city. But once there, he would sleep in his car to save money. Back home he would offer the car to homeless people to sleep in. The car itself became a running joke: how long could Hank continue to drive, and sleep in, that rolling scrap heap before it simply came apart.

Instead of partnering with me, he mentored me through my love affairs with others – one in particular, with a man who was marginally housed, teetering on a mental health precipice, and deaf. I don't think I would have entered that relationship without Hank's mentorship. Hank was completely unfazed by poverty, housing, disability, or mental health issues. In Hank's book, poor people, homeless people, schizophrenic people all need love, and can give love back. Just like the rest of us. No big deal.

After telling me of his cancer, and how much fun it was going to be, there was a long silence between us. At last, I told him how sorry I was to hear the news, how much I loved him, and that I wanted to care for him as I would care for a significant other. Those were the words I used. "I want to care for you as if you were my significant other." I had never used those words with him. I had never used those words with anyone. Not quite sure how I pulled those words out of the air. They have an odd formality about them. But somehow I reached, and those were the words I grabbed hold of.

Over the following months, the horrible progression of incurable lung cancer played itself out, and then he was gone.

In the end, I don't think I cared for him as I would have if he had been my significant other. No, scratch that, I am sure I did not care for him like that. I have a significant other now, a man I love deeply, with whom I share a bed and a life. If he was dying of lung cancer, I know what I would do for him. And I did not do that for Hank. I fell far short. But Hank found it difficult to ask for help from others, and even more difficult to accept help that was offered. Hank's way was to ask for nothing, sleep on the floor, live on air, and be of service.

The last time I saw him alive, he was close enough to death that he was able to talk about regrets. The Hank I had known would have found voicing regret too close to complaining, and Hank *never* complained. But the hourglass was nearly empty. He managed to tell me that his single regret was that he never had a real lover.

"Really? I never thought you wanted that."

On the verge of tears, he replied, "I would have liked to think that there had been somebody for me."

Oh Hank. Dear dear Hank. Are you telling me that we could have... That this was all a... That you were standing right in front of me all this time but I didn't see...

I have no answers to these questions. I never will.

Losing Hank was yet another lesson in how the departure of loved ones leave holes in our lives we will never fill. So we live full of holes. For me, in the empty place where Hank used to be, these questions linger. For years they held a nearly unbearable sadness. But life goes on, if we are lucky, and we make peace with our empty places, and I know now that if there was distance between Hank and I we might have bridged, the responsibility for failing to do so is not mine alone. Unlike my regret that I did not care for him better during his illness, which will go with me to my grave. But that too is OK. Our regrets are an important part of who we are. Hank too had a regret that was an important part of him, and I am grateful he shared it with me before he left.

Since Hank departed, I have thought long and hard about men. About their complexity. Our complexity. About their emotional distance. My emotional distance. About need and want and giving and taking and indulgence and abstention and more. I decided to write this book. I resolved that for the rest of my life, I would never miss an opportunity to love a good man. I have not always succeeded, but I have tried.

MARK

We fucked before we spoke. It was beautiful. And joyous. And in a crowd.

The first words I heard him speak: you missed the fireworks. But he didn't say them to me. He said them to a friend who had just flopped down beside us on the bed. The sex we had just shared was the fireworks he was referring to.

In my experience, gay male sex spaces are of two kinds. One is full of grim-faced men nervously moving about, saying no and no and no and no, avoiding eye contact, endlessly searching for that one guy who is one rung up the hotness ladder from them yet will welcome their approach, while refusing the approach of all men one step down the hotness ladder reaching up to them. It's not particularly fun. It feels a lot like work. Yeah this job sucks but someone has to do it. Men can spend hours in such spaces doing exactly that and never touch a single soul.

And then there are spaces that become joyous celebrations. Where the default answer is yes, and very few are left out. Where you can dive into an almost undifferentiated sea of masculinity and swim: breast stroke, back stroke, side stroke, butterfly, crawl, or tread water.

Where you simply can't believe your good fortune, that you are here at this time and place, partaking in this secret ritual which is not only forbidden but quite unimaginable to most people, unimaginable to you until you were in it.

Mark and I were at a winter solstice party organized by the radical faeries, a loose network of gay hippies dating back to the 1970s. And at this point in time, faerie solstice parties were almost always joyous celebrations. This was before cocaine and K and molly and poppers and E and G had flooded faerie parties, along with drugs whose names were corporate trademarks: Viagra for the boys on so much K and molly that they needed an additional drug to get their cocks hard, and AndroGel for those of whatever gender who wanted to butch it up. When you didn't need to keep Narcan close at hand for overdoses, or even pre-position EMT teams nearby if the party was a big one. Back when queers who weren't gay boys were happy that the gay boys could finally do their crazy gay-boy thing somewhere safe where they wouldn't get robbed or killed or arrested, instead of feeling oppressed by the gay boys because they weren't invited.

Hard to imagine now: a queer orgy that was not a chemical soup of smuggled or trademarked drugs. There wasn't even much alcohol at those parties. Just marijuana. Clouds and clouds of marijuana.

It was at one of these parties that we met, and fucked, and finally spoke. He was my height and age, but thinner and with a soft southern drawl and a winning air of kindness and calm. In a different world and a different life, he would have been the one, and my life after meeting him would have run in a very different direction than it has. But I wasn't ready. It was too soon after getting HIV. All signs pointed to an early and ugly exit from this world for me, and I was desperately searching for the love that would make the price I had paid for loving men "worth it." It would take me a long time to understand how deep a misunderstanding of love this thought entailed.

Mark would have preferred that I had a more mature understanding of love, so he kept his distance for some time to protect his own heart. A wise choice.

When we connected again, we were in another, much different, sexual space. The venue occupied the entirety of an enormous building. One floor was allegedly for straight people but in fact was for trannies and their chasers. (Yes, that was the language used by trannies themselves at the time.) The other floors were for gay men.

The place had a weird vibe. It was never that well-attended, so there was no way the owners were even coming close to covering their costs. Was it a tax write off? Was someone laundering money? Was someone too rich to care? Not my problem.

One reason the place was poorly-attended was because the sheer size of it undercut the first law of gay male sex spaces: get the party rolling by packing too men many into too small a space so that it is impossible to move through the space without being touched.

Come to think of it, I can remember two occasions, once in Sydney and once in San Francisco, when I was in a crowd of nearly naked men packed in so sardine-can tight that I was unable to reach down to grab the condom I had stashed in my sock. There was simply not enough room to bend over, even a little. Disappointing in a way, because I really wanted to fuck the guy wedged in in front of me, and these were the AIDS days when fucking without a condom was unthinkable. But the situation had transcended the bounds of sexual acts like penetration, and had become something else: something bigger, lighter, more out of bounds, more electric. A sea of bodies.

My Sydney experience was at an all-night party for 25,000 held at the state fair grounds. No cops allowed. The organizers got away with throwing a party of that size without police by organizing it as a private event held by a private club. When you bought your ticket you were also buying membership in a club of 24,999 others. Hosting debauchery at that scale without police required creativity and thinking outside the box. For example, over the preceding years a growing number of straight guys were showing up claiming to be bisexual but then hitting on the lesbians in ways that were definitely not cool. So the organizers revised the form everyone filled out when paying for club membership, asking the applicants to state if they were gay, lesbian, or bisexual. (This was before the word transgender had come into widespread use). It was a trick question. If you checked the bisexual box they would then refuse to admit you to the club. And thus they were able to have an outrageously debauched party for 25,000 without police and without a bunch a straight guys harassing the lesbians. Today, using a trick question to filter out the straight dudes posing as bisexuals would be considered offensive to bisexuals, and to all of our ever more fragile identities. So no more trick questions. That party still happens once a year, but there are lots of police to keep the partygoers in line, and no sex is allowed.

The other time I was in a room so crowded with naked men I could not reach my sock was in San Francisco, in a second-floor space above a large dance club. If you skipped the main door downstairs and went around the back and up the stairs, you entered a more private space with a bar, a dance floor, and several additional rooms. Once a month there was a gay party there that was one of my high holy days. Mandatory clothes check at the door, down to your underwear. All the patrons were gay men. They shut the door once six hundred people were inside, so that's six hundred gay men in underwear. All the staff were women: at the door, the coat check, and the bar. There were even women in cocktail dresses with trays of candy and cigarettes. The women clearly enjoyed their night. The gay boys who shared my sensibility enjoyed this too, found it kind of hilarious. For others, it worked their last gay nerve.

I remember being in a room packed wall to wall with men, lit only by a strobe light (no warnings signs about the strobe). A pool table covered with plywood occupied the middle of the room, and standing on the plywood was a young woman calling out in a high squeaky voice, "The San Francisco AIDS Foundation urges you all to have safe sex! Keep the condoms and lube coming, boys!" All the while throwing bunches of lubed condoms packet over our heads. She was a cheerleader for the gay sex team. If she had been wearing an actual cheerleader outfit with a big letter G on the front it would have not been out of place. The guy wedged in before me, the one I would have fucked if I had been able to reach my sock, or lucky enough to grab a flying condom, was furious at her presence. "What's *she* doing here?"

When he and I were finally pushed up against to the pool table he tapped her leg.

"Can I ask you a question?"

"Sure."

"Are you enjoying yourself?"

"Do you really want to know?"

"Yeah."

"*YESSSSSSSS.*"

The gleam in her eye could have lit the entire room. The whole thing just made me very happy.

Nowadays, queers go to sexual spaces and "practice consent." One must ask before touching. In the spaces I have been describing, touching many people you could not possibly have verbal contact with was unavoidable. In fact, that was the whole point. You gave consent by being there. Today, having a party with gay male patrons and female staff would require lengthy political discussions before-hand about who counted as male or female, who would feel left out, who would feel oppressed. By the time such a discussion finally ground to a halt many people would have lost interest.

And yes: packing so many nearly naked men into underground party spaces is fundamentally *not a good idea*. Yes: *something might happen that you do not like*. Yes: the fire marshal will be apoplectic, *and for good reason*. If the place catches fire... I cannot advocate for such parties. But I am so glad I attended them.

At a recent gay party in Mexico City that reminded me of the old parties in San Francisco, a Mexican turned to an American visitor, looked him in the eye and emphatically stated, "You are at a party with no rules. *Where are the exits?*" We used to have parties in San Francisco where it was up to you to have the good sense to know where the exits were. No more. It is much, much more safe. And less fun.

The faerie party where Mark and I met was in a league of its own: no rules and no cops, lots of exits, a reasonable amount of loving naked people in a very comfortable, not overly crowded space. Thank you, beautiful faeries.

It may seem odd that I started out writing about Mark, then digressed through the crazy spaces in which Mark and I had sex with who knows who. But this is one of the many deep connections Mark and I have. We not only met in one of those magic places, we were profoundly shaped by them. Our understanding of who gay men are and what gay life can be would be very different without those gatherings. Orgies of sex with people you don't know might seem shallow to you, but not to Mark and me. We continued to enjoy those magic moments over the years, and we look back on them now with a shared sense of awe and wonder which is part of our bond.

Anyway, back to the sex club where Mark and I reconnected. It was not a steamy crowded sexy space. It was cavernous and mostly empty. On one floor they had set up a bunch of backpacking tents so that one might have a bit of privacy. It was completely bizarre. No one goes to a place like that for privacy, there were never enough people present at this particular place to need privacy from anyway, and who wants to fuck in a little tent unless they are high up in the mountains? I never saw a single person go into one of those tents. Did the shady folks who ran the place collect a debt someone paid in tents? Who knew?

For a few months, drag queens took over the place for one night a month. Cabaret shows on one floor, fashion shows on another, and so on. Straight people would attend, fully clothed. They came in part for the drag and fashion, and in part out of curiosity to see what the inside of a gay sex club was actually like.

It was at one of those nights that Mark and I met again, almost bumped into each other. Immediately we were in a passionate embrace, lips and tongues intertwined. He felt familiar and strange, known yet new. AIDS and stress and my own immaturity and much more had kept us apart, and yet here we were, in each other's arms again, in another crazy, unimaginable sexual space. Nothing and no one was going to hold us back.

We soon became aware that we were being watched. We looked up to discover we were encircled by straight women, gazing in fascination. Look! Gay men exhibiting behavior! It was voyeuristic and odd and intrusive and kinda hot but not really but mostly it was funny. We took a look around, looked at each other, burst out laughing, and headed into one of the camping tents. I do believe we may have been the first people in all of history to actually go into a tent in that club. Pretty quickly we were naked and doing what gay men do best, when a mysterious hand unzipped the tent door from bottom to top. A woman's head appeared, three sheets to the wind.

"Mary, *is that you?*"

Our naked bodies were six inches from her face, but her eyes struggled to come into focus and failed.

"Mary, *are you in here?*"

We looked at her, stock still and speechless.

"OK, look, Mary, *I gotta go.*"

The head disappeared.

*

A few months later, the city busted drag queen night at that club. The owners did not have a cabaret license, so live music was not allowed. San Francisco to gay men: you guys can get naked and fuck and get AIDS and carry on all your debauchery in here, but if anyone puts on some clothes and plays a piano or sings a song we are shutting you down.

*

The other San Francisco club I mentioned, the one with the all-female staff, came to a sudden end one night when there was a fight

in the straight club downstairs and the police were called and came
charging through the wrong door. Oops.

*

Mark went on to find a loving man more capable of sustaining
a relationship than I was at the time Mark and I met. They are
now married, and I love them both. Recently, within a year of each
other, they both had strokes. Getting old is a bitch. There were some
years when I felt jealous of the relationship his husband had with
Mark, and I suspect his husband felt jealous of the connection Mark
maintained with me. But we are way beyond that now. Many of my
partners in crime from those days have either moved away or died,
and not just of AIDS. Mark and I are old enough now to have friends
dying of other things. When I go to his house for breakfast, I feel at
home in a way I feel nowhere else. Mark and I share such a similar
take on the world in general and queer culture in particular, we can
speak in an emotional shorthand that requires few actual words.
I treasure him, and his husband.

DONNY

Donny says, "I have been the most chaotic, random kind of person since I was young. My dad once told me, 'Donny can you be less extreme?' I didn't know what he was talking about. Is that a band?"

Donny is from Malang, a university city of eight hundred thousand in eastern Java.

"After school I got a job at a cell phone company doing online customer service. Then I watched this movie called *Big Fish* by Tim Burton. In the movie the father told the son a fish has to go to a bigger pond to be a bigger fish."

The educational system in Indonesia is abysmal, the result of three hundred of years of Dutch colonialism followed by an enforced ignorance imposed by thirty-three years of military dictatorship which sought to hide its own history. Donny, like many Indonesians, has pieced together his understanding of the world and his place in it from an eclectic assortment of sources that would startle anyone who received a formal Western education: fragments of religious writings, Hollywood movies, random shards of science and philosophy, punk rock, parents and family, friends, lived experience, advertising, and a particularly Indonesian kind of free thinking that comes from deep disappointment in present-day life in the country.

Donny set out for the very big pond of Jakarta, the capital of Indonesia. He got an office job at Chevron reporting on oil spills, and an apartment in a city of eight and a half million.

> I lived with my boyfriend I met on Friendster. I had lots of gay friends. Most are consumptive and hedonist. They have no money. They use credit cards to support their high lifestyle. So I took a job as a photographer at the Indonesian *Cosmopolitan* and met high class consumptive people, and they were also supporting their even higher lifestyle with credit cards. Then I saw a huge ad for a magazine that was a lifestyle guide for the modern male. I thought, "Geez, you need a magazine to tell you what to do with your life? Are you done with the Bible already?"

> A small fish going to the big pond meets a lot of sharks. I decided to go home. What I missed the most was I used to have a simple cup of coffee under a tree with the gentle breeze on my face. I enjoy that. In Jakarta you have coffee from Starbucks with the breeze from the air conditioner, and the coffee is expensive.

> I am very addicted to coffee.

> I got a job on a cruise ship as a photographer. I was a huge fan of Nirvana then, and the first stop was Seattle! Then we went to Alaska. In Alaska I would talk to strangers, indigenous people, we got along really well.

> Then I realized we were at the mouth of a big river, and I had seen that exact scene on a calendar in the sixth

grade, and I was there. And I realized that now I can die.
I had no more goals. My only goal had been to go to a
four-season country.

I lost the cruise ship job because Asian people work
harder because our cost of living is low. $1,000 a month
for me is a huge amount, so I have to do a good job
because they paid me so much money. You work for
what $1,000 means to you. So we became threats to the
people working on the ship with a higher cost of living.
And those people are the managers, so they just cut us
off. Asians were only allowed to work at jobs where you
are forbidden to see the customer. Only lowest level job.
Not photographer.

So I decided to go home and open a bar. First a coffee
shop. We had storytelling, some experimental music.
Some of the punk kids played acoustic music there
because it is too small for a punk band.

The social world that Donny was gathering outgrew the coffee shop
and became Houtenhand. Downstairs is a bar and cafe. Second floor
is a gallery, performance space, and bathroom. Top floor has an
office for Donny's distribution business, and a lovely outdoor patio
designed with lighting and decorations, all built by Donny.

Now we have three floors. The top floor is for distribut-
ing CDs and books. I call that floor "alternative economy."
I have so many friends who complain about their shitty
jobs. I am like, "Guys, stop complaining, *do* something."
So I provide a place for people to do things. So the place
becomes like a social movement.

But I am not a political person. I can't figure out what

I am yet. I used to choose to be a chaos, the fool in the tarot card.

A lot of people talk about this bar, and they are curious. "Why doesn't this bar have waiters? I am rich, I deserve to be served. And why do they play disturbing music?"

In most bars, the waiters come to you. A coffee shop or bar in Indonesia is a symbol of high class. Coffee is a status symbol. Coffee in a bar costs double what it costs on the street. Even KFC has become a higher-level symbol and that's junk food! But in here we sell the cheapest beer in the city. Here you have to come up to the bar and *talk to people* to get served. Then you are one of us.

All this activity around Donny's place brought the unwelcome attention of both the police and the Islamic Defenders Front (FPI), Islamist vigilantes seeking to impose sharia law in Indonesia, the world's most populous Muslim country. For most of its history, Indonesian Islam has been tolerant of diversity. The FPI means to change that. The FPI targets gays first and foremost. And the police still censor anything related to the massacre of more than a million Indonesian communists in 1965 that marked the beginning of the dictatorship. Danny has run afoul of both the police and the FPI.

This town had only one art gallery, provided by the government. But I like to disrupt people with art. I screened a movie about Indonesian communism. This is forbidden. The army and police came first to ask that I cancel the screening. Then the FPI came and asked me to cancel the screening.

I didn't cancel it. I just moved it forward. Instead of seven pm, I screened it at one pm. We switched the place of the screening to campus because my friends forbade me from doing it at the bar. The FPI came at seven to make sure I had cancelled the screening. They were yelling at my employee, who is lesbian. It's obvious. They were yelling at her, "Are you male or female?"

I came down to the first floor, and I said, "Oh, who's *that* one? The one with the muscles. He's so *cute*." I offered them a drink, though Muslims don't drink alcohol. I told them we should have a discussion about discrimination because it was *anti-discrimination day*."

Donny scheduled an educational event about HIV/AIDS, and again the Muslim vigilantes came and this time succeeded in shutting down the event. Donny felt that continuing with the event would have placed those in attendance at risk.

Now FPI's reach has extended into Donny's own social circle.

I had two friends, punk kids. They went to jail for selling marijuana. In prison there are a lot of FPI there to brainwash the criminals. The criminal is a character who has nothing to lose and nothing to do and is low educated. They were punk. They knew about socialists and communists. But they came out of jail Muslim extremist. They sold their books about Fidel Castro and Kurt Cobain, and they won't even come into my bar!

Donny's romantic life is as tumultuous as everything else.

I was falling in love and then I got broken heart. I thought I was an anarchist but this was not about killing a god, this was about killing a heart. It is easy to kill god any time, but killing love is hard. So I start to doubt

anarchism because I felt love. It makes me stay up all day
and take drugs and everything.

I was taking benzodiazepine for heartbreak, broke up
with my second boyfriend. I was a self-destruct kind of
person, always have been since I was a kid. I have the
scars from when I was a kid, being depressed because
I was kid with a huge secret other people are not supposed to know. I asked God and Jesus and the universe
about it and the universe didn't answer.

Then I went to my friend's wedding. The bride got sick. It
was Sunday. All the doctors were with their families. So
they asked me if I can call my gay doctor friend because
gays don't have families. I don't have kids or a wife, no
one to take care of. But I am still responsible for what
I become. Every human has to be responsible. At that
point of life I realized why am I born different, why the
universe made such an extreme character. I don't have
wife and kids. So I decided to give my life to my friends,
to art, and culture, and to everything I love. Guts is all
I got.

I always wonder about yin and yang, black and white,
and I am the grey area. I used to always have the impression that the grey is unwanted. But when the bride got
sick I realized that grey is not unwanted, grey is the connection.

Humans need some character which is neither male or
female. The universe needs a grey character which is
neither black or white. Grey is the bridge. I can be the
bridge, to fix things.

> Most of the time I fix things, perhaps without you realizing it. Some of my employees have wife and family so I provide them a job. I don't get married. I don't have a son. I have no one to take care of except my friends and music and art and coffee.

Donny's place is now the center of a large extended family of young Indonesian misfits: queers, punks, the angry and the isolated and the brilliant and the intellectual and the questioning. They gather every night and stay into the wee hours. One young lesbian told me she was bathing and sleeping there after she was kicked out by her family.

For most of its existence, the space has teetered on bankruptcy, not because of lack of customers but because of Donny's habit of giving everything away.

> My friends always ask me, "Why are you always giving away stuff?" And I say, "Because I want you to bury me when I die."

Donny doesn't know it, but the place in the world he has made for himself is the place that Harry Hay had in mind when he founded the Mattachine Society, the first post-WWII gay activist group in the US. Harry was a self-taught historian, and according to Harry, mattachines were characters from village life of medieval Europe. Something like a clown or jester, mattachines were single men who, having no family, could speak to feudal lords with less fear of reprisal than others. As a result, they were a social bridge, a go-between between lord and vassal. Harry believed they were gay and drew the conclusion that if gay men were to find social acceptance in twentieth-century America, they had better find a way to use their unique social position to contribute something useful to society. He left the Mattachine Society and founded the Radical Faeries as a vehicle for gay men searching for that role.

Hay developed these ideas while studying what he believed to be
a similar history in the indigenous cultures of North America.
Many included people who occupied a grey area between genders
and served as a bridge between male and female, often fixing things.
These people existed in both indigenous communities and in their
origin myths. Donny would be amazed.

Donny lives and loves and thinks completely outside of the current
international LGBT agenda. He is not interested in getting married
but is giving his life to his friends and art and coffee. He doesn't
want the right to serve in anyone's army; he is all about resistance to
authority. And he has no interest in transitioning to another gender:
he is fine with the grey area.

Talking with Donny means talking philosophy. Endlessly, relent-
lessly, and urgently. He can't stop. He does so without guile.
Absolutely earnestly. If Donny was a book he would be an open one,
though with a convoluted plot that is sometimes hard to follow. He
is very Indonesian.

> I think it was Pascal who said to be huge you have to be
> extreme on both sides, in black and white. You have to
> be very, very fucked up and very, very sane. I want to be
> that kind of person. I took my journey to the dark side.
> I took drugs. I rode my bike with my eyes closed. I took
> more and more Lexotan, very cheap weed, mushrooms. It
> took me to a level that... Einstein says you can never ever
> measure how dark is black. But at that point in my life
> I wanted to measure how dark black is. And now I will
> go to the white and measure how light white is.

I came to this city to play music at Donny's space. Donny met me in the early morning at the airport and drove me to my hotel on the back of his motorbike. Apparently, he thought I was sexy but straight, so after dropping me off he went on a Grindr hookup to release his pent-up sexual energy.

I arrived at my hotel and found him, once again on Grindr. Without Grindr we each would probably never have known the other was gay. We exchanged vague propositions but Donny regretfully explained that he had just had sex and didn't think he was up for more so soon.

Donny and I spent the late afternoon and early evening engrossed in the conversation I am recounting here. He was very disappointed we were not going to have sex, even though that was the result of his own Grindr hookup. "But does that mean I don't get to kiss you?"

He spoke of the sexual revolution Grindr has brought to this Muslim country. Suddenly gay men can have all the sex they want (which is a lot) right under the noses of the Muslim vigilantes. "Complete culture shock," Donny explained.

Donny wanted to spend the night together after my concert, my only night in Malang. I agreed, but by the end of the concert I noted that Donny had been drinking heavily with no end in sight. Furthermore, he could not leave until he closed down the bar, and there were customers who did not seem to be in a hurry. I told him I would retire to my room and he should come along when he was done, suspecting that he wouldn't make it. He showed up about ten in the morning, very hungover and embarrassed. Alcohol is his new drug. So much so that three months ago he was hospitalized with a liver emergency. In his judgement, enough time has passed that he can indulge again now. His alcoholism is sad. At least, it makes me sad.

As I said goodbye, I expressed my appreciation and respect for his ideas and his living example of how to be in the grey area in Indonesia. With more than a little annoyance, he replied, "I was kind of hoping you would disagree with my ideas."

"Why?"

"Because these are my ideas, and I am not happy with my life. And you have travelled far."

JOHN

He shuffled into the cafe, took a seat across from me, and grinned.

"Hi!"

I was not quite sure how to respond.

We had arranged the meeting through a personal ad in a gay paper. This was before the internet, before Grindr, before social media, before all of that. The personal ads of the day involved only text, no photos. He had described himself accurately in terms of height and weight, yet his appearance was not at all what I was expecting. His face was caved in. His skin was leathery. His feet had collapsed and splayed. He coughed a lot. He walked with great difficulty. He had full-blown AIDS. He was going to get a shunt installed in his chest soon so the doctors could just pour the drugs directly in. And yet here he was, *cruising*.

It's a lot to take in. The human tragedy. My repulsion at the thought of being physically intimate with him. Was I a horrible person for feeling that? I too had HIV, and was likely looking at my own future.

We talked. The conversation was easy, he was a naturally open and engaging person. He clearly got it that he was not most people's idea of a hot date, or even a conceivable date. My initial no, and my continued unease, did not bother him in the least. He was not there to shock or embarrass, or to make a statement. He was there because, who knows? Maybe I would have sex with him. Nothing ventured nothing gained. And if not, maybe I would turn out to be an interesting person to share a conversation with.

It occurred to me what a pity it is that I was just meeting him. He was obviously an extraordinary man I would like to know, but why bother when he was going to die any day?

*

That was how it was back then. When you saw someone like that, you assumed, fairly, that you would never see them again. And I thought that same thought, again and again, as I saw him, again and again, for the next twenty-five years.

A few years after meeting him, effective HIV drugs appeared, quite by surprise, which is why I am here telling this story. Those like me, who had HIV but had not yet progressed to AIDS, never did. Those who already had AIDS either died because they were too far gone or got better and went on with their lives. John was part of a very small group who did neither. Didn't die and didn't get well. He had full-blown AIDS for thirty years. I don't know how to convey what that is to those who have not been around it. One AIDS complication after another after another. Maybe you know what it is like to have terrible diarrhea. John had terrible diarrhea without a letup for thirty years.

We became close friends. Part Chippewa, he was a member of the Bois Forte Tribe in Minnesota. Older than me, he had been through several iconic political moments that I had watched from afar as a youth. He did campus organizing against the Vietnam War, then worked at a community kitchen run by the Black Panthers, a health center run by the Chicano Brown Berets, and then for an extended time with the United Farm Workers. He was at Wounded Knee.

Wounded Knee. That doesn't have much resonance these days, which is stunning to those of us who lived through the seventies, because Wounded Knee was the biggest armed confrontation between American Indians and the US state in the twentieth century. Look it up.

That is already an epic life, but for John it was just the prequel, because he was at the core of AIDS activism from the first moment: co-founder of ACT UP East Bay in 1989; the Berkeley Needle Exchange in 1990; and the list goes on and on and on. When effective AIDS drugs finally became available, the few AIDS activists from his generation who were still alive breathed a collective sigh of relief and moved on to other pursuits. Not John. He switched gears and went to work making the new drugs available to people who had no access to them. As in, collecting them, loading them up on planes, and just taking them to where they were needed. I believe there is an orphanage in Uganda named after him because of this work. I suspect very few people know about that, other than the staff of the orphanage and the kids who live there.

He took another bunch of drugs to Argentina, where he discovered he could sing like Carlos Gardel. Soon he had a new life in Argentina as a tango singer named Johnny Tango. Not only could he convincingly sing tango, but with his sunken face, leathery skin, shuffling gait, and the right hat and the attitude, he could come off as a very old man, perhaps a former boxer, singing of his long string of heartbreaks with Argentine women. He made it all part of the Johnny Tango persona.

More than anything, John was a fighter. And he was just unwilling to let AIDS take him out of the fight. There were AIDS profiteers to battle. Access to housing for people with AIDS to win. And so much more. If I were to look up *relentless* in the dictionary right now, I would not be surprised to find his name. John the fighter was simply not going to give an inch to AIDS. Not politically. Not socially. And not sexually. If staying sex positive during the worst of the AIDS epidemic was an Olympic sport, John would win every gold medal. There would be a larger-than-life size bronze statue of him in all his illness in front of the stadium.

Eventually all those years of AIDS did something to his brain, and all that fight that had been focused on social justice for so long became scattershot, a canon on the deck that came untethered and started shooting all over the place. It was just tremendously sad, but there was nothing to do about it.

When I think of John now, I picture him as a giant. Not metaphorically, an actual giant. Walking forward. AIDS takes his skin, his limbs, his organs, and finally his brain. And he just keeps walking.

JIM

I was sitting with my mother in her hospital room, telling her my final goodbye, and even then she gave away little of her feelings. She was a woman who asked for little and shared even less. He walked in, a tall, bearded man with a cowboy hat and a missing leg. Turned out to be my parents' new next-door neighbor in their little ghost town in the high desert. Very personable and presentable. A comfortable mix of formal and familiar. You could take him anywhere, introduce him to any parents.

After he left my mother told me I should get to know him. Said I would find him interesting. He might, she added, be a genius.

I saw him again at her funeral. And I did get to know him. And, well, I have no idea who is a genius and who isn't, but his art leaves me speechless. Which is fine. People talk about art too much. Henri Matisse said that all artists should have their tongues cut out so they can never talk about their art. The metaphor is too violent, but I don't disagree. Art schools spend more time teaching students how to talk about art than how to make it. I brought Jim to the university where I taught. The students got to spend an afternoon with him. He insisted on only one ground rule: they could ask him about anything except his art.

So I am not going to talk about his art here.

Each of Jim's works has a title, some running many pages in length, but none of them talk about the art. They are sort of companion pieces, poetry. Jim writes no placards or statements to hang by his art in galleries. His idea is more intimate and fleeting: you stand there and look at the art while he whispers the title in your ear. Here is one part of one title.

> Judgementa insecta am I
>
> Diptea Coleoptera, Lord of all praying mantises and mayflies,
>
> butterflies, dragonflies, houseflies,
>
> aphids and thrips by the millions of gillions
>
> of red ants and black ants,
>
> henceforth to be known throughout my realm as
>
> termites isoptera moptera ad infinitum
>
> I, Grand Patriarch of the West Field of Hudspeth,
>
> bow down in servitude to all living and dead
>
> short worms, long worms,
>
> wiggly worms and night crawlers
>
> bedbugs, stinkbugs
>
> black beetles and boll weevils,
>
> louse and lice,
>
> I, Willful Believer in the Weaver of Light

spin into a canopy of symphonies

all celestial centipedes, mantipedes,

mosquitos, magpies,

apple pies, cherry pies,

peach pies, lemon meringue pies,

for my eyes have eaten of the crust,

nothing is left on my plate,

lust unto dust without dismay

as the Sun moves across the sky this day

signing above the maddening swarm

so that from my hairy legs

springeth forth a buttocks

and a grove of tall Elders

as does the Earth enter the Earth

and the waters join the waters

so does my fear flow backward into my groin

as I supplicate the smooth roundness of your grace

and the soft curve of your forgiveness

so that dare I praise our stained bed sheets

even as the floodgates burst forth

into the morning fury unbuttoning my shirt,

unzipping my fly, untethering my belt,

melting into you, my mother

of Mathew, Mark, Luke, and John,

forsaken by a fifth lover,

recycled by a sixth,

legs spread-eagle,

mouth open,

ears unplugged,

your plump, pink bottom

splitting the sheath of my barstool

I, Luie-Lou-I,

repentant, repaired beyond all confines

and by thee, my holy moley tractor

bleeding the Earth with your blade

I know that in licking your song

my thong as sung no wrong.

Amen.

Jim and I created a very particular intimacy. We saw each other rarely, living far apart. We were never sexual. But we were in love and we both knew it.

We have a profoundly shared aesthetic in music and art and poetry. But there is more. Jim lived in New York City in its gay heyday, after gay liberation but before AIDS. I was in New York during those same years, but completely oblivious to all that. Those were the years I launched a music career, then began working with refugees from El Salvador, then dropped music entirely to immerse myself in the Salvadoran revolutionary movement. Jim was going to bars where men got fisted while suspended in chains over the bar, where if you had to piss you pissed on a man lying in the trough. I went to music rehearsal and political meetings. Jim got sick with AIDS before AIDS was an acronym. He watched AIDS decimate his community in New York while I watched people get shot and killed right next to me in El Salvador. Jim withdrew from the urban gay life to pass the remainder of his days making art in the desert in the American Southwest, by one chance in a million moving in next door to my parents. As Jim was withdrawing from the urban gay life, I was finding it. Over the years as his health deteriorated, he moved ever further from the urban gay life while I dove deeper in.

Jim is another one of these rare birds who neither died of AIDS nor recovered from it. How is it that I keep finding these guys? Oh right, I know: they are the ones who are still here.

Through Jim, I somewhat voyeuristically lived what could have been, should have been, my life with AIDS. And through me, Jim voyeuristically lived what could have been his gay life without AIDS. Fair is fair.

The years have been physically taxing for Jim. He lost his other leg, making him a paraplegic thanks to the peripheral neuropathy that was a side effect of the earliest AIDS drug. He got the "hump" on his back caused by the next generation of AIDS drugs. He got cancer and his bladder was removed. Then he got a second kind of cancer. Then heart disease. Then his spine collapsed from all that time in the wheelchair with two kinds of cancer, no legs, and no bladder. Then a third cancer appeared.

He now takes estrogen and testosterone blockers to keep the cancers at bay. He half-jokingly calls himself a eunuch. He loves to hear stories of my sexual adventures and to try, just try, to remember what sexual desire was like. I talk to Jim and wonder if I will be a happier person when the sexual desire finally fades. I almost look forward to it. I do look forward to it. But then the next beautiful sexual adventure unfolds and I drink it in and remember how lucky I am.

Jim has now lived so many years beyond what any of his multitude of doctors expected that he has become the caretaker of his last two lovers, one with Parkinson's, the other with dementia. There he is – wheelchair, collapsed spine, sunken face, three cancers – caring for those who until recently were in fine health. What's wrong with this picture?

For a brief moment Jim teetered on the edge of fame. *The Wall Street Journal* called him "America's greatest living unknown artist." The Chinese Minister of Culture flew to the west Texas desert to see his work. The owners of Sotheby's, a major New York City art auction house, decided they were going to make Jim big. They threw a private dinner at their home to introduce him to art collectors with deep pockets. Jim took me along for moral support. There were more servants than guests. A snippet of dinner table chit-chat: "Call me old fashioned, but I still think that when you spend more than a million dollars on a painting it's a lot of money." Stuff like that. But none of it took. Jim's moment passed without a single sale and the art world moved on to the next big thing. I don't think it was the art that failed to take, it was Jim. He is old. And he is a recluse. He is the antithesis of trendy. The makers of the art market didn't think the work of an old, quiet, thoughtful desert recluse with no legs would be a good place to park a million dollars. They were probably right. Jim barely spoke at the dinner where he was supposed to wow everyone. I stepped in to fill the void. Like when you are young and your date takes you to meet her parents, and your date is a mess because her relation to her parents is tense and fraught, but they are not *your* parents, so what the hell. And by the way, rich people drink really good wine, I'll take another glass please.

At some point Jim will die, and what will happen to all that art? The guy is an art hurricane, the most prolific artist I have ever known. For now, his massive output pretty much just sits there, filling many rooms, actually entire buildings, and a sizable stretch of desert. Maybe someday it will be "discovered," but I doubt it. Maybe it will move through the ravages of time becoming ever more unrecognizable, like Jim. Or maybe Jim will outlive us all. Maybe, at the end of the world, it will be Jim, alone in the desert with the snakes and spiders, surrounded by mountains and mountains of art.

*

Just before this book went to press, Jim died. He was 79 years old. He had lived through AIDS, heart disease, bone disease and four kinds of cancer. His legs, bladder, intestines, and stomach had all been removed.

I told him, "Jim, I know that aging is a process of letting go, but you are taking it awfully literally."

We could joke like that.

I had been worried about how Jim would die. He fought for life like no one I knew. He kept himself alive that way. If he had not been such a fighter, he would have died of AIDS thirty years ago. And then so many other times over the intervening decades, from one disease or another, he just refused to accept the possibility that his next work of art might not be made.

But at some point that journey would end, and I worried that Jim would die fighting for life, refusing to accept his end. The prospect filled me with sadness.

I have read that in the nineteenth century Americans placed great importance on being peaceful and accepting at the moment of death. That after the Civil War, the survivors would walk across several states to find the families of their war buddies who didn't make it, to sit at the family table and tell them even though their son died on the battlefield in the midst of unspeakable carnage, he was emotionally at peace at the moment of death.

These stories resonate strongly with me. That is what I want for myself, and what I wanted for Jim. The worst AIDS deaths I can remember were those who fought it to the very end, and died angry that life had been taken from them before they were ready. I feared that Jim would die like that. My last few phone conversations with him were not encouraging.

But that was not the way it went down. He chose to go to hospice. His sister, with whom he was extremely close, said that the last two days he was clear minded, at peace, and "absolutely radiant."

Jim was never religious, but he was an upper mid westerner through and through, and the long shadow of a very stern Shaker Christianity infused his art and his entire sensibility. "Those are my bones," he said, "in a river that runs, well, all the way back to Jerusalem." When he died I half expected the sky to crack open and lightening to be cast upon the land. But no. It was a day like any other, and Jim was just another person like any other. At the end of the world, the snakes and the spiders of the west Texas desert will have to make do on their own, surrounded by mountains of the crumbling art of James Magee.

ORI

"Hi, I have never had sex before and I would like to try it with you. I have twenty minutes."

"Whoa. Hold on. You have never had sex before?"

"No."

"Then we are going to need more than twenty minutes!"

Like most Javanese, Ori is small, and seems somehow overly sincere and a bit naive. Like he would hand you his heart in an instant and leave it to up to you to make sure it didn't break. Which he did.

He only had twenty minutes because, like many Javanese, he had almost no time away from work and family. But somehow he managed to return later that night and we shared an intimacy so tender it made a grown man cry. Soldiers put down their weapons. Policemen turned in their badges. Prison walls cracked open.

The next day he took me to meet his family.

For years onward, he would look back in amazement at this rash decision. "I took you to meet my *family*. What was I *thinking*?" In Java, family is everything. We say stuff like that in my country, but you don't realize how shallow we swim in that water until you see it in a place like Java. Once he got a voucher through his work for one night at an upscale hotel. He took his whole family. Mom, dad, all the siblings, cousins. Did grandmother come? I am not sure. They all piled into one bed together to see how rich people slept. I think there were nine of them in all. Later, in San Francisco, he would be absolutely dumbstruck at the sight of homeless people on the streets. "Where are their *families?*"

He introduced me to three generations of his family who lived in a single room with no bathroom or kitchen. Their sole worldly possessions included their few clothes, a propane burner with a few pots and pans, a tablet computer with a cracked screen, and a motor-bike. They survived like this: his mother would cook all night on the little burner while everyone else slept on the floor around her. In the morning, he would use the cracked tablet computer to take pictures of what she had cooked, then post the pics on Instagram. His mother would go to sleep and he would spend the day delivering the food on the motorbike to people who had seen the pictures on Instagram and bought it. At the end of the day he would return, wake up his mother, and they would go to the night market and use the day's income to buy ingredients for her to cook during the coming night. Repeat, and repeat.

It didn't leave a lot of time for losing one's virginity. It didn't leave a lot of time for anything. But somehow, every now and then, he stole a moment to log into Grindr and look for a man who is not from his place, not from his culture, who does not know his family, who will not tell any neighbor or villager or friend about the young man's secret, and who might, maybe, just maybe, take him to a castle far, far away where they will live happily ever after. But then he quickly logs off of Grindr and deletes the app entirely, leaving no trace on the family tablet computer. Can't be too careful about that.

So easy to screw up.

A neighbor who did piecework sewing on a nearly antique Singer sewing machine noticed Ori's little brother wasn't going to school and took him on as an apprentice. When his brother completed his first shirt, Ori, ever the social media entrepreneur, posted a photo of himself modeling the shirt on Instagram and sold it. That photo, in that shirt, was also Ori's only Grindr picture.

When a man offers his heart like that so immediately, wrapped with a bow, I am not one to turn it down. We fell in love. We each found our differences intoxicating: size, age, language, skin, culture, life experience, all of it. I grew up in small town America. He grew up a long motorbike ride from electricity. When he came to stay with me in San Francisco, he had never seen a machine that washed dishes or clothes. So many wonderful adventures and tender moments followed. I laughed when we went to Golden Gate Park and he asked if he needed to watch out for poisonous snakes or monkeys. He laughed when I let on that I was so mired in city life that I didn't even know that the world was full of ghosts which create a lot of the mischief in human life.

Everyone I knew fell in love with him. He is a man who puts his joy in life on full display for others to enjoy and share. My nephew said he could not imagine someone who did not like Ori.

But then the inevitable day arrived when the bill for our profound differences came due. We were in San Francisco. His US visa was about to expire. Getting another would not be easy. Rich Indonesians can just buy a plane ticket, get a visa, and come to the US any old time they want to, but not the poor. I had to move mountains just to get him that first visa.

It was a fine sunny afternoon when we sat down to review our options. I could move to Indonesia, but our love would have to remain hidden, we couldn't live together, and we could only be together occasionally. He could apply for asylum based on the homophobia in his home country. But once you accept asylum you can never return to your home country, and he was not remotely ready to say goodbye to his family. We could marry, but the cost of legal fees would total more than ten thousand dollars, and he would not be able to work legally in the US for two years. He could over-stay his visa and work under the table. He had actually held a job in a restaurant for a few weeks, but he had not understood he would have to lie about his legal status to get paid, and when he understood he refused to do so. His American friends explained to him that people lie about this all the time, and that half the restaurant employees in San Francisco were doing exactly that. But he would not budge. He could not lie. He went to his workplace, forthrightly told them that he could not legally work and that he understood he would not get paid for all the hours he had worked, thanked them for giving him a chance at a job, and left. So no, overstaying his visa was not in the cards.

Together we came to the understanding that we were not ready. That before asking for asylum and saying goodbye to his family, before getting married and forking over a pile of money and then wait-ing two years to work, and before telling any lies to employers, we needed to know each other more. Spend more casual time together. But there was no casual way for us to be together. Every option came with big life changes. The moment was easy and difficult and stressful and relieving and a loving coming together and already a stepping apart.

PART 6

CAMILO

We met in a strange new world I didn't know existed, and could not even have imagined until I was there. Or, until I was "there." A world full of beautiful people from all over the world engaged in sexual acts I had never dreamed of, for lengths of time I would not have thought possible. He was sitting in an office chair. Naked. One hand on his cock, the other on his computer keyboard, and a strange green thing protruding from his ass. He was extremely beautiful in a certain way. I could imagine him as Antinous, the young man so beautiful he stopped the Roman Emperor Hadrian in his tracks. The Emperor took him for a lover right then and there, and became so obsessed with him that when the boy died in an accident the Emperor ordered that temples be built to youth throughout the empire where his subjects were to worship the boy.

But we are not in ancient Rome. We are not even IRW (in the real world). We are at the bleeding edge of the merger of sex and technology, in a virtual world called Chaturbate. The basic idea is that you can log on, turn on the mic and camera on your laptop or phone, and masturbate. Others can watch you, and you them, and you can chat while you're at it. Chaturbating. There is even a way to give tips to masturbators you especially like. And if they have a

PART 6

green Bluetooth-controlled dildo up their butt, like he does, they get buzzed when you tip.

Given the way of the world, I suppose it is fitting to end this book with a man I only "know" virtually, and Chaturbate is a pretty riveting place in a poke-it-with-stick sort of way. It is future sex: we can get off watching each other get off, "chat" and make "friends," maybe even make some money, and not get HIV or HPV or Monkeypox or Covid or actually touch anyone or even get out of bed. Looking around Chaturbate, you see that a lot of people are on here for hours. Has anyone, ever, anywhere, in all of history, masturbated for eight hours? Did anyone know that was humanly possible?

We all know about "missionary position" and "doggie style," but here are lots of people sitting in chairs facing a camera, one hand on their genitals, the other on the computer keyboard, and a Bluetooth controlled butt plug in their ass. What should we call this previously unknown sexual posture, now assumed by so many for so many hours at a time? The Captain Kirk?

And there are tip goals: this much for the girl to put the dildo in her mouth; that much for the guy to turn around and show his ass. You can see couples poised at the point of sexual penetration, staring at the screen waiting for their tip goal to be met before proceeding. And everyone seems to have a cum goal. No orgasm unless the tip jar is full.

This brave new world is not some isolated little corner of the internet. As I write these words, it is the fifth most popular "adult" website, and the fifty-seventh most popular site of any kind, in the world. It has a user base of millions. Tens of thousands of people are online chaturbating at any given moment.

I cannot help but wonder what life would have been like if George

269

and Jerry and I had had access to something like this. We had no idea there were even hundreds people like us in the world, much less millions. What if we could have sat in our rooms and collected tips for being our faggot selves? If Chaturbate had been around, would George still be around as well?

And yet, when you look closely at Chaturbate there is clearly something amiss. People are there too long. Some seem to always be there. Like, really, all the time. And the bedrooms they are in are gaudy and excessive: what kind of person has a bedroom like that?

A clue can be found in Chaturbate FAQ, which explains that any account can become a "studio" account simply by creating additional accounts under its umbrella. As the FAQ says, "Studio accounts are an easy way to have all broadcaster earnings go into one account daily."

And with that, I present one last encounter with a man. I have "met" him but never met him, "know" him but don't know him. I feel very tenderly towards him, and I so deeply wish him well as he navigates a world that is not mine, will never be mine, and which I can only see from afar.

*

Hi Bob, I am interested in the topics you're talking about. The whole thing is complicated and simple at the same time. And it looks like you're honest, and genuinely interested in me, so we can talk. I always use pseudonyms for my security, so I will not say my name, but I am now nineteen years old, an Aries.

The basics: I'm a pretty normal guy haha, I'm not a party person, I don't go out much. I prefer staying at home and playing with my cats or spending time on the computer playing video games. So other kids think I am weird. I like Habbo, it's my favorite game. You meet other players and do stuff in hotels. I play in like seven hotels. I love the clothes you can buy in the game, virtual clothes. But they're expensive hahaha. Seriously I love Habbo. They just came out with new clothes in the game. I feel like a little boy hahaha.

To be honest, sometimes I can't stand still doing anything and I have to always be on the move. I have two real friends in the real world. They are both heterosexual. But most of my friends are in Habbo.

I knew I was gay from a very young age but I didn't want to accept it. I just thought that I liked to see the beauty in all people, not just girls. But I spent more and more time seeing the beauty in boys, so finally I let myself go and explore.

My mother is bisexual so there was no problem there, but she was afraid that people would hurt me. You know there are a lot of homophobic people in the world and they are mean. As for the rest of my family, I don't care what they think. I see the world through the eyes of my mother. She is the only one that cares about me, and I care about what she thinks. My father can go to hell. I don't want to know anything about him. He even denies I am his son.

I was never able to hide being gay. The other kids always suspected it. They treated me very badly. Believe me, I know what the word gay means. And the truth is I don't care. I don't really have close friends and I learned to be rude right back. But I had to change schools often. I studied at four schools and was kicked out of two of them for fighting. But there is a positive side to everything: I wasn't just fighting to fight, I was learning to defend myself. For example, one time there was this kid who was saying ugly things about me behind my back. So one day I told him to tell me all that to my face, but he wouldn't do it, and when he was going to leave he turned his back to me and said "faggot" between his teeth. I grabbed one of the classroom chairs and broke his arm with it. Now he and I are mature people, and he has apologized. Zero grudges. We were just kids then, about fifteen years old.

The first time I had sex I was fourteen years old. Big mistake haha. It was the worst experience in the world. I made a mistake and I won't talk about it anymore because there's nothing to say and that's it lol.

What do I want in a boyfriend? I want that he not be a bastard. And maybe also that he cares about hygiene, I've been thinking more about that lately. I like boys my age because things are calmer that way, nothing weird. I don't rule out the idea of dating men older than me, but it always seems to bring problems and they always want more from you, so I prefer not to get caught up in that drama. Being single, no one manages your time or gives you orders. Besides, I am really trying to keep my mind calm now, so I'm not dating anyone.

One day a fifty-three-year-old man invited me to dinner. I was eighteen years old. I said aww, it's nice that he does that, though it seemed a bit strange. I thought he had a wife. But as soon as I got in the car he told me he wanted to see me undressed. He got very angry when I refused, so I did it to avoid problems, because I hate problems. But then I said no more, now it's my turn to decide what happens. I don't accept that you pay for a date, I pay for my own things. I do not want to be a kept boy who people take advantage of, saying "How do I give you money but you don't do what I ask?" There can be so much anger. I have turned down many proposals that sound great but nothing in this world is free, everything has a value, and the value is you, your body, your youth. So better to do things alone and not owe anyone anything. I learned this from trial and error.

I don't know that I have exactly been in love, but I have been with people who left emotional marks both beautiful and ugly. For some reason the guys I have gone out with always leave me. I was recently seeing a guy who was really cool, but he had to leave the country. His whole family managed to go to the United States. But now he is in a shelter, those places that look like prisons, wondering what will happen to his life. He called me recently saying that everything is going to be fine, but really I don't know what's going to happen. Then there was a boy from France, fifteen years old. I felt so safe with him because he cared about me so much, so I opened up to him. Then one day he just disappeared. It was only a few months ago that I found out the truth of what happened, but that's another story and I don't want to talk about it.

When I was growing up, I realized that things in my house were not very good economically and I felt pressured to help. When my grandparents were alive they ran the family business, a few small stores selling basic food, and things were OK. After they passed away the stores closed and that was a hard blow. My mother works selling things in catalogs like Carmen, you check clothes and stuff like that. She has a boyfriend she's been with about ten years I think haha, a long time to still not be her husband. He works in a car shop. We are not poor, lol, thank God, there is always food to eat, and that is what matters. But from a very young age there was a lot of pressure on me to contribute financially. To at least pay for my own things, hopefully more. I have a lot of responsibility.

I looked for work but jobs in my country are not well paid. Just look on Google and you will realize what I say to you is true. The minimum wage doesn't pay for anything. And there aren't any jobs anyway. So you look on the internet for a job and you find one that says "webcam models: earn more than the minimum wage."

I knew that these pages existed since I was about fourteen years old, but I didn't really check them out because I was too young to do anything. I already had some idea of what the work was like but I did not imagine that it was a super giant industry. There are many things that I am still learning.

One month after my eighteenth birthday, I entered the sort of studio that is known here as a "garage studio," meaning it is very low budget. I started working with an account that was not mine, which now that I have been in the industry for a year I realize was wrong because it was identity theft. But I was so innocent of this world, I had no idea what was happening and I did not question anything. I knew the account was not mine because the ID on the account was not mine. On my second day Chaturbate they banned me for impersonation.

[...?]

I really have no idea why they put me on someone else's account, but I guess it was something to do with being just eighteen years old. I looked very childish.

[...?]

Well, yeah, OK, I started at seventeen. That's why I worked with an account that was not mine. I was under a lot of pressure to make money.

Well, I didn't last long in that studio. I was quite young, and they took advantage of my ignorance in these matters. They wanted me online for fifteen or sixteen hours a day, in front of the camera, which of course is exhausting. You should give it a try and tell me how you feel afterwards haha.

The second day I was there I said I wanted to go home to rest, but they wouldn't let me leave. I felt so lonely, but there was no point in crying. I thought OK, I will just obey their orders so as not to make

trouble, and wait for my chance to escape. It was terrible but I had
to pretend that I didn't care, and pretend that I liked being there in
order to earn their trust. I didn't have anyone to help me. I had to
solve the situation slowly but surely. There were only two other boys
working there and since they worked different shifts than I, I didn't
know anything about them. I was on my own. On the eighth
or ninth day I saw an opportunity to escape. The bosses weren't
looking, so I just ran out the door. I never went back. I didn't even
want to think about the place ever again, so I never said anything to
anyone about it.

But I believe you always have to see the positive things, and I thank
them for at least giving me a small sample of what this world is.
A somewhat strange experience, but we are formed by our experiences and I thought, well, I need to find something good to take
from all this, so I kept trying.

I looked for a decent studio with better facilities. I found one and
went for an interview. They told me that they had already created
an account I could use. They didn't tell me anything more about
it, and the truth is, I didn't ask anything either. I felt safe... a big
mistake haha.

They made me go into one of the seven rooms they had, and without
understanding what was happening I entered the room and they
told me, "Stay there and do what you want to do on camera."

I asked them if they were already broadcasting, and they said yes
and told me to take my clothes off. So I undressed and I was thinking that I was already doing well, but soon I realized that I was not
online, and that they were just recording what I was doing. That was
clearly wrong. They did not ask if they could record me or anything.
I have no idea what happened to those recordings.

At the end they told me that I could work for them, but with certain conditions which did not seem normal or honest to me, so I told them no and left.

I took a break from all that for a while and rested. And then I said, well, the third time is the charm, so I tried again, this time at a studio recommended by my cousin. The owner of the studio was a top trans model from Chaturbate and that gave me confidence. I went to the interview. I told them that I had been on camera and on some pages, and I already had an idea of what to do. She said super, you can start in two days. But I would have to pretend to be a trans girl.

Of course, there are real trans girls on these pages, but also others like me who are guys with wigs and women's lingerie pretending to be something we are not. I accepted the idea because I needed the work. I said, well, it will be something new for me. I felt comfortable knowing that my boss was one of the best on Chaturbate. I know pretending to be a girl sounds like an ugly thing to do. I approached it more like fantasy or acting, like I was in a theatrical production playing the role of a trans girl. The studios don't like hiring boys, because they are not always disciplined in fulfilling their connection hours, and they don't bring in as much money as girls or trans girls. Of course there are always exceptions. And there are also users who like knowing that you're a boy with a wig. Remember there is a wide range of tastes.

I worked there seven or eight months. My shifts were ten hours a day, always at night, six days a week. I always took Monday to rest. The money I made varied from week to week. The worst week I made less than ten dollars. On my best week people gave me $1180 of tips. But remember that Chaturbate takes fifty percent right off the top, and the studio keeps forty percent of what you earn. So Chaturbate kept

$590 and then the studio took their forty percent leaving me with $236 of the $1180 people had given me, and that was the best week.

Let me tell you some things about this webcam work. It is exhausting, and there is huge emotional and physical wear and tear. It is strange to turn on a camera and be so publicly exposed, completely naked, and everyone can see everything, and anyone can comment on anything. Everything that should be private becomes completely public, but you cannot even use your actual name haha. And on top of all that, it is a competition because there are thousands of others on camera doing the same as you. Literally thousands. StripChat has a section that shows how many models are connected at any given time and the number is never less than six thousand people: men, women, dwarfs, whatever. Of course you get bored. How are you going to entertain yourself for ten hours alone in a room in front of a camera? It's up to you how to make the time go faster.

Of course, not everything is bad. You find amazing people like you, people who are interested in you beyond the sexual. And the beautiful thing is, there are times when you feel like nothing but a sexual object, and then someone actually asks you how you are really feeling, and you reply honestly. But we cannot always do that because when we are on camera we must have a cute smile at all times.

Funny things can happen too. Once a user asked me to do a private show for him doing my workout routine. So I got paid to work out while we both looked at our cameras. He was very nice. That was the only time I saw him, but he said goodbye and told me to have a nice day. I was thankful and happy to know that he left happy. Then there was the time the guy asked for a private show and he wanted me to have a hard cock and my legs open signing Happy Birthday. It was actually a very complicated pose. He doesn't give me tips anymore but he is a nice guy and has become my friend. When his boyfriend broke up with him I was there for him.

There are also many things I have refused to do. Sometimes people want you to humiliate yourself for money. I won't do that. Another thing I don't do is insert a dildo in my ass. I wouldn't do that at this point because I don't know how to do it and it doesn't appeal to me.

[...?]

You think I always have a dildo in my ass because the Lovense is a dildo? Hmmm. Well, if it is, it is very small, and well, it's cool.

The emotional burnout can reach a sadistic level. The sites have an algorithm which wants you to be connected for at least six days a week for six hours a day. If you do that, your account moves up on the page and gets more visibility in the best categories. Categories like #twink, #young, #teen, etc.

There are three shifts in the webcam studios. Each shift is eight hours.

morning 6:30am to 2:30pm

afternoon 2:30pm to 10:30pm

night 10:30pm to 6:30am

Which shift you get depends on whether the person assigning the shifts likes you the best.

I had the night shift. I can tell you from experience that the night shift is the most exhausting because you are awake all night and you cannot rest until the next day. I left my house at eight pm and arrived at the studio at nine pm. I put on my makeup and the wig and went online at ten-thirty. I stayed online more than eight hours. I arrived back home at eight-thirty am. I went to sleep and woke up at six pm, so I only had two hours to do something I liked in my free time of two hours haha.

I did it exactly like that for about seven months and then my body just collapsed. I had a crisis of anxiety. It was something really strong. I was hospitalized. Before that, I was the one who would have said "Oh no, that's fake, that's just drama." And then I lived it in my own body, and learned what it was, and how strong it can be. So I learned to have more empathy for people. I have learned now that not everyone has or lives the same experiences, and to be more understanding of how others feel emotionally and mentally.

The anxiety crisis hit me because being in this industry was causing too much stress. Obviously I was making money but at the cost of what? My health. I had to think about this a lot.

I talked to my mother and made a decision to withdraw from all of this. But I was very afraid to leave the studio, because the studios don't like the models to work independently. They want you to always be there making money for them. And there are bad people in charge and they can ban your identity document, in which case you cannot broadcast on Chaturbate again. And on top of that, the studios make you sign a contract in which you cede the rights to your image for ten years or more, depending on which studio.

[...?]

How do they get you banned? It is so easy. The studio creates your account. It is controlled by the studio. They ask you for your ID to validate your identity. When you leave the studio, the studio still has copies of your ID and access to your account. All they have to do is make a different person broadcast on that account. Chaturbate will detect that it is not you, and will ban you from ever using your ID to validate an account on their site.

This studio worked under an even bigger franchise. I told you, it is a giant industry. So I talked to the boss of the big franchise and I told her that I wanted to "take a break." I didn't want to say "quit" because I knew that they could do me harm. I had seen that happen to others.

A lot of things happened while working at this studio, a lot of growth, both as a person and as a worker. There was a lot I was simply not prepared for, and I was under enormous pressure to help out financially at home. I learned more about how to confront this industry on my own, there are always people who try to hurt you or scam you or lie to you or take your money. You have to find your way through all kinds of disinformation, because most studios don't want you to learn how to do this yourself, so they make everything more complicated than it needs to be so they can keep you making money for them. I learned the basics in a supportive environment, and I am grateful to have been part of that studio.

My boss, the trans woman, gave good advice to all the models: be as independent you can. Those words stuck in my head. So I always had the idea of working independently from the comfort of my home, and to be able to really enjoy it and not see it as just a job. So I worked hard to save money so that I could leave to I don't know where. I had no clear plan, but I always wanted to do it.

By the time I left the studio I had saved enough money to buy a computer.

[...?]

No, the software does not let you broadcast from a phone, you have to have a computer. You can't do this without the necessary equipment: a computer, camera, microphone, lights, Lovense [the bluetooth controlled butt plug], a safe place to broadcast from, and a stable internet connection, which is nearly impossible to get where I live. Just the Lovense costs US$100.

So I figured I was done as a model. I took a break of about four months. I felt lost during those months, because I felt like I didn't do anything. And then, out of nowhere, a user I had met on Chaturbate gave me a camera so I could start from scratch at home. This gift was completely unexpected. Now he is a person who is very close to me, one of the closest people in my life. I have a lot of appreciation for him.

So I began my independent stage. My God, I was so afraid to do it. I had thought I more or less understood how to go about it, but I did not feel sure of anything at all. I had to research everything, about creating accounts, payment methods. Everything. It was a lot of information to learn, yes it was. Looking through my old messages I found a message from a guy who was offering to help me. We started talking and I told him about what was happening and he helped me, just like that, without expecting anything in return. It was so strange because I needed help and I didn't know what to do. I guess it's fate.

So I created an account on Chaturbate and another on OnlyFans. To this day I have not figured out how to get the money out of my account on OnlyFans, so I decided to just leave the money there and use it as a savings account.

The first day I broadcast independently I was so nervous I was shaking haha. I remember that day very well. My mother and my cousin were cleaning the house and I told them that I was going to connect, however I looked and come what may. I just turned on the camera and let things happen.

[...?]

If my mother knows what I am doing, we don't talk about it because I bring money in.

[...?]

Well, OK. So, if my mother knows, it's because she and I have a lot of confidence in each other.

That day, thanks to a user who is now also a friend but no longer enters my page, I made 2000 tokens. Chaturbate took half, but I was not in a studio so I kept all the rest. Around US$100. Thanks to him I felt sure that I could do well being at home, just having fun on camera. So my nerves were calming down little by little. I started connecting more and more often, until my account was at least in a decent position in the rankings.

I really feel like I "got it" now and I enjoy what I do. I see my regular visitors as real friends. We talk about normal things even though I am naked and masturbating. I enjoy the time I spend with them. I have also come to know some great people, people who really care about you, and that is something I have not felt for a long time.

My only real problem now is my wifi connection which is not ideal, but where I live there is no fiber optic coverage. I am working on resolving that right now.

This is also when I grew into an adult haha because I also created a bank account and acquired financial obligations like paying for the internet, paying for electricity and helping at home financially, which I had always wanted to do.

I thank all the people who with just one token or comment help us models feel better. We are people too, on the other side of the camera, and we have feelings. The users who treat us like real people have no idea how happy this makes us. Must users just sit and watch. They don't even give us a hello.

It is true that sometimes the work makes me feel bad, not because of what I do, because I like to talk and to touch myself. I just think oh God I can't do this much longer, I have to study something, but I have many responsibilities now in my life. Also, when you do this work you are always thinking "why does that guy get more tokens than me? Is it because of this? Or this?" You start to question many things about your appearance. You spend a lot of time watching others, to get ideas on how to improve your show. For example, I tried putting on a few articles of clothing but when I do that people leave. What I do now is this: you can always see my cock, but it will not be hard unless I get a special tip. And I don't cum unless my tokens add up to the cum goal.

I would love to find another way forward, but for that I need money to study. Remember that I am only a boy of nineteen without higher education. I would like to study to be a flight attendant but it's expensive hahaha it comes out at US$3500 dollars for two years of school. My other goal is to somehow get to another country and find work as a waiter, but the flights are expensive and they are now even higher hahaha. I am still young but already I feel like I am falling behind.

And, well, every day I'm learning more hehe. Do you have any more questions, Bob?

Author's note: The first royalties from this book were used to given to Camilo so that he could move to a different country and a better life situation. At the time of publication, he was still working regularly on OnlyFans.

ACKNOWLEDGMENTS

I would like to thank Christian Huygen, whose support and thoughts and criticisms and encouragements were crucial for this book, as is true for almost all my projects. Thanks also to Mark Lutwak and Y York. And to Alex DiFrancesco, Robert Glück, Brontez Purnell, and Jonathan D. Katz. To my primary editor, Adam Prince, and my publisher, Diane Goettel. Most of all, to all of the beautiful men I have mentioned in this book, minus Roberto D'Aubuisson and Sigifredo Ochoa, the two mass murderers.

Buster and Buddy first appeared in the September 2023 issue of the literary magazine *BULL*.

The Anesthesiologist first appeared in the 2024 issue of the literary magazine *The Baltimore Review*.

Bob Ostertag's work cannot easily be summarized or pigeon-holed. He has published more than twenty albums of music, eight books, two podcasts, and a feature film. His books cover a wide range of topics, from climate change to labor unions to estrogen and testosterone. His writing has won the "Most Censored Story of the Year" award from Project Censored and the "Most Important Book of the Year" designation from *The Nation*. He has performed his music at many of the world's great concert halls, including the Lincoln Center (New York), to Teatro Colón (Buenos Aires), Strozzi Palace (Florence), and the Shanghai Conservatory of Music.